BITTER TIDE

Pine Island Coast Florida Suspense: Book 3

JACK HARDIN

Nate & Sarah
Josh & Diana

Thank you.

CHAPTER ONE

Adoni-Bezek fled, but they chased him and caught him,
and cut off his thumbs and big toes.
Judges 1:6

"There is a tide in the affairs of men…"
Shakespeare

ON THE RAINED-OUT END OF A HOT AND HUMID August day in Southwest Florida, out of a dilapidated trailer park whose only appeal in the community had once been a thriving rose garden at its entrance, an old lady driving a run down Oldsmobile with no air conditioning stopped at the Red Rover convenience store and walked in to purchase a banana Moon Pie.

She stood at the worn and scratched formica counter for a couple minutes waiting for the attendant to appear, called twice, and finally, after a mutter of frustration and a last look around, slapped two crinkled dollar bills on the counter and walked out with her treat.

She stopped where her car had been. She looked

around and then turned back to stare into the empty space. This is where she had parked. Last week, she had forgotten where she had placed her television remote. Her granddaughter found it the next day in the freezer. And the week before that, she had misplaced her eyeglasses. Those, as it turned out, were sitting right where she always kept them, on her nightstand. Also found by her granddaughter. But the car? She had just driven out here. This is where she had parked. And now she was staring at a cracked, sunbleached parking space with a large oil slick in the center and a crushed styrofoam cup straddling the faded line.

Her Oldsmobile was gone.

———————

The building had a fresh coat of paint, a bright orange that would sear your eyeballs if you were staring at it in midday without sunglasses, the color matching the furious palette selected for nearly every other clapboard building on Matlacha: cornea-melting blues, purples, yellows, and greens.

Ellie O'Conner walked up the two front steps, opened the door, and was hit with a refreshing blast of air conditioning when she stepped in. The gallery was small, no more than four hundred square feet, and quiet. Easels stood on unstained pine floors, and coastal paintings of all sizes clung to the walls. Shelves dotted the floor space, showcasing jewelry, postcards, and ceramic figures of local wildlife: manatees, dolphins, fish, and pelicans.

The space belonged to Jean Oglesby, a local artist who had a cult following of sorts, composed of people from nearly every zip code in the state and many from abroad. She was an exhibitionist painter who couldn't produce originals fast enough. Tourists would come just to visit her shop and take home something that would remind them of the old charms of Florida's southwest Gulf Coast and slow living.

Jean had been Ellie's fifth grade art teacher, and it turned out that, at least in Ellie's situation, Jean was a much better artist than a teacher. Ellie still couldn't draw a half-decent stick figure and had no idea how to go about doing otherwise. When it came to artistic expression, Ellie had failed to advance beyond the unmodulated doodles of a recently weaned toddler.

The gallery's back door was open, and the faint smell of cigarette smoke lingered inside. Ellie walked to the rear and stepped out onto the decked porch that looked out over the waters of Matlacha Pass.

Jean was leaning over the railing with a Virginia Slim tucked between her skilled fingers. She was slender and tall—a half inch short of six feet—and wore a white bohemian skirt and a multi-colored tank top of her own design. Her long, graying hair was pulled back into a loose ponytail and ended just above her tailbone.

"Hello, Jean."

The older lady's body jerked, and she straightened. Cigarette ash drifted to the wooden deck. "Ellie! Good Lord in heaven, you just about scared me off into the water, hon."

Ellie smiled. "You should put up a chime in the shop so you don't have an early heart attack. Sorry to have scared you."

Jean waved her off. "Don't worry about it." She drew down on her cigarette, and the tip glowed a hot orange before it darkened against the release. She blew out a hazy line of smoke. "That's not a bad idea about the chime. Haley Perkins mentioned the same thing to me the other day. I think I may have a simple setting I can program into the alarm system." She looked at Ellie through clear lenses set into bright pink cat eye frames that had a small nameplate embedded near the earpiece. It read *Tom Ford.* Her eyeshadow matched the color of her building, except the orange over her eyelids was infused with a metallic glint that made her eyes look otherworldly, alien even, especially when she blinked. *Flamboyant* was the best word to describe Jean Oglesby's style, but it was all built upon a stunning ability to capture the essence of the indigenous plant and wildlife she saw around her.

"You're alone here today? Where's the help?" Ellie asked.

"Carol's mother is sick, and I told Clayton to take the day off. He was aching to go fishing. I don't mind. What brings you in?"

"Major's birthday is coming up. He's turning sixty-two, and I want to get him a painting. He loves your stuff, you know." Major was Ellie's uncle—by relation-ship, not by blood—and along with being one of the most well-liked and well-known patriarchs of the local community, Warren Hall happened to own the most frequented bar on Pine Island, The Salty Mangrove, located at the southern tip of the island.

"Don't I know it. He finds his way in here to look around every couple of months. What do you have in mind?" She took in another hit of nicotine. Her hand was shaking.

"Jean, are you all right?"

Jean followed Ellie's gaze to her trembling hand and quickly brought it down to her side. "Oh, fine. Just a little bit of a nervous tick."

Ellie eyed her. "What's going on?"

"Just family stuff. I don't want to concern you with it." She stuck the cigarette back in her mouth and sucked in more smoke.

"Jean." Ellie's tone sounded like a mother warning her child not to play in the mud. "Out with it. What family stuff?"

When the artist turned to look at Ellie, her eyes were rimmed with concerned tears. "It's Ronnie, my boy. I haven't heard from him in a couple weeks. He calls me every Friday at lunch, you know. Has for years. It's been two weeks, and I haven't heard a peep or a tweet."

"What do you think is wrong?"

Jean huffed. "He's been involved with the wrong crowd, that much I know. He got in with some group a while back, and he seems to think of them as family. I don't know what they are really: a gang or a cult. But they all follow the teachings of this old man who was always talking about national pride and the 'Real America,' whatever that means. I never could understand Ronnie when he tried to explain it to me." Jean shook her head. "I feel like a terrible mother, not taking the time to understand."

"Jean, you're not a terrible mother. Ronnie, he's my age, isn't he? Mid-thirties?"

"Sure."

"He's a grown man. You can't beat yourself up for him going with the wrong crowd."

"I don't know, Ellie. It's more than just that. He has this friend who had been selling marijuana for some time and Ronnie got involved too, there for a while. Ronnie told me he got out of the whole drug thing a while back, but now he's acting strange again." She paused. "I know this all makes him sound bad—he really is a good man, you know."

"I'm sure he is, Jean."

"He just never did have any great role models. He grew up with his father in Ohio, and he was the one with all the money at the time. He and I divorced when Ronnie was little, you know. He's still this big-shot lawyer up there in Cincinnati. He won full custody, and I lost my boy, but he never spent any decent time with Ronnie. Was always too busy in his office or his wood shop. I've done what I can over the years to be there for him and love him, but a mother's love still can't fully compensate for that of an absent father."

"Jean, no one can predict what kind of choices kids will make when they grow up. Do you know where he is now?"

"No. He moves around so much." Jean stabbed her cigarette into a palm-shaped ashtray. "I'm so sorry, hon. This is not why you came in here. You want to go in and pick out something for Warren?"

"Sure, let's go see what you've got." They walked back in, and Jean shut the door behind her. Ellie slowly walked the shop, gazing at the handbags, shirts, dresses, watches, earrings, and men's neckties that all bore Jean's art. She walked along the wall and stopped at a three-by-four foot painting of the Norma Jean pier, looking strong, sturdy, and a little weathered as it had before the airplane crashed into it over a month ago.

"Jean, this is great. Is this the original?"

"Yes, it is. Painted it just two weeks ago."

Ellie looked at the price tag and almost cringed. "Has Major seen this?"

"I don't think so. He hasn't been through here for a perusal in over a month, I suppose. Harvey came in and scanned it last week, so I should have prints and trinkets with that image in the next few days."

"He still has your *Ancient Shrimp Trawler* hanging over his living room fireplace. He'll love this one." Ellie reached up to take it off the wall and winced. She brought her elbows down a few inches to relieve the pain before trying again. Three weeks ago she had been repeatedly punched in the ribs by an ex-Navy SEAL intent on not being arrested for drug trafficking. Ellie had won out with a little help from her butterfly knife, but her ribs still had a couple weeks of healing before they were back to normal, pre-punch conditions.

"Are you okay?" Jean asked.

Ellie smiled across the fading pain. "Just a little sore."

"I'm getting a bunion removed tomorrow," Jean said. "I hear that recovery isn't all sunshine either. Would you like to get it? The painting?"

Ellie disregarded the price and nodded. "He will love this."

"Then here, let me grab it." Jean stepped in and lifted the frame off the wall, then walked over to the checkout counter. She gently laid it down and wrapped it in bubble wrap. "You get the favorite person's discount. Forty percent off."

"Oh Jean, you don't have—"

"I know I don't, but I want to."

"Thank you, friend." She swiped her credit card in the card reader. Jean handed her the receipt and then the painting. The ladies walked in tandem toward the front door. When she had come in, Ellie had missed the small table set up against the wall. "Are you hosting a book signing this weekend?"

"I am. Artie Kaepernick just came out with his Pine Island Cookbook. I told him he could put his stuff out, shake hands with the incoming, and see if he can move anything. I hope he does. Anyone who hasn't tried his Key lime grilled chicken is really missing out."

"If I don't make it in, grab one for me, will you? I'll pay you for it when I see you next." It had been Artie who had once suggested to Ellie that a requiem should be held, a dirge sung for the old Florida country that had, over the last couple of decades, been dissolved throughout the state by commercialization, fanfare, and tourism. But such a mournful song would not be sung here. Matlacha and its neighboring communities of Saint James City, Pine Island Center, Pineland, and Bokeelia all congealed to make up the laid back and naturally rural culture of the greater Pine Island area that was cherished for its serenity, ample mangrove-fringed coastline, and abundant fishing. It was Florida's version of Mayberry, and tourists came back year after year to sit on bar stools and fish off docks with locals who always made you feel like you were a part of the family.

"Of course," Jean said. "That will mean a lot to Artie. I'm glad you came in, Ellie. Always good to chat with you, hon."

"You let me know if you don't hear from Ronnie and if I can do anything to help."

Jean nodded. "I will."

CHAPTER TWO

THE OLDSMOBILE RAN OUT OF GAS FIVE MILES BACK. He couldn't understand it. The gauge said it was just over half full. Maybe it was the gas pump. He didn't know, and after three minutes of trying to turn over the engine and slapping and cursing at the dash, he gave up, got out, and put his soles to the steaming asphalt shoulder.

What he didn't know was that, had he simply asked the old lady back at the convenience store for a ride, she would have obliged him and asked where he needed to go. When he answered "Arcadia," she would have scrunched her face, thought about it, and said, "That's over thirty miles away, but I suppose I could manage. Don't have nothin' better to do." Then at some point during the drive, she would have commented that her gauge was on the fritz and never went below the halfway mark and that she should probably stop off at the Sunoco on their way up there.

But that's not what happened. He had stolen the car and never did see the pocket notebook on the passenger seat with her large, messy scratchings that kept track of her mileage. Even if he had noticed, he wouldn't have guessed what it was for. Maybe tax purposes. Maybe the old lady had a little business where she made quilts or crocheted potholders or sold organic seeds. But then he wouldn't have really cared.

His hands were balled into fists as he walked, not from anger but from fear. He was tired of feeling them shake, so he curled his fingers tightly into his palms like a turtle into its shell. Every time he heard the far off drone of a car coming up the highway behind him, his throat thickened and his stomach curled and he would turn to make sure they weren't slowing down for him. Surely they couldn't find him out here? He had taken the back roads, and they didn't know where he lived. At least, he was pretty sure they didn't.

So he walked for an hour while the sun beat down on his denim jacket and his feet sweltered in his black combat boots. He mumbled to himself as he tried to process what had happened. There was no way they would think he wasn't a part of it. He shouldn't have run out like that. But now he had fled, and there would be no doubt. He couldn't go back. He had stolen that car, and the cops would be looking for him.

He threw a nervous glance over his shoulder to look for any police cruisers down the road. But what he saw instead was everything he'd seen in his waking nightmare this last hour. He saw what he hoped would never materialize into reality: an orange Mustang a half mile behind him. And it was coming toward him at a crawl, moving more and more onto the shoulder. That was the moment his loins turned to water, and along the back of his spine and up into his teeth he felt a rush of cold blood. He turned his whole body around so he could keep an eye on the car and continued walking backwards. The car was coming faster now, its supercharged engine beginning to growl. Squinting, he could make out two figures through the windshield. One large, one larger. Grown men weren't supposed to wet their pants. Not unless the switch at the end of the green mile was about to be thrown and you were strapped in, about to ride the lightning. But maybe he was. Maybe this was his green mile. He swallowed hard and then shot quickly toward his left, his feet leaving the asphalt and running down the grassy slope off the road as he bolted for the tree line.

The Mustang screeched to a stop on the shoulder. A door clicked open, and one of the men called out to him. He knew that jesting voice. Oh boy, did he know that voice.

He ran faster.

A gun discharged near the road, and the bullet smashed into the cypress tree directly to his right, sending flecks of angry wood into his cheeks and eyes. He ducked and entered the cover of the tree line.

And there was that voice again, that voice that made him want his mommy and wish that he had driven that Oldsmobile south instead of north, east instead of north, anything but north. His heart was drumming into his ears now, and he struggled on, criss-crossing trees like a mad spider until the moment the toe of his boot snagged an exposed tree root and sent him tumbling forward. When he landed his cheek fell onto a small rock which gouged him beneath an eye. Ordinarily, he would have felt an extreme amount of pain, but as it was, adrenaline was entering his veins faster than a post-surgery morphine drip, and he scrambled back to his feet and kept running.

They were both coming now. He could hear them calling for him, wooing him back in that sarcastic way that they had.

More gunshots, more woods chips in his face.

His lungs were burning now, coated with liquid fire, but he didn't notice so much because all of a sudden his feet sloshed into stagnant water, and with every step his boots stuck a little harder, a little longer. Water reflected the broken sunlight at the base of the trees and told him he was heading into moderate swampland.

The water was now above his ankles. There would be alligators in here. Lots of them, he knew, their hooded eyes protruding from the black water, waiting patiently for some unsuspecting creature to slip on by. And yet, strangely enough, this knowledge did not induce fear.

It didn't even bother him.

He would rather take his chances with the alligators in front of him than the crocodiles behind him.

CHAPTER THREE

ANDRÉS SALAMANCA SCROLLED DOWN THE WEB PAGE, browsing images of surfboards as they passed, musing to himself over color and size, wondering what beach on the eastern coast of the state he should choose and whether or not he might end up being any good. He had never surfed, and the internet said that a beginner board for a man his size should be at least six inches longer than a board for someone who actually knew what they were doing. He could rent one, but he preferred to purchase one instead. He had no hobbies of his own. Ringo had his books, his boats, and his businesses. Chewy, his tall, hairy coworker, had his motivational talks and liked to go on long walks on nature trails.

There was another shipment coming in from Mexico this weekend. Now that their biggest competition was out of the way, business was really ramping up. Once things settled down and new systems and structures were put in place to accommodate the growth, Andrés would take a vacation and go surfing. Take one, Ringo had urged. You never take any time off. And that was when, for the first time since he was a teenager and Maria Ortiz kissed him underneath the mesquite tree in his uncle's backyard, Andrés felt a tingle of excitement.

He had grown up on the dirty, blood-stained streets of Ciudad Juárez, where the only wave to be ridden was a cocaine-induced high or the thick blood lust that hit you the first few times you entered a strip club. Andrés never had tried the stuff he sold. He, like Ringo, knew a good business when he saw one. But in Andrés's estimation, trying your product while selling it seemed, to him, much like farming piranhas and deciding one day to take a swim in the pond.

He thought briefly of his former associate, Scotch. How he had broken one of Ringo's rules, nominating himself to be a taste tester of their cocaine, and how he had subsequently met his fate with a twenty-foot python in a sealed room not fifty feet from where Andrés now sat.

Andrés's phone was sitting on the desktop next to the mousepad. It rang. He scrolled past a few more surfboards and answered without looking at who was calling.

"Is he there?" the caller asked.

"Yes." Andrés stood and walked to the end of the main hallway and into Ringo's office. The room was lined with built-in bookcases fifteen feet high. The higher shelves had to be accessed via a rolling ladder. All the books were hardback, clothbound. Classics of history, philosophy, and fiction from the Romantic and Victorian era, all of them a gift to Ringo from Andrés's former employer, Ángeles Negros, the Mexican cartel that was the single supplier of Ringo's cocaine.

He walked across a thick Oriental area rug woven in

a pattern of two dragons facing off. Two dark leather couches sat in the center of the room, a large mahogany desk near the far window that looked down on the perfectly manicured lawn that terminated at the Caloosahatchee River beyond. Ringo sat behind the desk, leaned over, examining satellite photos of the area.

Andrés stepped close and remained silent. Ringo finally looked up from the photos, took note of the phone in Andrés's hand, and nodded. Ringo had a policy not to personally talk over the phone. He didn't trust encryption and masking. The best way to keep a long-standing anonymity was to simply keep your voice off the airways. He paid others enough so that they were willing to do it themselves. Andrés punched the speaker button on the cell phone. "Okay," he said, and handed it to his boss.

"We're all set," Aldrich said. "Five hundred is scheduled and will run into the Alcove and the Cave." Ringo understood the code. He had conceived it himself. Alcove was Georgia; Cave, Virginia. "Now that Nunez is gone, we can fill his empty routes. Make sure you keep them stocked. I'll do what I can to keep eyes elsewhere." Silence, and then, "I heard that our newest associate is running guns now? I thought we had a mutual understanding?"

Ringo muted the phone and spoke to Andrés. "We do. I'll be dealing with him soon enough. I may want your help with that." Andrés took it off mute, put it on speaker, said, "We do. I'll be dealing with him soon enough. I may want your help with that."

"Fine." A pause, and then, "We need to be very careful about the Manatee."

Again, Ringo put the call on mute. "I'm fully aware

of that. I never liked doing business with the Manatee from the beginning. That was your idea, if you recall. I suggest you're the one who remains careful." Andrés repeated the words into the phone.

"Yeah, I know. I'll be in touch." The call ended. Andrés slid the phone into his pocket. "What are those?" he asked, observing the photos.

"I'm scouting new delivery locations." He chose two of the large photos and handed them to Andrés. "I've circled three areas on there. You and Chewy go check them out. I think they'll be good. I want us more sure than ever on exit points, not just receiving."

"Okay, *Jefe*." He scanned the images. "These are south?"

"Yes."

"Okay." He looked up, looked like he had something on his mind.

"What is it?" Ringo asked.

"There remains the issue about César. Are you going to provide him a date you can meet again? His man called me again this morning."

Ringo smiled. It was a crooked, sinister smile. He removed his white fedora, the one with the black band, and set it on the edge of the desk. He ran a hand over his buzzed and graying auburn hair. Then he sighed. "I believe it was Chaucer who said that patience is a conquering virtue. What do you think about that?"

Andrés typically demurred with questions like this. He wasn't intelligent like Ringo. He wasn't smart like Chewy. But it wasn't his boss's intention to shame him when he asked such things. It was Ringo's way of communicating his philosophy, and it was his meticulous philosophy that helped him build a localized drug empire that almost no one knew existed.

It was how he lived two very different lives.

Andrés gazed through the window at a palm and considered the quote. "*Jefe*, I think that it might mean that it is good to be patient." He thought some more. "That maybe the patient man is stronger than the man who is not?"

Ringo nodded, satisfied. "Yes. Precisely. César is too eager. His existing influence, given to him by the cartel, makes him feel powerful. I suppose it should. But the irony is that in his power he has become impatient and overzealous and because of that, less powerful. Impatient men make mistakes, Andrés. I don't like working with people who make mistakes. That's why I'm still here, and men like Mateo Nunez are not."

"What would you like me to tell him? That you won't meet with him?" Andrés had spent most of his life in Mexico working for César's people, for Ángeles Negros, Mexico's most ruthless and, arguably, most successful cartel. Only three years prior had César recommended that Andrés go and work for Ringo. And so he had. It was the best decision Andrés had ever made. Ringo had been good to him. Very good. And Andrés, no longer doing maritime runs across the Gulf, was able to keep a low profile and live somewhat of a normal life. But he knew that the leaders of the cartel were not the kind of men that you blew off or promised to get back to. Always genial on the surface, they turned you into minced meat—literally—if they sniffed you undermining them, taking your business elsewhere, or simply disrespecting them. They were of the most feared men in their industry, marble tombs spread over lavish Mexican acres a sober testament to it.

"No. Don't tell him that I won't meet with him," Ringo replied. "I will meet with him. But I'm not ready yet. This will be the third time in a year. In the past he has respected my prudence in only meeting face to face once each year and no more. In addition, the last time we met in Cuba he once again pushed me to move into something other than cocaine. I'm done."

"Done," a surprised and intrigued Andrés repeated. "What do you mean?" he asked cautiously.

Ringo smiled and shuffled the remaining photos into a small stack. "You'll see, my good man. In the meantime be...patient. I'm working on something. I'll let you know soon. Send Chewy in, will you? I need him to run somewhere for me."

"Of course, *Jefe*."

CHAPTER FOUR

THE PARKING LOT HAD JUST GOTTEN A FRESH COAT OF paint, its deep black contrasting against bright white lines marking off each parking space. Ellie parked her Silverado in her usual spot at the far end of the lot and stepped out into the warm morning sun. Her appointment, five minutes from now, was with Garrett Cage, the Special Agent in Charge who headed up the DEA's Fort Myers office and an old friend who went back to her high school days. Garrett had brought Ellie on with the agency three months ago, during which span Ellie had managed to bring down an elusive drug ring, doing so with brevity and style. Thereafter, Garrett had ordered her to take three weeks off, said it wasn't a suggestion, and that between a couple bruised ribs and a successful bust she deserved it. Today they were meeting to discuss her next course of action. They had taken down Mateo Nunez's organization, and that was something to be celebrated. But celebrations were hard to come by and quickly passed. They knew that, at a minimum, there remained at least one more local kingpin hovering unseen below the surface. Someone who they knew absolutely nothing about.

Ringo.

After scanning her badge on the front door's card reader and getting through the metal detector, Ellie rode the elevator up to the fourth floor. She walked across a sea of cubicles and knocked on the glass door to Garrett's office. She didn't see him behind his desk. Sandra, his receptionist, told her to go on in, that Garrett would return in a few minutes.

The glass door shut quietly behind her, and she walked in, stepping up to the wide window that overlooked Fort Myers. When Ellie left the CIA over nine months ago, she would never have imagined that she would end up back home working for a completely different agency. But these last three months with the DEA had been unexpectedly satisfying. Ellie was good at her directive and found, to her surprise, that she actually enjoyed it. She stepped away from the window and over to a wall filled with pictures, diplomas, and certifications. There was a picture of Garrett with several members of his FAST team on tour in Afghanistan five years ago. They were posing in their desert BDUs, eyes encased in sunglasses, helmets on, rifles in hand. Garrett had left FAST a year after the picture was taken and accepted a post at DEA headquarters in Springfield, Virginia, before being offered the helm at Fort Myers almost a year ago now. It was one of life's ironies, she thought. During the four years that Ellie and Garrett had gone to high school together, the senior class had endowed Garrett with the unofficial title of being the most committed to smoking marijuana. As Garrett told it, a wake-up call had come soon after they graduated in the form of his favorite cousin dying of a heroin overdose, convincing Garrett to quit smoking posthaste, which he accomplished cold turkey. After being drug free for several years, his veins had been clean long enough for the Army to take him in, where he served four years before getting out and making a transition to the DEA. Still scanning the wall, Ellie took note of a framed photo of Garrett in a suit, standing next to the agency's Principal Deputy Administrator, Timothy Jackson. The men were looking into the camera, shaking hands.

Garrett had done well for himself over the years. For the time being he was at the helm of the Fort Myers district office, but Ellie expected him to continue climbing the ladder to the top. It wouldn't surprise her if he ended up in Virginia several years from now as a division chief.

The door whispered over the carpet as it opened. Garrett walked through. He was a handsome man with a strong forehead that didn't detract from a well-defined face. He kept his jet black hair finger-combed to the side, and his blue eyes were bright and piercing, his eyebrows thick. Ellie saw him for a man who would age well, someone who would look distinguished well into his golden years.

She motioned to the picture of him in Afghanistan. "You ever miss being over there in the field?"

He glanced at the picture as he maneuvered around his desk. "I guess." He gave a weak shrug as he sat down. "I haven't told you much about my time over there. On one hand, yes, I loved it. Some of the best men and women I've ever had the opportunity of working with were over there. Some of them still are. But as you know, it's all opium over there. Nearly a million acres in Afghanistan alone are seeded with the stuff, and it produces thousands of tons every year. We did good work over there, but it was especially difficult to make any sustainable progress. The DEA is trying to arrest the kingpins and destroy their stockpiles, the CIA is trying to buy them off so they can use them to rat others out, and other agencies have their own conflicting agendas. I got weary of all the competing objectives that tended to keep the wrong people high on the hog. Anyway," he said. "Enough of that. How are you feeling?"

"Not bad. Still a little sore but nothing broken." She took a seat.

"Good. That was a heck of a fight you were in." He folded his hands on the desk and leaned into them. "So, are you ready to get back at it? Or do you want some more time?"

"I wouldn't be here if I wasn't ready to go."

"And this is the same Ellie O'Conner that I couldn't beg to join me at the first? Now you're raring to get back out there?" He smiled.

"My father trained me to expect success. We've had some, and now I want more."

"Well, your father was right." He leaned back into his chair and flipped an ankle on top of a knee, clasped his hands. "So, this is your investigation. Since we got Nunez, I've been tied up with way more things than would interest you, so...what's on your mind in terms of our next move?"

She didn't hesitate. "I want to go after Ringo."

Garrett frowned, nodded. "Ringo? You mean the Casper the Ghost? I don't think we have anything substantial on him, do we?"

"No, we don't. But that's my job, isn't it? We didn't have anything substantial on Nunez until Mark and I started sniffing around. Ringo's name keeps coming up. There must be something to it. On top of that, whoever called us and gave us the lead on the drug swap on Norman Hardy's island—I think it was the competition trying to gain ground. I can't help but think we made it easier for them to succeed."

Garrett drummed a set of fingers over his knee. "All right," he finally said. "But I want you to keep me up to speed every step of the way. Anything you find out, every jot and tittle, I want to know about it. I've already got my higher ups breathing down my neck about having you on board without their authorization. They like what you did with Nunez, but I'm still on thin ice now that everyone down in Miami knows what I have you doing. When asked, I need to be able to tell them in real time what you're seeing out there. Also, if you don't find anything quickly, then I want you to move on to something that might furnish results a little faster. I hate to push you that way, but, as you know, that's the world we inhabit around here."

Ellie nodded. "I got it. Did Mark ever get any interviews with the guys we arrested at the Ridgeside property?"

"No, he didn't. None of their lawyers will let them talk until a decent plea bargain is reached with the DA's office. So that option is weeks away, if not months."

"I figured as much. Any further word on where Trigg Deneford and Eric Cardoza slipped off to?"

That got a huff out of Garrett. Three weeks ago, less than two days after they arrested a couple men working the local drug scene, the men had disappeared.

They had been locked up, and then were set free. "No idea," he said. "I've put in calls to my superiors, and they've said it's way outside my pay grade. Theirs too."

"Theirs too?" Ellie repeated, astounded.

"Yeah. Bizarre, isn't it?"

"So two men who had a hand in bringing tons of cocaine into Lee County have been released from prison, and no one can tell us anything? Does that sound right to you?"

"Of course not." He turned his palms up. "But what am I supposed to do? I've been told to stay out. I've even had Glitch dig around through the networks, and he's saying it's like Deneford and Cardoza never even existed. All he could find was the arrest record written by our own office."

"No way."

"I've never seen anything like it. Whoever these guys were working for must be at the top of the food chain."

"And you're not getting any more support from Miami after our bust?" Ellie asked.

"You would think so, but no. No, I'm not."

"Why? That just doesn't make any sense."

"Look, because of what you and Mark did, our office got a nod from the top, but they're standing firm on their MO for the year, and that's focusing on Miami-Dade. Budget talks begin at the end of the year. You know how it is. If there isn't a thick line item in the budget for it, then it has no philosophical or operational weight."

"But we just did all this on a shoestring," Ellie said.

"Don't I know it. And it looks like that's the way it's going to have to stay for at least the next six to nine months. So for now, run your Ringo angle and anything else you think will get you somewhere. But, and I can't stress this enough, keep me up to speed every step of the way. If I get questions, I need to have answers. I don't want to hear that you've known or intuited something about Ringo without letting me in on it. Clear?"

Ellie stood. "All right. I'll get with Mark, and we'll figure out the best way to move forward."

Garrett said, "I won't be in on Friday, but call me if you need anything. Angela's coming into town tomorrow night. I got us tickets to go see *Les Misérables* up in Tampa this weekend." Garrett's wife spent most of her time in New York City. She had created a fashion line that was getting off the ground and came down to see her husband a couple weekends a month. Garrett had expressed a wavering hope that the tiring arrangement wouldn't have to go on much longer.

"I should probably meet her one of these days. Don't you think?" Ellie said.

"I do. Maybe next time she's down we can have you over for dinner. You both would get along well, I think." His desk phone rang. He grabbed it up, and Ellie stepped out.

CHAPTER FIVE

THE TOP STEP OF THE FOOTSTOOL JIGGLED A LITTLE, and Ellie grabbed a rafter to steady herself. She ducked and reached to the string of Christmas lights hanging across the inside ceiling of The Salty Mangrove's tiki hut. A red bulb had blown and caused half the run of lights that followed to go out as well. Gloria and Fu Wang sat with their backs to the marina, he wearing shorts and a red polo, she stuffed into a black one-piece swimsuit that looked as if it had reached the manufacturer's limits on stretchability.

Ellie unscrewed the small bulb, replaced it with a fresh one, and the dark lights came to life, restoring the funky, tropical ambience that Major, the bar's owner and Ellie's uncle, liked to maintain around Pine Island's favorite bar. Ellie stepped down and tossed the old bulb into the trash before putting the footstool away. "That's much better," Gloria said, looking up at the lights. Her husband nodded approvingly, leaned in, and mumbled something to her. She nodded, said, "I'll ask. Ellie, what was the name of that champagne we all had at the ceremony last week? Fu liked it and wants to get a bottle to celebrate our anniversary next week."

"Your anniversary?" Ellie replied, stepping up to the sink behind the bar and filling a glass with ice. "How many years?" Fu and Gloria were as odd a couple as one would find. And yet, in some strange way, they seemed right for each other. They lived on a Gibson houseboat not two hundred feet from The Salty Mangrove—where they spent most of their passive income and drank enough alcohol each day to fuel a small jet.

"Six years," Gloria beamed. "It still feels like we're on our honeymoon."

"Congratulations, you guys." Ellie held her glass under the spout, filled it with water, and squeezed a lime wedge into it. "As for the champagne, I don't remember what it was. I can text Major and ask him."

Last week, after completing repairs on the Norma Jean pier, Major had held a rechristening ceremony. Council members, local business owners, members of the Rotary and Lions Clubs, and a couple hundred other people from around the island had come for a quick celebration. Six weeks prior, a small amphibian airplane carrying nearly a ton of cocaine had crashed into the southern end of the pier, not a hundred yards from where they were now sitting.

Sharla Potter sat a couple stools down from Gloria. "You two met on a boat tour, didn't you?" she asked.

"We did," Gloria blushed. "Providence sat me right next to him. You know, with as large as I am sometimes I get nervous about who I'll be seated next to on a plane or a boat. But Fu," she turned and smiled at her husband, "he liked me being pressed into him. It's been nothing but good times and fireworks ever since."

"Well, I'm with Ellie," Sharla said. "Congratulations on six good years." She nudged her wine glass toward Ellie. "Let me get another pinot, Ellie. If you would be so kind." Sharla was the mango matron of the island, who, along with her husband Gary, owned The Groovy Grove, a fifty-two acre mango plantation in Pineland. She wore a wide-brimmed straw hat, her straight gray hair hanging untethered behind her, her delicate nose turned slightly upward at the end. Sharla was loved by anyone who had the good fortune of meeting her and was the perfect embodiment of Southern hospitality and grace. The Potters, along with Ellie's uncle, were pillars in this community, small business owners who gave back their money and time to ensure that Pine Island retained its slow, sequestered way of life and kept greedy industrialists, who would seek to build seaside penthouses far into the sky, at bay.

Pine Island was the largest island in the state of Florida, its southernmost point sitting not three miles north of Sanibel Island, and stretched seventeen miles northward, its widest point no more than three miles. The island had managed to keep a lower tourist profile than its nearby neighbors like Cayo Costa and Sanibel, in part because it was lacking their powdery beaches, a point that none of the locals viewed as a negative.

Gloria jabbed her elbow into her husband's ribs. "Honey, we need to go pick some mangoes up at The Groovy Grove sometime."

Fu nodded intensely. "Yes. Yes."

"We'd love to have you," Sharla said. "Right now

things are a little hectic, but plan on coming out after Mango Mania."

Mango Mania was a late summer festival that saw Saint James City shutting down for three days as thousands descended upon the southern end of the island to celebrate and enjoy the golden fruit. Dozens of local merchants and vendors would set up along south Oleander Street and spill out onto The Salty Mangrove's boardwalk and halfway down the Norma Jean pier.

"Ellie," Sharla said, "I hear your sister and niece are coming back home. I am so glad to hear that. I've missed them more than my granny's gravy."

"They are. I can't wait," Ellie said.

"She's renting the old house out, isn't she? Are they going to stay with you?"

"No, her renters just completed their lease and vacated last week. Katie and Chloe will be moving back in."

"Wonderful."

When their father died, Ellie was knee deep in an overseas career with the CIA, and Frank O'Conner's will placed the home in his youngest daughter's hands. When Katie moved to Seattle last summer, Major had convinced her not to sell it.

Sharla took a sip of her pinot grigio. "I hate that Katie and Chloe are going to miss the festival again," she said. "Chloe was only a little thing then, but that year before they moved she would stay at our booth and hold out a paper plate of mango slices to passersby. Of course, she would when she wasn't busy helping herself to the actual samples."

"Well, the festival is my all-time favorite weekend of

the year," Gloria said. "Music, mangoes, and seeing everyone pack this place out."

Fu straightened up. "Fun," he said. "Be fun."

Ellie froze and stared at Fu, her mouth nearly hanging open. "It will be fun?" she repeated. "Fu! Are you actually speaking English?"

"Yes, yes," he smiled.

"I keep telling him he would have more fun if he decided to speak the native tongue," Gloria said, and winked at Ellie. "I think he may be coming around."

"Well, what do you know," Sharla muttered, stunned on her own accord.

Fu, almost anticlimactically, muttered something in Chinese again.

"Oh, yes," Gloria beamed. "I completely forgot. Guess what we did last night?" Fu mumbled again, and his wife flushed. She smiled coyly and waved him off. "Oh, not that." She looked around at their friends, still reddened as with sunburn. "We finally ordered a drone!"

Sharla tilted her head. "You don't say."

"It should be here in a couple weeks," Gloria said. "I can't wait to use it. We'll be able to fly it from right here and see this whole end of the island up close. The remote has a built-in color screen."

"Gary got one so he could fly it over the Grove and put it on YouTube," Sharla said. "They sound like large mosquitoes. Drives me nuts."

"That's why we chose this one," Gloria said. "It's nearly impossible to hear once its thirty or forty feet overhead. Something about a raked wingtip, but I don't really know about all that. But it can go up to seven or eight miles out on a single battery if there isn't a lot of wind."

"Fun," Ellie said. Her phone rang, and she fished it from the pocket of her jean shorts. She noted the caller and answered. "Hi, Jean."

"Ellie, how are you, hon?"

"Fine. I've got the painting all wrapped up. Major's going to love it."

"Good. Good. Listen, would it be too much trouble for you to come over to my place later this evening? If you have some time." Jean's voice was heavy with worry.

"Tonight? Sure I can. Everything okay?"

"I don't really know, Ellie." She paused. "It's about Ronnie. He called me earlier. Ellie, I think he's in some trouble, and I don't know the right thing to do."

CHAPTER SIX

Jean Oglesby's home sat on two acres at the north end of Pineland, up against Big Jim Creek Preserve. She purchased the place five years ago after Teddy Baxter—a giant of a man who had pioneered blue crab fishing in the area—died and his big-time city kids had put it up for sale. At the time, Jean had been looking to upgrade from her small home in Saint James City, and she grabbed it up within a week of the sign getting jammed into the front yard. Unlike most local artists who still floundered about on the murky financial bottom of an artistic ocean, Jean had found a measure of stardom after making a painting based off Daniel Hagerman's 1944 picture of Ernest Hemingway.

Several years ago a big-shot winegrower from Spain, who also happened to be a fan of Hemingway, was visiting Matlacha and bought Jean's Hemingway painting on the spot. When he took it back home to Spain, several of his friends decided they wanted Jean to make them custom paintings of their own, and, in the way that a cover band has that one song that garnishes a cult following, Jean came into a modest international following that continued to grow.

Local sales at her shop in Matlacha represented only a fraction of what she brought in. She kept an office in Bokeelia, just a mile from her house. It was staffed by three full time people and, in the busier winters, a few more part-timers. Her renown and style had spread, and dozens of online orders for prints came in each day.

Jean's neighbors, like herself, were the island's cultural gatekeepers of both past and present. Archie Holland's lot was to her east. Archie was the president of the Chamber of Commerce and known by the locals as the Creative Coast's charming bulldog. Charming, because he could groom just about any interested party to set up shop or business on the island. In his twelve year tenure, the area had blossomed with more artists, charters, and liquor licenses than ever before. Bulldog, because he could run off a big corporation intent on over-commercialization faster than you could say Matlacha.

Gertie Fenwick's house sat to Jean's west. Gertie was the vice-chair of the Historical Society. She was vice and not chair because of her quick and flaring temper that would leave her opposition driving home with singed eyebrows. They kept her around because of her zeal. But the chair eluded her due to her inability to be winsome or polite.

Ellie stepped out of her El Camino, walked past sixty-year-old oaks and a cluster of leather ferns, and went up the broad, wood-plank steps to the front door. She knocked and waited and caught herself smiling as she stared at the door. It was painted in a base color of bright yellow with tarpon and manatees stenciled across.

The door stuck out from the rest of the exterior, which was clothed in a muted off-white and olive green. The door opened, and Jean motioned inside. "Ellie. Come in, hon. Thank you for coming over." Jean's eyeshadow was a cobalt blue and dusted with a fine layer of glitter. Ellie hadn't seen her without the makeup extravaganza since she was in grade school and couldn't remember what she looked like without it. It would be strange if she did. Jean Oglesby without her gaudy face paint would be like seeing Dolly Parton without a wig. And no one was quite sure they wanted to see that. Jean was clutching a cane, and a surgical boot adorned her left foot.

"How did your surgery go?" Ellie asked.

"Fine, I just have to try and not be on my feet too much for the next couple of days. I have to wear this silly thing for the next couple of weeks."

Ellie followed Jean through the wide rotunda and into the kitchen. The kitchen boasted a large stainless steel gas stove with matching vent hood, a refrigerator built into the cabinetry, and white quartz countertops. Jean was one of the area's most successful artisans, and her living arrangements were a clear testimony to that. The front of the cabinets matched the front door: palms, tiki huts, and dolphins painted over yellow.

"You want a drink? Got plenty of just about everything." Jean refilled a nearly empty martini glass from a pitcher on the counter.

"I'm all right."

Jean left her cane leaning against a barstool, took her glass, and walked across the dark wood floors into the living room. She took a seat on a pink loveseat and propped her booted foot onto an ottoman. Ellie positioned herself on the matching couch. "So what's going on with Ronnie? Is he all right?"

The older lady huffed and shook her head. "He swears that he is, but I have that motherly instinct that knows when your little boy is sneaking a cookie two rooms away and when that little boy grows into a man and is running around with the wrong people. Ellie, I know you're not a mother yet, but when you are you'll just know some things. Things that you have no explanation for. It's like the hair standing up on the back of your neck, except somewhere deep on the inside. I know I'm not aware of everything he's ever gotten himself into. But that tingling...it's there."

"Did he say why he hadn't been calling?"

"I asked him. He wouldn't say. Blamed it on a cell phone problem and said he's been busy. But you don't work Jean Oglesby that way. I'm not a nagging mother, never have been. That's one reason why Ronnie and I are so close. But you'd better believe I pressed him. Ellie, you should have heard his voice. All I could do was picture him huddled down into a corner with his arms wrapped around his knees. He sounded scared if I've ever heard a scared man."

"Did he say where he was?"

Jean took another sip of her martini, swallowed, then did it again. She set her empty glass down. "In so many words. I inherited a bit of land from my father out near Archbold. A dozen acres an hour and a half from here. Before my father died and before Ronnie left home, we used to go spend Christmas up at a tiny hunting cabin out there. Just the three of us. Ronnie and his Gramps would go hunting and brought back a deer more than once. Anyway....I'm rambling, Ellie, I'm sorry."

"Take your time, Jean. I'm in no hurry to be anywhere else."

Jean's shoulders relaxed, and she settled further back into the plump cushions. "Thank you." She sighed. "So I asked him where he is, and he tells me he's celebrating Christmas. Ellie, that scares me. If he has to talk in code, then he's afraid someone is listening. That cabin must be what he meant. He lived with his father up in Indiana, you know. I got him during the summers. His father gave him everything he wanted: an ATV, guns, trips to Central America for spring breaks, even a boat. But what Harry failed to realize was that what Ronnie really wanted was his father, not his father's stuff, and he never did get that."

"Do you want me to go out there and try to talk with him?"

"Ellie, I would. I really would. I'm just his mother, you know. If I go out there, he'll just get mad at me and clam up." She motioned toward her foot. "Plus, I can't drive for the next couple weeks. Maybe you could get something out of him, I don't know." Jean rubbed her forehead and closed her eyes. "I'm sure I sound like a paranoid mother—an old mother at that—but I don't know where to turn, what to do."

"Jean. You know I'm DEA."

"Sure, hon."

"I'm not saying I won't help or that I won't go out there. I'm happy to do that. I only want to be transparent. If I find something that I need to report, that will put me in a dilemma."

"I understand."

"I'll tell you what. If I find out anything, I'll let you know what it is and will keep in you the loop. Okay?"

"Just help him, Ellie. Whatever this jam is he's gotten into...just help him out."

"I'll do my best, Jean. Does he have a number I can call him on?"

She shook her head. "He said he's keeping his phone off except for when he calls me."

Ellie stood up. "Get some rest. I'll head out there tomorrow afternoon, and we'll get all this straightened out."

CHAPTER SEVEN

ELLIE SHOT OFF HER LAST FIVE ROUNDS IN RAPID succession, and they all pierced the paper target thirty yards down range, all within four inches of center. She pressed the magazine release, and it fell into her hand. She set it on the concrete counter and slapped in a fresh one. Fifteen more rounds. She raised the gun, found her sights, and got off three more bursts of five each: five at the head, five at the chest, and a final five to the head. All but two shots had entered the red spaces she had aimed for and those, just a couple inches out.

She brought the gun down.

"You missed two. I can't believe it. What a letdown."

She smiled. She cleared the chamber and set down the weapon. She lifted her ear muffs, slipped them around her neck, and turned around. Tyler Borland came up and gave her a firm hug from the side. The hug was something new over the last couple weeks whenever they saw each other. Ellie found that she liked it very much.

"How was your class?" she asked. Then she frowned and said, "Your hat. It's not red."

"You know what? I knew there was something different about me today. I just couldn't place it." He shook his head.

Ellie didn't know if she had ever seen him without his red Hornady ball cap. She wasn't sure what to think. This one was dark blue and had Reticle's company logo stitched above the bill in white. "Why the change?"

"My mama. She thought it would be nice to have a hat with my logo on it."

"You ordered hats for the gun shop, didn't you?"

"I ordered hats for the gun shop," he said sheepishly, and then perked up. "Do you like them?"

She examined the hat. "I'm not sure. I'll have to get back to you."

"What? Really?"

"Of course I like it. It's a great idea."

He smiled, like he was relieved, like her opinion was the only one that really mattered. "Good, because I ordered branded koozies and t-shirts and keychains too."

"Koozies? That's big time, Tyler. You have a koozie with your logo on it and you're made."

"Stop it…"

"I want the first one out of the box."

"Done. They'll be here next week. Hopefully in time for Mango Mania."

"I thought you weren't doing the festival?"

"Someone dropped out, so it opened up a space. I've got a couple employees running the table for me. They've got Reticle set up right next to Wild Palm's table. Have you had their rum? Oh, man."

"I have. Major likes it too. That's the only rum he pushes at The Salty Mangrove now. Speaking of Mango Mania, I'm going to walk the festival that Saturday morning and then go fishing at Blind Pass." She jiggled her eyebrows, hoping to convince him to come out on the water with her.

His expression flattened. "Nope."

"Come *on*. It's just a boat, Tyler. Jaws isn't going to jump out of the water and grab you up."

"You don't know that. Besides, there's all kinds of stuff in those waters. I'm just fine with my boots in the dirt."

"I don't like your hat anymore. It's dumb."

"So we're six years old now, are we?" He winked at her and went off to oversee a private lesson on the long range.

Ellie reloaded her empty magazines, slipped her ear protection back on, and fired away.

CHAPTER EIGHT

JEAN OGLESBY'S TRACT OF HUNTING LAND SAT IN THE southeast quadrant of the intersection of State Road 70 and US Route 27, ten miles west of Lake Okeechobee, the Sunshine State's largest freshwater lake. Ellie had turned off Route 27 onto a silted road that cut through a thin forest of scrub oaks, hickory, and sand pines reaching upwards amongst clusters of cordgrass. Spanish moss hung lazily from the trees' fronds and branches, like old abandoned laundry still drying in the breeze. Ellie turned her Silverado left at the dead end and drove another mile before seeing a cabin on the right, tucked back into the trees. She slowed to five miles an hour, and her tires moved over exposed roots and small rocks dotting the long sandy driveway. She parked, grabbed a brown paper bag from the seat next to her, and got out.

The cabin's exterior was made of uncut cedar trunks split in half. Long strips of thin, aging bark hung off the wood, and cobwebs ran sporadically in the cracks between the posts. There was no awning, no porch. Just an aged pine door with a wooden handle. Ellie stepped up to it and knocked.

A commotion ensued behind the door. She heard someone scuffle to her left and then to the right, then the floorboards creaked as they came close to the door. "Who is it?" a man's voice snapped.

"Ronnie, it's Ellie O'Conner. Your mother sent me over to chat with you. She's worried about you."

"I don't know you. You need to leave. Right now."

Ellie had anticipated this. Almost down to his exact words. "I have Marlboro Red 100's in a soft pack. A whole carton, Ronnie. What else do I have in here?" She opened the bag and looked in. "Coke Zero, jalapeño bologna, and Twizzlers. Your mother says it's all still your favorite. So, the deal is you have to open the door. I'm not leaving this stuff on your doorstep."

There was no noise, no sound from inside for nearly half a minute. Finally, "How do I know you're friends with my mother?"

"Because I have jalapeño bologna."

Another five seconds and the door slowly opened. "Careful now," he said, stepping back with the door. Ellie walked in. She stepped over to an old farm table. The place smelled musty, a combination of sweat, dust, and old wood. She set the bag down and turned to see Ronnie shutting the door with his foot while training a .38 revolver at her chest. She raised her hands and stepped back. "Whoa there, Tiger. Ronnie, I'm only here on your mother's request. She's worried about you."

"Well, I told her not to be."

"That's not really the way it works."

His expression steeled. "Well, I know that, but what

else was I supposed to tell her?"

"Why don't you put that down and we can talk about it? Look," Ellie pinched the edges of her t-shirt and pulled it up until he could see her waistline. She slowly turned all the way around. "I'm not armed."

He pointed the gun to a high back easy chair in the corner. "Have a seat over there." Ellie complied. The cabin was tiny: one room consisting of the table, a couch, and the chair, a short kitchen counter with a stainless steel sink, two double beds at the far end. A deerskin rug sat on the floor in front of the couch. Two makeshift end tables summed up the furnishings; no refrigerator, not even a fireplace.

Ronnie sat on the couch across from his unexpected guest and kept the gun trained on her. He was an average looking man. His deep brown eyes looked tired, and his scraggly brown hair was uncombed. He wore a Ron Jon tank, and a thin gold chain hung from his neck. Days-old scruff covered his face, and a round pink scar the size of a dime sat right between his eyes, reminding Ellie of the bindis that Hindu and Jain women wore, only much larger. Yesterday, before Ellie had left Jean's house, Jean had showed her a picture of her son and had explained the scar. Ronnie had been eleven, bouncing a tennis ball on the wall of his father's work-shop while his old man, tipsy on Crown, was busy with a drill press, punching holes in a piece of pine intended to be part of a nightstand he was building. No one noticed that the press was loose, and his dad didn't see his boy running toward him, chasing the rogue tennis ball. Ronnie's father pulled down on the handle, the press slid off the table and right onto his kid. The boy's face ended up wedged between the press's table and the tip of the auger. The auger—a carbon-steel bit, its sharp point like a screw—was still spinning when Ronnie shifted and the feed level mashed onto the floor. That auger started in on him and went right to the bone, stopping just at the other side before getting into the gray matter. One in a million chance, his father had said. Ronnie, it seemed, was the one, and twenty-some years later he still had the bright scar to prove it.

"You know my mama?" he asked. "Then what's her favorite painting in her house? One she painted herself."

Ellie resolved herself to answering whatever questions he asked. "*The Dolphin on High Seas*. But I think she's gotten to calling it *The Jumping Dolphin*. Her original is framed in briarwood and hangs near the back door."

If he was impressed, he didn't show it. "Where did she work before she became a painter?"

It wasn't a very good question. That was public knowledge, probably on Jean's website. "She taught at Pine Island Elementary. She was my art teacher as a matter of fact."

He nodded like that impressed him more than her previous response. "What did she say about me?"

"You mean, did she tell me about you calling every Friday around lunchtime, that you missed a couple weeks, that you told her in code you were holed up out here?"

He still didn't look satisfied, but he stared at the floor and nodded to himself as if someone inside his head was telling him to trust her. He lowered the weapon and set it on his leg, leaving his hand splayed on top of the steel. He kept his stare on the floor. "You can't help me. It's ridiculous that you came."

"Maybe it is, but I don't have anything better to do.

So why don't you humor me and give me an idea as to what kind of trouble you're in. You're shut away in here like a scared fox, so unless you think this is just going to blow over, then at least give me something. If not for me, then for your mother." She watched him as he sat there, his nose flaring, his lips drawing a hard line while he decided whether or not to let the cat out of the bag. When he sighed and his shoulders slumped, she knew the proverbial cat was getting out of the proverbial bag.

"It's just all messed up," he said. "Was never supposed to be like this." He stood up, walked a few paces to a cabinet above the sink, and took out a bottle of gold Bacardi. He set the gun on the counter and poured a generous measure of rum into a plastic cup and had it down in two chugs. He wiped his mouth with the heel of his hand and leaned back against the counter. "After Harlan died, we started selling pot." He shifted his eyes toward her to gauge a reaction. She presented none. Ellie had already decided she was going to keep her cards close to the chest. Ronnie didn't need to know she was DEA; not yet. It would only spook him, and she would be on the other side of his cabin door within a few seconds. She kept listening.

"It was just a little at first. It's how we started funding ourselves. I didn't think it was all that big of a deal. It's not like we were selling heroin to kids. But then Oswald, he called a meeting one day and said we're going to be moving guns now. Now I know it ain't right selling drugs at all, but I drew the line right there. See I'm not talkin' little .22 plinksters or .410 shotguns. I mean the mothers. Military grade crap. Anti-materiel crossovers like Barrett XM500s and short-stroke SIG MCXs."

Ellie shot up an eyebrow. She had never shot the MCX; it had been procured a year after she left Brussels. But the Barrett she had fired on many occasions. It was a .50 caliber designed to penetrate armored vehicles and concrete barriers.

"And no way in hell I'm messing with black-market firearms," Ronnie continued. "Dawson felt the same way. That's all a whole 'nother level, and then you have to start dealing with the people that are willing to find that kind of stuff. I'm talking the kind of people that you don't double-cross; and if you do, the kind of people where someone has to change out the carpet when they're done with you."

"Ronnie, back up for me a little bit. Who is Harlan?"

"Harlan Tucker." He said the name confidently, proudly, like she would know who he was. When all he got back was a blank stare, he said, somewhat quizzically, "Harlan Tucker, the Enlightened Cowboy?"

She shrugged. "I'm sorry...I've never heard of him."

Ronnie rolled his eyes. "Harlan was the truest purveyor of wisdom and national honor America has had in decades. He wrote this." He stood, walked over to an end table, and picked up a paperback book. He handed it to Ellie.

She read the title out loud. "*The Patriot's Handbook of Anarchy.*" The back cover had a small black-and-white photo of an older man sporting a trimmed white beard and wearing a leather vest complete with a bolo necktie. The book was dog eared and creased all along the spine, worn like it had been read and reread a dozen times.

"That there is the best book written in the last century." Ellie wasn't sure Ronnie had all the qualifications to make such an assessment, but she didn't push back. He stuck his hand out, and Ellie gave him back the book. He returned to the couch.

"Harlan fought in Vietnam for a cause he couldn't get behind. When he got sent back stateside early because of a shrapnel wound—'home alive in sixty-five' he used to say—he realized he was a mockery to his countrymen. And after everything he saw over there, he quit life and became homeless for twenty years before some guy in a downtown mission gave him a talking-to about purpose and change. It lit a fire under him, and Harlan started speaking against the injustices of our government and the need to bring back the national pride as conceived in the early days of the Republic. After a while of leading a small grassroots movement, he wrote this." He held the book up again. "It's his magnum opioid."

Ellie grit her teeth to keep from outwardly smiling at the misnomer.

Ronnie kept going. "Harlan spoke about things that a lot of us always felt but could never put words to. Like how the government keeps taking our liberties instead of being the institution that protects them. Harlan was different than a lot of these other guys like him who lead groups like ours. He didn't hate blacks or Jews like the skinheads do. He wasn't interested in harassing people or looting like the Hells Angels. To him, liberty was not found by getting rid of ethnic groups but by bringing harmony between them." Ronnie lifted his shoulders, and his chin followed. He said, "'We are a distracted people. Television, entertainment, concerts, and video games are robbing our youth of the beatific vision of our country's founders. We were meant to make a better world for all that shall come later, not squander what we have so there is nothing left to leave behind. We must stand up and fight for righteousness, to fight for freedom, to fight for truth. Our society remains in a rapid state of decay, and men and women no longer understand how to work together for a common goal. Unless we act, no one else will.'" Ronnie looked back at Ellie with moist eyes. "That's from the book. I memorized that last year. Page one hundred and seventy eight."

Ellie took note of a simplicity about Ronnie. It wasn't stupidity. Unrefined maybe, but from all she could tell, Ronnie meant well. The Enlightened Cowboy had given him something to believe in.

"You mentioned a Dawson," Ellie said. "Who is that?"

"Dawson…" Ronnie's voice trailed off. He started picking at the little fuzz balls in the fabric of the couch cushion for a little too long. Maybe the rum had kicked in. He had probably been enjoying some prior to her arrival.

"Ronnie," Ellie said.

He head jerked up. He blinked. "Sorry. Sorry. Dawson...right?"

She nodded.

"He's my friend. The best friend I've ever had. Dawson Montgomery. I was supposed to meet him at a truckstop in Arcadia a few days ago and then we'd roll out here together. But he never showed, and I'll tell you what, Dawson always shows. Always. You could set a watch to him." Ronnie looked at her suspiciously, as if he was deciding whether or not he wanted to tell her something more. "What I'm gonna say now you have to swear this stays here. I don't want my mama finding out. Deal?"

"Sure. Deal."

He sighed. "Dawson got busted last year for moving pot. They never tied it back to our group, and it wasn't anything more serious than that, and it was only a second offense so he didn't get the whole book. So he was out in seven months, and as it goes with parole requirements he had to get a," Ronnie made air quotes, "'real job.' So he did. He got a 'real job.'" Finger quotations again. He paused and looked at Ellie once more with untrusting eyes, then kept on. "He's had this job at a convenience store in LaBelle for a few months now. Red Rover, they call it. Problem is not long after Dawson gets out, then he revved up the ol' easy money engine again. Only this time it wasn't pot, it was cocaine." Ronnie put up two defensive hands. "I didn't know he was. I swear. I quit dealing anything myself after Dawson got nabbed last year. Until I bolted and came out here, I'd been putting in forty hours a week doing the night shift stocking shelves at Winn Dixie. Anyway, Dawson said they had this particular shipment coming in that was hidden in repurposed dairy boxes. Cocaine at the bottom, and a layer of packed cheese—like Kraft or something—over that." Ronnie nervously rubbed the back of his neck. "Dawson called me in a panic. Said that he had gone to the back section of the Red Rover to check the boxes and what had come in a few hours earlier had been changed up."

"Changed up? How so?"

"So Dawson...one time every month he gets the closing shift at the Red Rover which ends at midnight, and then he has to turn around and open up at six a.m.

So on that night he just stays there with the lights out, and they come in through the back and drop off the goods. Then a little while later the distributor comes in and grabs it up. But this time," he shook a finger, "he receives the boxes then happens to fall asleep behind the front counter. He wakes up at around three and hears a sound in the back, and when he gets back there ain't no one around. He opens the back door, ain't no one around outside either. So for good measure he checks the boxes again and notices that the packets of cheese had been disturbed. He digs further, sees the cocaine, digs further and sees...guns. *Guns*. Not only that, some of the coke was gone to make room for the weapons. And that's the moment the distributor gives their little rap on the back door. They're there for pick-up. So he lets them in and takes them back to the walk-in cooler and tells them what's in the boxes and can't explain the guns or the missing drugs. Near twenty kilos, man, just—swish—gone. The distributor is pissed and doesn't take anything. I guess them and Dawson got the ol' bamboozle. The distributor left empty-handed."

"So it was after that when Dawson was going to meet you at the truck stop?" she asked.

"Yeah. Right after. He calls me from the store *fuh-reaking* out and I tell him to just play it cool and not to saying anything until we could figure something out. But he called me back a few hours after the store opened and said he was too scared to stick around." Ronnie had started pacing and ended up at the Bacardi again from which he proceeded to help himself to another couple fingers. "I tell him to just call Oswald and be honest and tell him what happened, and that's what he does. He finally gets in touch with him a little after lunch, but apparently Oswald accuses him of lying and said he was sending someone up there to get him so they could have a little chat."

"So he bolted," Ellie said.

"Yeah. So he bolted; rings me up right before, and I tell him where to meet. Dawson didn't have a car, so I don't know what he was talking about when he called again and said he ran out of gas and now he had to walk it. I think his phone died in the middle of him talking. Anyway, he doesn't show. I wait a few hours and he still doesn't show and I think the worst and jet. My car is in the shop, so I hitched a ride to the exit and walked out here and haven't heard anymore from Dawson. I put the battery back in my phone and walk toward the highway every morning so I can get reception and check voicemail, but I haven't gotten any calls except from my mama and my landlord." Ronnie stopped pacing and sat on the edge of the couch. "They got him. I know it. I don't even know if he's still alive."

"Tell me about this Oswald fellow you mentioned?"

Ronnie blinked a couple times, and a light entered his eyes. "Wait, you said you brought smokes?"

"I did."

He walked over to the brown bag on the table. Peering in, he stuck his hand down and brought out the carton of Marlboros. "Damn if I forgot you said these were in here." He popped the flaps, drew out a pack, and went over to a drawer near the sink and pulled out a blue Bic lighter. He opened a pack, withdrew a stick and lit it up, and closed his eyes as the nicotine hit his blood. He breathed out a thin haze and plopped back onto the couch.

"So toward the end Harlan—Harlan died a couple

years ago—he took Oswald under his wing and spent most of his time with him, grooming him as it were to carry the torch once he was gone. But as it turns out Oswald wasn't too keen on any of Harlan's beliefs. He just liked the idea of being able to rally people to a cause. So when Harlan died, Oswald pulled all literature —posters, pamphlets—and canceled campus gatherings and rallies. He's a smart guy. Smarter than I gave him credit for at first. He sifted us until only the faithful were remaining. Those faithful to his new vision."

"Which was what?"

Ronnie drew down on his cigarette again. "Pretty simple now that I look back on it. He said that in order to really change things you have to have influence and that the surest way to have influence is to have money. Money and power get things done. The quickest way to get the most money the fastest is on the black market. He's eccentric and a little weird sometimes, but he's," Ronnie tapped his head with a forefinger, "a really smart guy. Most of us just fell in line. You know the whole, 'the ends justifies the....the…things'?"

"The means?"

"Yeah. That. The means. He wanted to turn things around and start building cash flow, so he started kicking people out of the group and only inviting those of us to the meetings who were willing to put the old ideas on pause for a season so we could have more influence later. And Dawson, he kept on— say, you want a smoke? I haven't even offered you one."

"Thanks. I don't smoke."

"Okay. Sure. So Dawson, he kept on believing. I got out a few months ago. Started seeing it for what it all was—that ol' Oswald had no interest in returning to

Harlan's ways." He picked the book back up and stared at the small author photo on the back, then turned it over and clutched the book hard, like it was his best friend in the world, holding onto it as if it were a Bible, he a preacher criss-crossing the sawdust trails, prepared to hail the faithful word underneath the windswept flaps of a makeshift tabernacle.

Ellie remembered what Jean had said about her son. How his father had never been there for him. Ellie had seen the negative effects of such relationships up close when she was in Albania five years ago. She was three weeks into an insertion, gathering intel on a shoemaker suspected of being a middle man; selling U.S. secrets on behalf of the highest bidder. During her time there she'd seen the many teenage boys and young men with an eagle's wing tattooed on the top of one hand; the mark of the feared Lushnja Gang, one small appendage of the country's growing mafia presence. Albania was known to have one of the highest crime-generating elements in the world, and they stuffed their ranks with young, fatherless men looking for meaning, purpose, and a sense of belonging.

Ellie never would forget the snowy evening she was in Tirana, walking back to her flat with a takeout bag of tavë kosi—baked lamb with rice—when a young man stepped from an alleyway, jabbed a gun into her ribs, and told her to keep walking. Ellie got a look into his eyes and saw the fear in them. He was probably no older than sixteen. She could feel the muzzle of the gun vibrating in her ribs as his hand shook nervously. It was a rite of passage for this boy. If he brought her back to their lair, he would be in; one of them. They would let him have his way with her, and then the rest of them would too. Then they would sell her into another country as a sex slave, or possibly cut her open and harvest her organs on the black market. The boy barked at her in his native tongue and kept an arm across her shoulders to make it look like he was a loving boyfriend shielding his girl from the cold. "You don't want to do this," Ellie whispered.

"Yes. Yes, I do. Shut up," he replied in haltering English.

Ellie stole another glance at his uncovered face. He hardly had black fuzz for a mustache, his round cheeks, pink in the cold, looking like ripened peaches. It was not the face of a hardened man who kidnapped unsuspecting ladies off the street. He led her down an alley and was just about to open the back door to a vacant restaurant when she doubled over, faking a sharp pain in her abdomen. She groaned loudly, and, as the kid leaned down to see what was wrong, Ellie brought her knee up hard, and it connected with his nose. Blood gushed out onto her jeans, and he fell back into a pile of dirty snow. She took his gun, removed the chambered round, removed the magazine, and then dismantled the slide before dropping it all at his feet.

"Bad boy," she said, and walked away. The kid was probably executed for his failure. The Albanians were not known for their mercy. They were ruthless and vigorous in their violence. She wouldn't have been able to do anything for him. He had chosen his own path. She wasn't there to save the world or protect young punks, just her country's secrets.

Harlan Tucker would have been the father Ronnie never had access to in his youth, Oswald the older brother. Ronnie would have imbibed whatever Tucker was selling, and in this case it happened to be a neo-patriotic worldview. Tucker would have been a charismatic man who not only gave these boys something to believe in but also gave their hands something to do about it. It was the perfect combination of passion and ability. Only they had lost their father too soon, and their older brother stepped in to lead them astray.

Ellie stood up. "Ronnie, why don't you come back with me?"

"No. No way. I'm fine right here. I mean, food is running a bit low, but I'm not going anywhere."

"Your mother is worried about you. It would make her feel a lot better if you came back and stayed with her for a while."

"No. No way," he repeated. "It would be too easy for Oswald to find me."

Ellie wasn't certain that Ronnie wasn't being overly cautious, but she conceded. "All right. Look, why don't I come back in a couple days, and I'll bring you some real food? If you've changed your mind, then you can come back with me."

"Thanks." He opened the door. "Why are you doing this for me?"

"Like I said, your mom is a friend of mine." She stepped outside, slid her sunglasses down off her forehead, and turned around. "Ronnie, we've all made poor choices from time to time and come out the other side wondering how we even got there. You seem like a decent guy." She looked into his eyes. "I hope I'm not wrong about that."

He returned her gaze, the expression holding a measure of the simplicity that Ellie had noted earlier. "You're not."

CHAPTER NINE

RINGO'S HOME WAS NESTLED ON THREE AND A HALF acres in west Iona on the southern edge of the Caloosahatchee River. His seven thousand square foot mansion sat in the center of perfectly manicured lawns and gardens and was hedged in by eight foot high laurels that provided ample privacy on either side. The front of the property was graced with generous groupings of tall slash pines, white oaks, and royal palms, through which a sand lime brick driveway snaked in thirty yards off the main road and ended in a broad semicircle at the front door. A white marble fountain of three jumping dolphins sat in the center of the turnabout, surrounded by a bed of yellow tulips and bright pink gerbera.

He loved being here, here on the water with direct and easy access to anywhere he wanted to go along Florida's eastern seaboard. There was a downside, however. It was his proximity to Saint James City, which lay only seven miles to his west off the mouth of the river. But being further away would be cumbersome. This was the best location from which he could run his business, but it meant that he had to be careful when coming out on his dock during the daylight hours, couldn't present himself to those cruising the river or even friendly neighbors. The neighbors, however, were not much to be concerned with. To his right and his left, along with most of those in the immediate area, the neighbors came down to vacation only a couple months out of the year, their mansion in Iona was one of two or three that they kept around the world. Any interest they might have in knowing their neighbors was generally mitigated by a greater desire to get out on the golf course or a fishing boat that was heading out to deep waters.

Ringo sat in a cedar Adirondack chair, staring at the river before him, its surface reflecting the full moonlight, its waters flowing like liquid coal. The tip of his cigar glowed against the darkness, making a searing sound as he puffed patiently on the end and the dry leaves were eaten by the fire.

Far behind him, Andrés and Chewy came out of the back door of the home, walked past the pool and the honeysuckle-covered trellis, and made their way out to their boss. He could hear the padding of their feet when they hit the dock. They stopped next to him. Ringo motioned toward two additional chairs. "Have a seat, gentlemen."

They sat. Andrés looked at Chewy, then out to the water. A ways out, a catamaran slid through the river, heading to open water. A salty breeze was present, but soft, gentle, welcomed after a hot and humid summer day.

Ringo took another slow draw off his cigar, let the smoke curl in his mouth, and then released it without haste. He kept his eyes on the water. "Eli Oswald has become a problem."

"Guns?" Andrés asked.

"Yes. Guns. Was our understanding not made clear to him?" Ringo asked.

"It was," Chewy said. "Very clear. As always. What kind of guns?"

"Military grade. Moving it along with our product. In the same cases. Six weeks I've been working with this man. Six weeks and he already breaks one of my rules. What is wrong with the world that people can no longer keep their agreements?"

Twenty minutes went by. No one spoke. Ringo finished his cigar. He looked at Andrés, who was now leaning forward with his elbows on his knees. "What do you think the consequences should be?"

"He broke rule number one." He said so in a way that made the conclusion obvious.

"But he's not a part of my organization," Ringo said. He had already made up his mind, and the two men sitting with him knew it.

"When someone does business with you, they are a part of your organization," Andrés replied. "He needs to go."

"I want us to lay low for a while," Ringo said. "I trust you both. If we need to pull back somewhere, then pull back. We didn't come this far by being greedy or foolish. Aldrich would like us to wait a couple weeks to give him room to work an angle with Eli Oswald."

"What kind of angle?" Chewy asked.

"A consequence for breaking one of my rules and increasing our exposure."

Chewy stood and took a couple steps to the edge of

the dock. He flipped up the collar of his wool trench coat, scratched at his beard. "This could get ATF involved if they ever find out about him."

"Hence Aldrich's plan," Ringo replied. "The last thing we need is two agencies scanning the horizon for us."

Five minutes of silence. Finally Chewy, soberly and reflectively, said, "Yesterday is not ours to recover, but tomorrow is ours to win or lose."

Ringo nodded. He smiled broadly. "Amen. Amen indeed."

CHAPTER TEN

ELLIE, known to her six teammates simply as Pascal, stood at one end of the ping pong table, waiting for the ball to be served. Faraday, the other woman on TEAM 99, said the score and served. The thin plastic ball shot over the net and landed on Ellie's side of the table before speeding off at an angle. Ellie reached for it but missed getting her paddle on it by a quarter inch, giving Faraday the point.

"Good one," she said.

They were in the large common room on the second floor of the compound, where a fully equipped kitchen stood in one corner with an eating area adjacent. The other half of the room consisted of a pool table, the ping pong table, a few leather couches, a flat screen TV, and several different gaming consoles. A neglected dart board hung near the pool table.

Cicero was on the couch, clutching a bottle of Gatorade, streaming an early episode of *24*. Virgil—the largest, most muscular member of the team—walked into the room and opened the refrigerator, said to the food, "Hey, I'm not telling you anything unless you give me immunity."

Ellie and Faraday snickered. Cicero rolled his eyes but kept silent.

"Trust...me," Virgil quipped again. Cicero sat up, turned around, and threw the remote at his teammate. Virgil swiveled and snatched the device from the air before it hit him. "You throw like a girl."

"Hey," Faraday said defensively, and brushed her dark bangs from her eyes, "I can throw better than that."

A sigh from the couch. "Would you guys shut it? I'm trying to watch this."

Virgil grabbed a rotisserie chicken off a shelf and shut the refrigerator door. He set it on the counter, grinned, and said, "Nobody says 'hit me' when Jack Bauer deals blackjack."

"When life gave Jack Bauer lemons, he used them to kill terrorists," Ellie said.

Faraday: "When Google can't find something, it asks Jack Bauer for help."

And so it went that whenever Cicero opted to watch *24* in the common area, he got a communal ribbing. Every time. Someone had suggested he was a sucker for pain, but the truth was that Cicero was the foremost extrovert of the group and didn't much like watching television in his room. "Come on, you guys," he said.

"Bauer is like the best character ever. I'd even stick him a notch above MacGyver."

"Whoooa!" the room said in unison.

"Dude. Not cool," Ellie said.

Virgil had torn a leg off the chicken. He pointed it at Cicero. "You keep making comments like that, and we might be less motivated to watch your six next time. Better than MacGyver? Please…"

At the ping pong table it was Faraday's serve again. With a quick release of the ball and tap of her paddle, she sent it across the net. Ellie reached out and punched it back over. It bounced into the far corner and out of Faraday's reach. "That's the game," Ellie said. She set her paddle on the table, stepped up to the whiteboard on the wall, and put another tick mark next to her name.

"One more game?" Faraday urged. "Come on."

"I think I'll end on a high note," Ellie said. "Keep practicing. You'll get me one of these days."

She walked across the room and patted Cicero's shoulder as she passed the couch. "Hey, you should make a commitment not to say stupid stuff anymore." He shook his head and waved her off. Ellie went over to the fridge and brought out a cold bottle of water.

"When does Voltaire get back?" Faraday asked.

"Tonight," Virgil said, still tugging meat off the chicken and putting it on a plate. "I think that's what Mortimer said. Why?"

"He's the only one around here I can beat in ping pong," she said.

Ellie chugged the water down in one go and tossed the bottle in the garbage. She noticed a thin gauze wrap on Virgil's right hand. "Did you cut yourself shaving again?" she grinned.

"I wish. No, got it last night when I was adjusting the timing belt on my truck." He winked at her.

Over half of the missions the team were given, they went together—all seven of them. The other missions were delegated and assigned as matched their individual abilities, skills, and strengths. When the latter, they were not allowed to share details of the operation with anyone else. If two other teammates were assigned to go out with you, that's all who knew about it. "Not your mission, not your business." It was one of the ground rules and one that would swiftly get you booted off the team if broken. As yet, no one was willing to test the boundaries.

Virgil didn't have a truck. None of them, in fact, had personal vehicles. Not here in Belgium anyway. His reply was his way of saying that he couldn't talk about it. "Well, I hope the truck is all right." Ellie smiled back. She liked Virgil. He walked a proper line between serious and jokester, always knowing when the best time was to exercise which quality. In contrast, Voltaire, their team's leader, was sober-minded, generally serious and thoughtful. It was one of the qualities that made him good at his job, what made him such an exceptional leader. It was also the quality that reminded her the most of her father.

"It's on the mend."

"I'm going to go be productive," Ellie said. "I'll see you guys later." She exited the common room and turned down the hall. A door clicked shut at the other end, and hard-soled footsteps echoed down the concrete corridor. Two men appeared from around the corner, both in suits and ties.

She easily recognized one as her boss—TEAM 99's director. Mortimer was a wide, pear-shaped man who, in spite of the extra weight, had a distinguished appearance: strong cheekbones, well-placed nose, and low eyebrows that were set over piercing eyes. The other man she knew by reputation only, having never met him in person. He was Scott Reardon and served in a leading role at the Directorate of Mission Services for the Defense Intelligence Agency, a position that had him coordinating the dissemination of counterintelligence to the DIA in particular and to the Department of Defense in general.

Both men acknowledged Ellie with a nod as they passed. No words were exchanged.

It wasn't the first time Ellie had seen a high ranking member of the government walk these halls. As it was, the compound was located at the north end of an airplane hangar at the U.S. Army Garrison at Benelux, just five minutes from NATO headquarters in Brussels. On top of that, TEAM 99 was engaged in the most clandestine of operations sanctioned by the U.S. government, and it wasn't a strange event to see the men making decisions come to speak with the team's director in person.

Ellie walked into her economically decorated room and shut the door behind her. A small desk was on the wall opposite her bed. She pulled the chair out, sat down, and fired up her personal laptop. For the thousandth time her eyes went to the picture pinned to the wall: her father, Major, and her younger sister Katie huddled together down at The Salty Mangrove, holding half-empty glasses, the three of them making goofy faces. Katie had sent Ellie the picture earlier in the year. Ellie's family didn't know where she was stationed, but they had an address at Langley where they could send things to her. From there, the mail would be forwarded to her here at the compound.

She missed them all. Deeply. One day, she knew, she would leave all this and go home and be with her loved ones. But that day wasn't now. And it wouldn't be tomorrow either. For the foreseeable future she was doing exactly what she had been made to do. Not only was she exceptional at it, she loved it as well. There were missions, of course, that were more challenging than others. And they didn't always go as planned. Sometimes the wrong people were caught in the crossfire or the bad guys got away. It was rare, but it did happen. Even the members of such an elite group as TEAM 99 were human. Sometimes you did everything right—trained, planned, strategized, researched—and the dice just didn't fall in your favor.

Her laptop chimed, and she navigated through her browser to her Gmail account. She had a new email from Major. They wrote to each other at least once a week, sometimes more, never less. She heard from her father and sister as much too. Katie had recently broken the news that she was pregnant. The baby's father, it seemed, had no interest in hanging around. It wasn't ideal, but that baby would have everything it needed in its grandfather and Major, the two best men on Earth in Ellie's opinion. Ellie was going to be an aunt, and she smiled every time she thought of it.

She read Major's email, clicked reply, and started typing.

MORTIMER WALKED into his office and shut the door behind Scott Reardon. The two men had cordially shaken hands on the helipad three minutes prior but as yet had not spoken. Neither man had a reputation for initiating or enduring small talk. They had each gotten to where they were, respectively, because of their repudiation of trivialities and formalities. Both were company men and, as such, were swift to get down to business. Mortimer walked behind his desk and sat down. He extended a hand toward a chair. "Have a seat."

Reardon did not have a seat. Instead, he walked to the expansive window behind Mortimer and looked out, his hands clasped lazily behind his back. He was of average height, his brown hair peppered with gray. He looked down on a double barbed wire fence that formed the perimeter of the Army garrison and then beyond, where a forest filled with elms and English oaks grew tall.

Mortimer waited for him to speak. Reardon's visit to the compound was unusual; unexpected, although not completely out of the ordinary. The men represented the interests of two different agencies: Reardon, the DIA, which was the principal source of foreign intelligence for combat related missions; Mortimer, the CIA, which, historically, had been focused on providing intelligence to the President and his Cabinet. In the upper echelons of the agencies, such lines became fuzzy, if non-existent. The two men's paths did cross from time to time, as intelligence exchanged hands, when personnel or information needed to be shared across agency lines. There were very few within the CIA who even knew of TEAM 99's existence. Reardon was one of the even fewer outside of the Agency who was privy to that knowledge.

Reardon unclasped his hands and casually slipped a large photo from his suit jacket. He turned it upwards and laid it on the desk, pointed to one of the three people in the picture. "That's you, isn't it?" was all he said.

Mortimer was now fifty-nine years old, and during his distinguished intelligence career he'd held positions at the Pentagon, the NSA, and, for the last twelve years, the CIA, opting four years ago to head up TEAM 99 over an appointment as the Deputy Director of the National Clandestine Service. Ever a pragmatist, less a politician, he ended up choosing the former on the principle that he would be more effective in the field. Now, the color crawling up his neck and reaching for his hairline matched the red in Reardon's tie. "Where did you get this?" Mortimer growled, not taking his eyes off the image.

"I'm not sure that matters." Reardon, now that he had Mortimer's attention, walked around to the front of the desk. He sat down in one of the two armchairs. He crossed a leg over the other. He folded his hands and rested them on a knee. "The way I see it is that you don't have many options. There are a couple more of those too. Different dates, in case you're wondering."

Mortimer didn't glare at him, although he wanted to. His expression was flat, unreadable. Unfortunately, in this circumstance it didn't matter. He knew it didn't matter. He was now in the inescapable net of the most politically ruthless American he had ever met. "So what do you want?"

It was the question Reardon had come all this way to hear. His expression, too, was flat and hard eyed, but inside he held a slight smile. "I have a proposition for you."

Mortimer stood. It was his turn to look out the window. His throat felt constricted. He wiggled a couple of meaty fingers behind the knot in his tie and pulled out on the collar. There was no sense in getting emotional about the photos. What was done was done. He couldn't go back and change it. And Reardon, in cases like this, was not to be bargained with. If Mortimer knew anything about the man, he knew that much.

He turned back around, his face set hard, his eminent career—his life—now in the hands of one who was surely more viper than human. "Let's hear it."

CHAPTER ELEVEN

Ellie rapped her knuckles against the cabin door and immediately heard a shuffle from inside. "Ronnie, it's Ellie." Silence, and then the door cracked open, and all she could see was an eyeball set against the darkness of the interior. "See? Just me," she said.

"You're alone?"

"I am. Your mother wanted to come out, but she just had her foot surgery and can't drive right now. That, and she's planning for the mango festival. It's her busiest time of the year, you know."

The door swung open. "Come on." She went in, and Ronnie took a lingering and nervous gaze outside before stepping back in and quickly shutting the door behind him.

The only light was a gas-burning lamp set on the small table in what could be deemed the kitchen area. "You need more light in here, Ronnie. You're going to go crazy without it. At least keep the door open."

"I'm fine," he shot back. "I'm not keeping that door open. Not taking any chances if Oswald figures out where I am. He looked at Ellie's empty hands. "I thought you were bringing me some stuff."

"I did. The bags are in the car. I can bring them in if you decide to stay."

"I told you when you were here the other day that I'm not leaving. Oswald don't know about the place."

Ellie pulled the only card she had. The only one she needed. "You know, Ronnie, you say that, but wasn't Dawson going to meet you here?"

"Yeah. That's what I said. What's it matter?"

"Well, if I go along with your suspicion that Dawson got nabbed by this Eli Oswald, then isn't there a chance that your buddy might talk, might give you up?"

A connection registered behind Ronnie eyes. His shoulders visibly straightened. "Ah, hell. I hadn't thought of that." He rubbed the back of his neck and started pacing.

"You've been here nearly a week now, so maybe Dawson hasn't talked...yet."

Ronnie groaned.

"Look. Come on back. It's probably not best that you stay with your mother if they really are looking for you. You know The Salty Mangrove, don't you?"

"Sure. Who doesn't?"

"My uncle is the owner. I had a talk with him about your situation, and he's agreed to let you stay at his place."

"Your uncle is Warren Hall? *The* Warren Hall?"

"Yes."

His mouth unhinged, and he stared at Ellie like he now considered her to be from royal descent. "I can stay at *his* place? Really?"

"He's a good man and doesn't have anyone living

with him. He's happy to help you lay low until all this blows over."

"But what if Oswald finds out? Does your uncle have a house alarm?"

His naiveté forced Ellie to contain a laugh. From all that Ronnie had said about Eli Oswald, it didn't appear that he might be the kind of person who would allow a standard residential security system to stop him. "He won't find out, Ronnie. The only people who will know are myself, your mother, and my uncle."

"You swear?"

"Yes. I swear."

He chewed on his bottom lip, thinking. "All right. Fine," he conceded.

Ellie motioned to the couch. "Have a seat, Ronnie. Just for a second."

"Um, okay." He went over to the couch and sat into it. Ellie took a chair next to him. "So here's the deal. I need to tell you something before we leave. Something you should know before you agree to come back with me."

"Okay…"

"Let me say first that your mother trusts me. So let's get that out there."

"What are you trying to say?"

"I'm getting there. But I want you to know that I'm here because, more than anything, I want to help as a friend. With that said," she paused and watched his expression, "you need to know that I'm a contracted investigator for the Drug Enforcement Agency."

Ronnie bolted from the couch like the cushion had just morphed into a red hot eye of an electric stovetop. "What? You're with the DEA?" He let out a string of curses. When he turned back around he wore a menacing glare. "You said I could trust you!"

"Ronnie. Calm down. I'm not here because I'm DEA. It just so happens that I work for them. But I wanted you to know before we got a week or two down the road and you found out from someone else."

"But I didn't do anything."

She extended a reassuring hand. "I know that. But in the interest of full disclosure you needed to be aware. If your old group of friends are in fact still moving drugs, then I'll need to notify my office of that. As long as everything you've told me is the truth, then you have nothing to worry about."

It took five more minutes for Ellie to calm Ronnie down, another five to get him to gather up what little he had and get into her truck. They put the little cabin behind them and bumped along the sandy road for a half mile before turning right and heading in the direction that would lead them to Route 27 two miles ahead. In the distance Ellie saw the bright glare of the sun winking off what she assumed to be a windshield. Soon the vehicle was near enough for her to see that it was a car. An orange car. Ronnie, who had been squinting down the road, suddenly tensed. "Is that a Mustang? Can you tell?"

"It looks like one from here. Why?"

"Curtis has a supercharged orange Mustang." Ronnie's breathing quickened, and his voice went shrill. "Oh man. Oh man, they found me. They found—"

"Ronnie!" Ellie's quick, harsh tone shut him down. "Relax, okay? It's all right. My truck sits a lot higher than the car. Just duck down by the floorboards. They'll think I'm alone. Now hurry before they get close enough to see your silhouette."

He nodded frantically. "Yeah. Okay." He unbuckled and slinked down and tucked his head below the seat.

"What does Curtis look like?" she asked.

"Uhh...creepy. Got his brow pierced and a few gold teeth. Got one of those expressions that makes you think he's in deep with the devil. Which he is," he added, laying emphasis on each of the last three words.

The Mustang continued its approach, and Ellie slowed and moved as close to the edge as she could. The road was narrow, fringed on either side by forestry and shrubs. Her windows were rolled down, as were the ones in the Mustang. She locked eyes with the driver and gave him a short but polite nod as they slowly passed each other. He had bleach-blonde hair, a stud piercing his left eyebrow, and a couple gold teeth glimmering behind a curled lip. He wore a gray wife-beater, and a tattoo swept down his neck. With her truck riding as high as it was, the passenger was out of view. He smiled at her—more like a menace—and Ellie brought the Silverado back to the middle of the road.

"Was it him?" Ronnie asked.

"Yes."

Another groan. "Oh, Jesus on a donkey. They found me. Dawson, he...he must've talked. That must mean they have him."

Ellie kept her eyes latched on the rearview to see what direction they would turn when they arrived at the end of the road. Ronnie stayed down near the floor but lifted his head. "Where'd they turn?"

She waited. "Left. They turned left. They're gone. You can get up now."

When Ronnie returned to his seat, his hands were trembling. He didn't seem to care that she noticed. "The only place down on the left is my cabin."

"I know. But you're not there, okay? Relax. I'll get you back safely, and they won't find out we've got you at my uncle's. Just be glad I didn't show up a half hour after I did."

Then Ronnie said, in a moment of hopeful, if not naive, optimism, "Maybe they won't know I was there, and it will be a dead end for them."

"The lamp will be warm. It doesn't matter. Buckle up."

"What did they do to him to make him give me up?" he asked himself out loud.

Ellie turned off the dirt road and drove south on US Route 27. Saint James City was nearly two hours away.

CHAPTER TWELVE

If you asked the locals where you could get the best cup of coffee around, they'd hit you with The Perfect Cup, nine times out of ten. The nine would, of course, be right, and the one could be properly accused of possessing taste buds that had never quite fully matured. Ellie sat at a corner table in the small, cozy restaurant and took down her last spoonful of seafood chowder before nudging the bowl to the other side of the table. She stood up and went to the self service bar at the back wall to refill her coffee. Selecting the blonde roast, she added cream and went back to her table. The empty chowder bowl was gone. She looked at the time on her phone. She had arrived here a half hour early for her meeting with Mark and Garrett. The three of them had a meeting at the office set for earlier this morning, but Garrett ended up having to push it back a few hours and offered to come closer to Ellie.

She picked up the copy of the Pine Island Eagle she had brought in with her. The cover featured stories on hurricane preparedness, some road construction in

Bokeelia, and a lead article remembering the life of Jim Dodgers, a long time resident who had fought with the 23rd Infantry/Americal Division in Vietnam and had been deeply involved with Post 136 of the American Legion. Jim had a fondness for the water, and on several occasions Ellie had chatted with him down at the marina. Jim had been one of those rare people who, after spending only a few minutes with you, had you walking away believing that he really did like you, whoever you were. And of course, he did. Jim could make you feel like a million bucks because he thought you really were a million bucks; he just didn't discriminate. Ellie remembered him telling her once that love is what made the world a better place. Not a hippie kind of love, but true affection that was grounded in a belief that sometimes all a person needed was for someone else to believe in them. Men like Jim Dodgers weren't replaceable. They could only be missed.

Ellie opened the paper. Page two featured a full list of vendors for Mango Mania and a map of where each one would be positioned at the south end of the island. The adjacent page was dedicated entirely to Jean Oglesby and her art. A captioned picture of her smiling next to a bright painting of Jimmy Buffett acknowledged Jean as the queen of exhibitionist art in these local waters. Ellie had set the painting she had purchased for Major in her guest bedroom closet. Citrus was a good dog, but he was still a dog, and the last thing she needed was to come home one day and see bits of canvas hanging from his lips. Katie and Chloe would be back next week, and they all planned on having a small family party for Major soon after their arrival. Ellie was happy to say that the painting was from all three of them.

An older couple stood up from their table and waved a thank you toward the counter as they walked out of the restaurant. They spoke to each other too loudly, their hearing in dire need of assistance, and were commenting to each other how much they loved this 'cute little town' and that, of course, Ruth, we can come back next year, and yes, Harold, I have my purse, and do you want to try and get in a final view of the sunset on the pier tonight before we head on back to Amherst in the morning? Ellie watched them fondly as their clamorous voices waned into the parking area. Maybe one day she would have someone like that to grow old with. She had to agree with them. Matlacha was indeed a 'cute little town,' a serenely colorful coastal village that served as a perennial gateway into Pine Island.

The front door opened, and Garrett and Mark walked in. They acknowledged Ellie, ordered their drinks, and then, after filling them at the coffee bar, came over and took a seat with her. Ellie folded the paper and set it down.

"Cool place," Mark noted, looking at the mural of the water on the far wall. "I've never been here before."

Garrett checked his watch and took a sip of his coffee. "Thanks for being flexible and rescheduling with me," he said. "So, what do we need to talk about?"

It was mid-afternoon, and they were the only ones on this side of the restaurant. Ellie kept her voice low and for the next ten minutes filled her partner and her boss in on the situation with Ronnie and his connection to Eli Oswald. She told them about the drugs and weapons, about Dawson and how he had yet to turn up, and the orange Mustang that passed them as she was bringing Ronnie back. When she finished, Mark looked intrigued, Garrett sober. He asked, "So what are you proposing?" Garrett was always looking for solutions, not just facts. It was why his office was getting things done.

"To start with, Mark and I need to see what we can find on this Oswald guy and his little crew. From what Ronnie says, there's less than a dozen people left who have fallen in line behind him and do his bidding. But those folks are all in and are moving cocaine. If that's the case I don't want to let this just slip on by."

"Where are his stomping grounds?" Mark asked.

"Don't know yet. Ronnie said Oswald recently moved out to the country and has what he now calls his compound."

"That sounds promising," Garrett quipped. "I've never had good associations with the word 'compound' when used in a domestic context."

"Yeah," Mark said. "Sounds cultish. Makes me think of Waco."

"So that's what we're dealing with," Ellie said. "I've called Dawson's parole officer, and she says Dawson is on her whisk list."

"Whisk list?"

"I took it as a cute way of saying that once they find Dawson he's getting whisked back to prison. Anyway, she didn't have anything for me. I did get the license plate off Curtis Smith's Mustang when he passed me yesterday. It was registered five months ago in his name. Smith spent three years in juvie for physically assaulting his foster mother. Oswald spent two years in the federal system for leading an illegal protest in Tallahassee, burning the American flag, and resisting arrest. Both of those incidents were nearly twenty years ago when both men were still teenagers. The only other item of interest on either of them was a DUI suffered by Smith six years ago. All that aside, their records, as far as the government is concerned, are clean. I think Mark and I will start working on visiting known residences and hot spots."

"Good," Garrett said. "Make it happen. I am going to throw out a caveat though. If we find these guys and it really does look like everything your friend Ronnie says is true, then we now have an interagency investigation on our hands. Ellie, you haven't been involved with one of those yet, but let me tell you, they're about as fun as asking your cousins to help you plan a family reunion. It moves slowly, inefficiently, and everyone starts fighting for what they think is priority. Guns? We're talking about looping in ATF. Kidnapping? The FBI. I'm not sure I want to get involved in something where the ATF will want to tag along too, especially if you're not even sure that any drugs these guys might be involved with are being moved through my jurisdiction. Are we sure this Dawson fellow has been kidnapped?"

"No," Ellie said. "It's speculation at this point, but since they obviously know where Jean's cabin is and Dawson has skipped probation it's certainly feasible."

"He could just be hiding out somewhere," Mark said. "You know, trying to stay abreast of these people he thinks he's upset?"

"Sure," Ellie said. "It's a possibility. You know how these things go. He's a grown man and no one saw him get nabbed, so there isn't a lot of gusto in anyone's sails to go out and try to find him. Anyway, it sounds like he was responsible for ensuring that a lot of cocaine swapped hands. The sooner we start looking into it the better."

"Make it happen." Garrett said it with finality.

Ellie looked out the window, saw a father and son heading toward the bridge, poles bouncing on their shoulders, tackle box and bucket in hand, and it reminded her who the three of them were really working for.

CHAPTER THIRTEEN

THE "M" KEY WAS BROKEN. KYLE ARMSTRONG pounded it several times in a vain hope that it might start working again. Nothing appeared on the screen. Frustrated, he muttered under his breath and pressed the speaker button on his desk phone. It beeped. At least that button worked. "Laurie?"

"Yes." Her voice was strained.

"My keyboard is kaput. Can you get me another one by the end of the day? A wireless one, please?"

"I can, yes. Um...Kyle?"

"Yeah."

"There are some people here to see you. They just walked past me and are heading to your office."

"Okay…"

At that moment Kyle's office door opened, revealing a tall, hairy man in a wool trench coat and another man of Spanish-looking descent, the sides of whose head were shaved and the longer hair on top pulled back into a short ponytail. A lady in a dark dress suit and heels followed behind them. They entered, shut the door, and stopped in front of his desk.

Laurie, still on the speakerphone: "Kyle? Is everything all right?"

Kyle answered, all the while keeping his eyes on the intruders. "Uh, yeah. Yeah, Laurie. Just fine. I forgot that I had called and invited a consulting agency to come over. Just get me the keyboard, please."

"Okay…"

He disconnected and stood up. "What is this?"

"Well, hello to you too," Chewy said. "Ringo asked us to come over and say hello."

Kyle grit his teeth and whispered through a clenched jaw. "You guys can't just show up like this. I can't have people asking questions or getting suspicious. You just freaked my receptionist out."

"Ringo knows what he is doing, so please, sit down." It was Andrés who spoke, and he leaned over the desk until Kyle could smell the scent of a musk cologne. "Sit. Down."

Kyle complied and Andrés smiled, leaned back. "Thank you. Kyle, we would like to be on good terms with you. So far you have managed to get our product across state lines in a very comfortable fashion. Ringo sends his thanks."

"Well, you can tell him this last truck going to Birmingham is it. After that I'm done. If I'd had any idea I was getting involved with this kind of stuff, I never would have borrowed money from him."

"But you did," Chewy said. "And I believe he forgave that debt."

"He made me move his drugs on my trucks," Kyle growled.

"He did no such thing. What you did, you did of your own free will."

"He threatened my family, you jackass. Quit acting like I had a choice in the matter."

"But you did, Kyle. At any time you could have gone to the police and turned us all in. But you did not. Now if you did, we have enough of your documented involvement these last couple months that, even with a plea deal, you would end up in the clink for at least a solid ten. How old will your son and daughter be in ten years? I wonder if your wife would decide to remarry instead of waiting for you to get out."

A vein, like a centipede, worked its way across Kyle's forehead. "Shut up! Just shut up." He gathered himself and then asked, "What do you want anyway? What did you really come here for?"

Andrés turned toward the lady that had come with them and in a show of courtesy declined his chin. "This is Yolanda. Your newest employee."

Kyle looked at her suspiciously. She was calm, composed. Her long black hair was pulled into a tight ponytail that started high up on her head. She had a long neck and long, smooth legs that stood out of a short skirt. "I'm not hiring right now. Not unless she can drive a forklift."

"This is Yolanda. She is your newest employee," Andrés repeated. "From now on she will be helping with your books. Your...accounting." Andrés's broad smile seemed to indicate that he thought he was doing Kyle a favor.

"I already have an accountant. Laurie. She works up there at the front, doubles as our secretary."

"Kyle. I will say that Ringo expects Yolanda to work

here. As an accountant. He has hired her, and she is good at what she does."

"But I don't need—"

"You do not know what you need. Kyle, you have partnered with Ringo to move some of his product. However, he has identified an additional way in which the two of you might...work together. You move much rum, and, well, that is good for us all. You can help us by selling more rum than you currently do. Yolanda will make sure that happens."

"Make sure that happens? An accountant? That's a job for a sales—" The moment Kyle's words ceased was the same moment that his synapses fired off and his brain made the intended connection. The color in his face shifted to a sickly hue of ash, and his eyes, rather than widening, drooped down in horror and landed on an unused glass globe paperweight. Kyle said to the paperweight, very slowly, "I'm not laundering money for him too." His tongue felt unnaturally heavy, like wet cotton, and his throat was now too parched to swallow.

Andrés's brows drew together. "Launder money? Kyle, what kind of men do you think we are?" He looked quizzically at Chewy and then toward Yolanda. "We want everything to be above board. That is why we are coming to you. Yolanda is the best, and she will make sure everything is in working order."

Kyle ran all ten fingers through his sandy brown hair. He kept his face toward the desktop, closed his eyes, said, "For how long?"

"As long as you and Ringo are in business," Chewy said. "Which if I had to guess—and I don't like to guess, I never win in Vegas—I would guess indefinitely."

Kyle rose from his chair. "You tell Ringo I want to see him. If he's going to do business with me, then I don't want his henchmen coming around here making trouble."

"Trouble? I don't think we're making any trouble. And I don't know what kind of movies you watch, but we're not henchmen." Chewy resettled his coat on his shoulders and drew his arms across his chest. He looked liked he was shivering.

"You're cold?" Kyle asked.

"Yes. Very."

Kyle stared at him, bewildered. It was eighty-seven degrees outside, and here in the offices the thermostat was set to seventy-two.

Andrés set a hand on Yolanda's shoulder and gave it a gentle squeeze. "We will leave you and Kyle to chat. Kyle, you might tell Laurie that Yolanda was a referral from a good friend. Or something. I am sure you will spin it right. That was Laurie that we met coming in, yes?"

"Yes." When Kyle gazed past Andrés, his eyes fell on the framed one dollar bill hanging on the wall beside the door. The symbolic first dollar the distillery ever made. But what got his attention right now, and what made him think that his eyes were playing tricks on him, was that George Washington's face was no longer a creamy green. It was turning darker. And now it looked black. No, it *was* black, and not a Frederick Douglass kind of black either; more like coal black, like someone had spilled over the contents of an inkwell.

"Kyle...are you still with me?"

And now the ink, or whatever it was, started running

out of the small frame and making two thin tracks down the wall. The two tracks grew wider and then branched out into little rivulets, thickened, and Kyle could see that they had now taken the shape of someone's hands. Not just anyone's hands. George Washington's hands. Well, no, that wasn't quite right. He knew whose hands they really were. They were his, black and sodden with the filth of dirty money.

When he looked back to the frame, the ink had gone and ol' Georgie's complexion had returned to normal, but now he was looking at Kyle with disdain, shaking his head at him the disappointed way a mother might do when she finds out you've been clandestinely smoking a little reefer behind her hibiscus.

Oh, great. Now he was hearing voices. Or, more precisely, just one: George's. *"You wouldn't tell a lie now, would you, Kyle? Surely not about something like this? Washing someone's dirty money? Don't tell me all that talk you heard as a boy about me chopping down that cherry tree did you no good at all, Kyle."* George Washington's voice was far deeper than Kyle had imagined it might be.

Chewy snapped his fingers in Kyle's face. It worked. Kyle gave a kind of shivered jolt and took an unsteady step backwards. "Good. You're still with us. You had Andrés here worried for a second."

Kyle needed to rest. Or a drink. Or both. Yes, certainly both.

"Laurie looks like a nice lady," Chewy was saying. "I would hate for her to get nosy and for something unfortunate to happen to her, so handle this wisely. Yolanda will be our eyes and ears from now on. I would suggest you don't underestimate her." With that, Andrés and

Chewy put their backs to Kyle and walked out of his office.

Yolanda turned her attention to him, offering a cold, professional smile. "So, where is my desk?"

CHAPTER FOURTEEN

WHEN ELLIE APPROACHED THE SIDE DOOR LEADING into Major's home, she heard a rhythmic thumping coming from inside, varied and discordant. She opened the door, walked through the kitchen and across the living room, and then took the carpeted stairs up to the second floor. She poked her head into the first room on the right. Ronnie was behind a full drum set, focused and maybe a little irritated. A large poster was pinned to the wall behind him: the Beatles walking across the zebra crossing near their Abbey Road studios. Major was standing to the side, his back to the door, his head moving slightly with the beat of the drums.

"Hey!" she called out.

Ronnie looked in her direction and lifted his chin to her by way of a greeting, but he kept playing. When Major turned and saw Ellie, his face brightened, and he walked over and gave her firm hug from the side. They watched Ronnie for a while, and when he finally stopped he was breathing heavily.

"Not bad, Ronnie," Ellie said. It was, in fact, very

bad. But her father had brought her up to be polite. He had also raised her not to lie. In this case, the latter assisted the former.

"I was texting with a couple old buddies last night," Ronnie said, "and we got to talking about maybe starting a band. I use to play these things, you know. The drums."

"You don't say."

"Yeah. I didn't realize how rusty I'd gotten. Been years since I played." He paused. "Did you need something?"

"I wanted to give you an update. Based on the information you've provided, my partner and I are going to work on locating Curtis Smith and Eli Oswald."

"That's good, Ellie. That's real good. It's like I said, Eli is something else. If you find him you've got to be real careful. It took me a while to realize he was no good, but when I did…" He jerked his thumb over his shoulder.

"And you have no idea where this new place of theirs is?"

"Nope. He only let a handful in on it."

"Well, if by a long stretch you do hear from Dawson, make sure I'm the first to know."

"You got it." He twirled a drum stick through his fingers, and it came loose, flew across the room, and hit the floor lamp. He looked guilty at Major. "Sorry."

Major walked over and picked it up. "Don't worry about it." He handed it back to Ronnie, said to Ellie, "Want to get a drink downstairs with me?"

"Always." Ronnie was playing again before they had made it to the top of the stairs, and they went down and into the kitchen. Major pulled a couple Landsharks from the fridge and popped the tops. He handed one to Ellie, and they each found a place to sit in the living room.

"You're doing a good job, you know."

"With what?"

"Your work at the DEA. You helped take down that network we all read about in the paper. That's a big deal."

"Thanks. It does feel good to be doing something meaningful."

"Oh, so pouring drinks at my bar isn't meaningful?" He winked at her.

"Totally meaningless. Can't see how anyone could enjoy that." She winked back.

Major took a pull on his beer. "Ronnie's a good kid. He can stay here for as long as he needs to. Just...be careful out there, okay?"

"I will. I always am."

"You're tenacious," he said. "You got that quality from your mother, you know."

"Yeah?"

"Yeah."

Upstairs, the drumming stopped, and they heard the bathroom door shut.

"I'm going to the Caribbean for a few days after the festival," Major said.

"No kidding. Where?"

"Not sure yet. I'm meeting up with an old friend who's going to be out that way. Somewhere in the Bahamas if I had to bet. He's one of those people who doesn't decide exactly where until he gets close."

"I'm glad you're finding time to take a break," she said. "You work too hard."

"Thanks, kiddo."

"How long will you be gone? You'll be back to pick up Katie and Chloe from the airport with me?"

He grimaced. "No, but I emailed Katie a couple hours ago to let her know. I'll be back just a day or two later."

"No worries. Don't forget about your birthday party. Just the four of us."

He smiled. "Can't wait."

When Ellie left a half hour later, Ronnie's rhythm had somehow managed to have gotten worse, the cacophony spilling all the way down the street like a clunky truck.

CHAPTER FIFTEEN

ELLIE AND MARK HAD SPENT ALL MORNING AT THE office combing through printouts of anything they could find on Eli Oswald and Curtis Smith: past residences, old credit and debit card statements noting where purchases were made and how often, utility bills, ISP information for their internet connections, and smartphone geo-locations. The only bank account between the two was with SunTrust and still active, but it had a zero balance, no transactions in the last four months, and when they called the bank had informed them that the statements started coming back last month.

Ideally, they would have another team working through additional information on the other names Ronnie had provided, the names of those who were still counted among Oswald's little following. But it was just the two of them—Garrett couldn't put anyone else on this—so for now, their focus was narrow.

So, they had come away with very little. Eli Oswald, it seemed, had ghosted. The last phone number they had for him now belonged to a Charles Hinkle in Bonita

Springs, and no title, utilities, or real estate transactions surfaced with his name on them. And the same with Curtis Smith. The Mustang was registered in his name but remained under an address that he hadn't lived at in nearly a year. They knew that because that had been the first location they visited earlier today. It was an apartment in Estero, and the mother of four now living there hardly spoke English and had never heard of either Oswald or Smith. The front office was no help either, although Mark was content to grab a couple cookies intended for potential residents on his way out.

The second location had taken them to a mobile home in Immokalee. It was vacant—gutted really. Nothing there but the carpet. Even the stove had been taken.

Now, at their third and final stop, they sat on the back porch that belonged to Eli Oswald's older brother, Drew. The home sat on the west end of the Golden Gate Estates community in Naples. Eli's brother had done well for himself. The three-acre lot was endowed with dozens of pine and fruit trees, an enclosed pool, and a small barn.

Drew Oswald was of average height and looked like he might be carrying around two-twenty. His face was full and elongated, not dissimilar to a horse, albeit less pronounced. He hadn't looked surprised when he opened his front door, glanced at Ellie's badge, and heard the topic of conversation. He escorted them to his back porch where he was grilling and directed Ellie and Mark into a couple lawn chairs. He stood near the grill as he spoke. "I'd be lying if I said I didn't expect you guys, or someone like you, before now."

"Why's that?" Ellie asked.

"If Eli's in trouble, it doesn't surprise me. What's he gotten himself into?"

"Unfortunately, I can't provide specifics," she said. "But we were hoping you might have an idea as to his whereabouts."

Drew huffed. "I wish I did. He never tells me, and I never ask."

"When was the last time you saw him?" Mark asked.

"I guess that would have been about three, maybe four months ago?"

"Is that typical?" Ellie asked. "So much time in between visits?"

"Oh sure. Sometimes longer. You never know with him. And 'typical' isn't a word you would use in the same sentence with Eli. He's unpredictable. Eccentric."

Ronnie had also used that last word to describe Eli. "Eccentric?"

"Just, well, I would say flamboyant, but that holds a certain connotation these days. He has a...colorful personality."

"What about any contact when he's not here? Phone calls? Emails?"

"No. He's not so great about any of that stuff." Drew lifted the lid to the grill and flipped the two chicken breasts. He shut the lid again.

Ellie asked, "What you know about Harlan Tucker?"

Drew blew a long puff of air from his cheeks, lowered his brows. "I don't know," he finally said. "I never met the guy. Eli left me a copy of his book a couple years ago." He pointed inside with his head. "It's on a bookshelf in there. I'd be lying if I said I'd read the whole thing. It's not bad...just not my thing. I think Harlan Tucker was probably a good guy and meant well. Don't know that I could say more than that. Eli liked him though."

"So your brother was close to him?"

"Couldn't say. I'm not sure Eli is all that close to anyone. But if it suits him, he'll let them think he is."

"Does that apply to you as well?"

"Absolutely. Eli and I aren't close. I love him, and he's always welcome here, but it's hard for me to trust someone who hides behind an ever-changing exterior."

They spent the next several minutes inquiring about Drew's own career, how long he had lived here, and his and Eli's family. Drew had spent his entire adult life with an agricultural engineering firm, never married, and he and Eli were the only children of parents already passed.

"Here's the thing you have to keep in mind about my brother. He's smart. And he knows he's smart. He can put up a front better than Howie Mandel. On one hand he's talking with you and laughing with you, but all the while," Drew whirled an index finger near his temple, "he's got something going on up in here."

"As in crazy?" Mark asked.

"Oh no, no. Not crazy at all. Brilliant. The cogs are whirling, and you couldn't tell that he was scheming something if you got up close and stared deep into his icy blues. I won't say I got the short end of the stick because I've done well for myself. But Eli, he got an extra stick altogether."

"Does he have any favorite hangouts that you know of?"

"I don't."

"This address is on your brother's driver's license." Ellie left the question implied.

"My home is a constant in Eli's life. He knows he's always welcome, and from time to time he sticks his head in for a few weeks."

"Did he say anything out of the ordinary or look any different the last time you saw him?"

"So something you need to know about Eli is that he's always saying things out the ordinary. Like 'I do wish it would snow tonight,' or 'When the saints come marching in heads are gonna roll.' I know it sounds like he's nuts, but he's speaking to himself in his own vernacular. He just says and does random things all the time. Last time I saw him he had just gotten a tattoo of a parrot on his shoulder. A purple parrot." He shook his head. "Big eyes, deep purple feathers. I don't get it, but then that's Eli."

"Does any mail come for him?"

"Oh sure. But I just toss it out. He'd never open them." He lifted the lid again and poked at the meat. "I don't know if someone else pays his bills or if he just doesn't pay them. He just never gives attention to it. He'll leave after staying a month or so, and a thin stack of envelopes with his name on them will still be sitting on my kitchen counter, untouched."

"Would you hold onto anything that comes in?"

He shrugged. "Sure."

Ellie stood, and Mark followed suit. They thanked Drew for his time.

"Look, I don't know what he's into," Drew said. "I wish I could say you're barking up the wrong tree, but you may very well not be. If I hear from him, you'll be the first to know."

They said their goodbyes, and Ellie and Mark got

back in her truck. As they were pulling onto Collier Boulevard, Ellie said, "Strange, isn't it?"

"What's that?"

"How two people can basically have the same upbringing—the same rules, parents, and experiences—and yet turn out completely different from each other."

"Yeah. After what you relayed to me what Ronnie said about Eli, I half expected his brother to be some weirdo. Seemed like a pretty normal guy though."

They compared notes during the half hour drive back to the office. As they were pulling in Tyler had called and informed her that his swag for Mango Mania had come in, and asked her to come up later that afternoon so they could open the boxes together. After she dropped Mark off Ellie went home and took Citrus on a five mile run to clear her head and work through the conversation she had with Eli Oswald's brother. When she got back to the house she had just enough time to make herself a green smoothie and take a quick shower before leaving again to meet Tyler.

CHAPTER SIXTEEN

THE SILVERADO'S ENGINE TICKED AS ELLIE WALKED away from it. She made her way across the earthen parking lot and over to the cinder block building that contained Reticle's offices. Tyler was up front near the stalls talking with his range boss and, by the sound of the conversation, a patron interested in a monthly membership. Ellie dipped inside and walked down the hall to the gunsmithing shop at the back. The room was broad and boasted several tables and tools: a mini-milling machine, belt sander, bolted table-top vice, and a grinder. A 14" x 40" gunsmithing lathe sat on the rear wall, Reticle's newest piece of equipment. Rifles of all types were racked on tables, ready to be custom altered or cleaned by a pro. Two cardboard boxes sat on the table in the center of the room, one large, one small. A blue and yellow logo was stamped across the sides: "Genius Print." She walked over to them and resisted the urge to open them. She thought it was cute that Tyler already had a successful business but could get so excited about a couple boxes of trinkets with Reticle's logo on them.

The sound of boot heels echoed down the hallway. Tyler asked as he walked in, "You didn't open them, did you?"

"Of course."

He slipped a pocket knife from his jeans, flipped the blade out, and it clicked as it locked into place. He looked at Ellie with bright, anticipatory eyes. "Ready?"

"No. Can we build the suspense a little more?"

"No...we can't," and with a few quick motions Tyler had severed the clear tape. He closed the blade and returned the knife to his pocket. Ellie slid the small box closer, and Tyler grabbed the large one, both of them peeling back the flaps and looking inside. Ellie's box was filled with metal keychains bearing Reticle's logo, available, it seemed, in three different colors: blue, red, and black. She pulled a red one out and examined it. It was circular, a little smaller than a half dollar. It was dense, heavier than Ellie had anticipated.

"These are great," she said.

Next to her, Tyler sighed.

"What's wrong?"

He shook his head, said nothing, and handed her a koozie.

She gave it a once over before a laugh slipped out that she couldn't suppress. She set her fingers to her mouth to stifle the next one. "Oh, Tyler." Tragedy and hilarity had coalesced into a koozie. She laughed again.

"This is funny?" he asked.

Ellie looked back down on the koozie. Genius Print, as it was, had misspelled Reticle's name, replacing the "R" with a "T": "Teticle."

"Do you know what that word looks like?" he said.

"Certainly," she snickered. "And everyone else will too."

"Unbelievable." He reached into the box and dug through the rest of them. "They're all like this. Every one of them. What am I supposed to do with these?"

"You could donate them to that guy who has his billboards all over Fort Myers. That doctor who claims to have done over ten thousand vasectomies."

"How do they get the keychains right and get the koozies wrong?"

"Genius Print," Ellie said slowly, and then laughed.

"Genius Print, my butt," Tyler said. "I'm not going to be able to get them to fix this in time."

"A lot of places do overnight."

"I don't want to pay the extra," he said. "I'll just get these folks to refund me."

"At least the keychains are nice." She handed him one.

"Yeah. At least these aren't named after a body part."

"I want that one," she said.

He gave it back and sighed again.

CHAPTER SEVENTEEN

HE KEPT HIS EYES CLOSED AS THE WAKING NIGHTMARE descended onto him once again. He thought that this must be how people feel the morning after they wake up in the slammer with a pounding headache and a charge hanging over them for vehicular manslaughter, all because they had left the party too late and told Dougy they didn't need a designated driver and then drove away, swerving down the street with a BAC of .23.

But Kyle Armstrong wasn't drinking last night—he was tonight though, oh boy, was he—and he hadn't hit anyone with his car. No, but what he had done was wait until *Yo-lan-da* left the office this afternoon and then booted up her laptop. He knew the password; Laurie was the one who had created it. It was a company computer after all, and Kyle had every right to access it. He spent the next two hours looking at spreadsheets and document revisions, digging through accounting software, each passing moment growing more and more paranoid, until Carlene had called him, mildly frustrated that he wasn't home yet and informing him that dinner was on its way to getting cold.

Now, Carlene was inside, the kids asleep, and Kyle sat on his porch swing with a bottle of Evan Williams at his feet and a mason jar a quarter full of the stuff firmly in his grip. His entire adult life, whenever stress got to him, he went for whiskey before rum. He didn't know why that was. He always woke up feeling about a full barrel worse than he did with the rum.

Early last month, when Ringo approached him about moving his drugs, he thought that would be it. Sliding some of his packages into a few boxes of rum, sending it north, picking the skin off his thumbs until there was no more left, having the product delivered safely; do that three or four times and he would be done with the grimy pollutant that was Ringo. But Kyle had been accused of being myopic more than once before. Yet somehow, in spite of this weakness, he had built a highly successful business in an industry that was quickly becoming oversaturated. Even today, he had gotten an email from California. A chain of liquor stores called Golden Agave wanted his rum. And not just a little bit; more than he had on hand. This stuff didn't just appear out of thin air. It took time: three, six, twelve, fifteen years, et cetera, et cetera. But Wild Palm had only been cranking along for five years now. He wasn't one to speed the process or add caramel color to his batches to deceive the very deceivable masses. His father had taught him to do better than that.

His father.

A kindly but strong man's man who had turned a small hardware store in Kansas into a chain across the Midwest before he sold out to Ace Hardware thirteen years ago for millions. Kyle had inherited his father's ability to create and sustain something meaningful.

Kyle had taken the family home to Kansas for the holidays last year, and after presents had been opened and all the wives and kids went into the kitchen for hot chocolate, Kyle's father looked over at him from his high back chair near the fireplace and said, "I'm so proud of you, son."

Kyle had never been the soft type, and, like his old man, he never cried. Ever. But in that moment—one of those moments that a young man seems to yearn for and forms the basis of all his work on—after his father had said those words, his emotional furniture was rearranged, and he swallowed the rock in his esophagus, turned his head, and blinked four times. He was successful. The tears never came.

"Thanks, Dad." In those eight words a full conversation had elapsed, one that sent Kyle back home to Florida with the energy and self confidence of a high school quarterback in front of the cheerleading squad.

But all that had changed after Ringo showed up and forced Kyle's hand. Kyle was now using this business as a means to move cocaine into the heart cavities of his country. And as of three days ago he was laundering money too. Laurie was going to ask questions. She had already started after Andrés and Chewy left, after Yolanda stayed and he had to tell her someone else was now handling the accounting.

"But I handle that," Laurie had said. "And what I can't do Vic Hapner handles. He's the best accountant in the county, you know that, Kyle. What'd you go and hire someone else to do it for?"

And all Kyle could say was that they were growing

and he wanted to bring it in-house. That seemed to satisfy her. Except Yolanda was not the most genial of people. Yolanda was all business. Flat expression, didn't say much, got her work done, and left. Laurie liked to talk—grandkids, Florida State football, local gossip—and soon she would figure out little Yolanda wasn't interested in being her friend or yapping about why Tina Caldwell didn't make it to the Silver Ladies luncheon. Once Laurie got stale about all that, she would start poking her nose into things. It was all a little too much.

The words reverberated through the air, just as they had when Kyle's father had spoken them eight months ago.

I'm proud of you, son.

The happy tears did eventually come; they had come later that evening as Kyle sat alone on his father's front porch with a glass of Glenlivet. They were the kind of tears that you could quickly wipe away if your wife opens the front door and comes out to ask you if you had brushed the kids' teeth. Still though, they were true tears. His dad had told him he was proud of him, and now Kyle was nipple deep in the dark underworld of drugs and dirty money. And that didn't happen to be the worst of it. No, the worst of it was that Kyle let Ringo threaten his family, let Ringo wiggle his mangy hands down his crotch, down past his belt line, and grab him tight by the balls. Kyle had the resources to hide if needed. Somewhere far away even. He could have called the cops and told them who it was that was black-mailing him and what other product Wild Palm had been distributing. Sure, they may not have believed him at first, but they would have come around. Until then

Kyle could have taken the family and driven up to the Finger Lakes and disappeared, waiting for it all to blow over.

But he didn't.

It would have been nothing to get in Ringo's face that Sunday when he came over and told Kyle he would be using Wild Palm to move some of his blow.

But he didn't.

He could have given Andrés and Chewy the finger two days ago, told *Yo-lan-da* to scram, and then hauled tail to New York.

But he didn't do that either.

And the most afflicting thing about it was not that he had failed to stop it before it started. No, the worst part about all of this was that Kyle Armstrong was a coward. His spine was made of papier-mâché. No one could be proud of a coward, and wasn't it Shakespeare or Julius Caesar who said that cowards die many times before their deaths; that the valiant taste death but once?

Kyle felt dead.

It would be the first of many.

His wife, with whom he shared all, was inside checking email on her laptop, maybe watching reruns of Parenthood. Her husband was a drug dealer.

His son and daughter were in their beds asleep, dreaming of whatever innocent kids dream about— Optimus Prime and Elsa? Their father was a drug dealer.

Worse, even. He was the guy who made sure the drug dealers' businesses thrived. Without men like Kyle their operations simply limped along, no wind in their sails.

He downed the last of the bourbon and wiped his

lips with the back of his hand. He couldn't speak up now. It was too late. The last six weeks had seen him move hundreds of kilos across state lines. They would cut him a deal for squealing, but Andrés had been correct when he noted that Kyle would still be looking at ten years easy. Maybe twenty. He knew because he had Googled it, and Florida case law in this instance was easy to come by.

Somehow, in just a very short amount of time, Kyle had managed to fall into a nightmare of grand proportions. He was a drug dealer now. Another cog in the grand ol' machine that kept the cartels high on the hog.

His glass was empty. He needed another drink. He reached for the bottle of Evan Williams and bumped it. It fell out of reach. He stood up, too fast, and felt the space between his ears turn to fuzz. He reached out and grabbed the porch swing for balance, but the swing, as porch swings tend to do, moved beneath his weight. Kyle pitched forward and, with nothing else to grab onto, planted his face into the pine floorboards and saw a spangled flash of tiny starlight before sleep came early.

CHAPTER EIGHTEEN

THE MANGO MANIA FESTIVAL WAS HELD THE THIRD weekend of August and saw the celebrated fruit being brought in by the truck load, most of it coming straight from the north end of the Island.

Local growers, besides furnishing mangoes, brought along every possible mango dish and fixing. Tables and pop-up tents were filled with dried mango, mango ice cream, mango soup, mango mustards and jams, mango curry, and dozens of other recipes. Trying to list off all of them brought to mind Bubba Blue on the bus, rattling off to Forrest Gump all the possible ways there were to cook shrimp. The festival brought Saint James City its busiest weekend of the year, with nearly all of the island's ten thousand inhabitants showing up to take part and thousands more pouring in from all over the state.

Fish houses set up tables with fryers, offering up local catches of crab, fish, and shrimp. Merchants selling festival t-shirts, conch shells, and fish were perched all along the southern tip of Oleander Street and halfway down the Norma Jean pier.

Jean Oglesby had a large pop-up tent set up right next to The Salty Mangrove, the most sought after location for merchants on this busy weekend. Jean had once confided in Ellie that every time the festival came around she made enough money selling her art and merchandise to pay her mortgage for the next twelve months. Judging by the size and location of Jean's home, that was not a small amount of money.

Tyler and Ellie walked up the ramp that led to the bar. Tyler had driven in from Cape Coral, parked at her house, and they walked down to the marina together, navigating congested parking and whining golf carts. With the crowds came traffic. Cars would line Stringfellow Road for a mile on each shoulder, and the island's governance ran shuttles all the way from Pine Island Center seven miles north.

Ellie had considered bringing Citrus but had finally decided against it. Citrus didn't do leashes. He would have gotten down here and been so excited that this many people had come out to see him that he would have run off the end of the pier in sheer, uncontainable excitement. And there was no doggie ramp.

Live trop-rock music greeted them as they walked past The Salty Mangrove and out onto the wider boardwalk. Joel Henderson's laid-back tunes sounded like a musical marriage between Jimmy Buffett and Glenn Campbell and that, along with the suds being poured freely at the bar behind them, had everyone in a relaxed mood, feeling as if they were in their own slice of paradise. Major was moving at a near-frantic pace behind the bar like a mother trying to feed a gaggle of toddlers at snack time. He beamed when he noticed her and waved just before a patron stole his attention away. Ellie had offered to help him this weekend—his busiest of the year—but he had insisted otherwise.

"Hey, look at this," Tyler said. Ellie followed him over to a couple children juggling mangoes. A small crowd had gathered and was oohing and aahing over their skills. The children, a boy and a girl, no older than ten, were in a coordinated rhythm, flicking mangoes to each other. Ellie counted nine in the air at a time. "I can do that," Tyler said.

"Sure you can."

"I mean, really. I juggled chainsaws in Texas. At spring bluebonnet festivals. People ate it up."

"You can't even hold your truck keys without dropping them."

"I said chainsaws, Ellie. Car keys...those are a whole different beast. Very slippery. Lots of pieces."

She shook her head. "Come on. Let's see what else there is."

Tyler fished a couple dollars from his jeans and tossed them into a bucket at the children's feet. He caught up to Ellie, and they made their way down the pier, finally stopping at a table that sold beach-themed jewelry. The young owner was busy talking to another couple. The table was filled with necklaces made of shark teeth, tiny shells, and sand dollars, small lockets filled with sand, and wire earrings molded into every kind of sea life. A necklace made of green and blue sea glass caught Ellie's attention. She pinched at the thin silver chain and held it up. Ellie didn't own much jewelry, locally made or otherwise, but she liked this one.

She waited for the owner to finish with the other couple and then asked, "How much?"

"Twenty-two dollars."

Tyler reached into his back pocket and grabbed his wallet with one hand while the other slipped the necklace out of Ellie's hand. "I've got this."

"Hey, I'm a big girl. I can get it."

"I know you can. But I'm a bigger boy, and I've decided to get it for you." He threw her a wink, and Ellie conceded, a flutter crossing her stomach. He fished out a twenty and a ten dollar bill and handed them over. "Keep the change."

The girl behind the table brightened. "Thank you. Do you want me to wrap it for you?"

"Nah." Tyler stepped in front of Ellie and maneuvered the chain through her hair and around the back of her neck. He was close, and Ellie felt the warmth of his strong chest radiating onto her cheeks. He stepped back, assessing her. "That's nice. Pretty necklace on a pretty girl." He looked down. His green eyes filled her blues.

A warm, muted crimson crept up Ellie's neck. "Thank you." She pulled her eyes away and looked down on the jewelry. "It's nice."

"Come on," he said, and started walking again. They kept going, scanning the vendors, both of them silently reflecting on the moment that had just passed between them. They came to a white pop-up tent on their left. A banner hung at the front: *Wild Palm Distillery*.

A man that looked to be Ellie and Tyler's age greeted them. He was tall, slender, had short brown hair and a strong forehead. His eyes were kind.

Ellie said hello and asked, "Are you the owner?"

"That I am. Kyle Armstrong." He reached out and shook both their hands.

"My uncle loves your rum," Ellie said. "He always has a couple bottles at his house and sells a ton of it at his bar." She noticed a big knot on the right side of his forehead, like he had whacked into something, wondered how he had gotten it, and decided not to ask him about it.

"Yeah?" he said, smiling. He grabbed a bottle from the table and twisted the cap. He poured a little into two plastic shot glasses and handed one to Ellie, one to Tyler. "Who's your uncle?"

"Warren Hall. He's owns The Salty Mangrove." Ellie tilted the tiny cup back, and just before the clear liquid entered her mouth she saw Kyle Armstrong's expression change. It was hardly noticeable, but Ellie had been trained to notice hardly noticeable. It was a quick descent of the eyebrows and, behind them, worried eyes. Kyle recovered in an instant.

Tyler hadn't noticed. He lowered the cup and winced against the burn of the rum. "So good," he said.

"Glad you like it," Kyle said. A small girl popped out from behind him and waved at Ellie.

"Hello," she giggled, and then said, "you're pretty."

"Thank you," Ellie said. "You're pretty too."

Kyle set a gentle hand on the crown of the girl's head. "This is my daughter, Sophia. My best employee."

"Nice to meet you, Sophia," Tyler said. "Are you the taste tester?"

Ellie sent an elbow into his ribs, and he coughed. He looked at Kyle. "Sorry, just kidding."

Kyle laughed, patted his daughter's head again.

"She makes sure that the table has enough cups on it."
A couple men dressed in biker leathers approached.
Kyle excused himself and gave the newcomers his fresh
attention.

Ellie and Tyler continued on down the newly
repaired section of the pier, passing more vendors and
stopping at a tent whose owner Ellie knew well. "Sharla,
you're not out of that mango ice cream yet, are you?"

"Ellie. Hi, sweetie." Sharla came around the table
and gave Ellie a hug. "It's always so good to see you."
She stepped back and looked at the man beside Ellie.
"Tyler, right?"

"Yes, ma'am. That's what my mother named me,
even if I didn't have a say so in the matter."

She gave Tyler a hug too and then returned to the
shade of the tent. "Gary went to go get more ice cream
out of the cold storage. We made twice as much as we
did last year, but it's going twice as fast. Here." Sharla
reached into an ice chest and pulled out two paper cups
with lids on them. She extended them, and Ellie and
Tyler each took one. Sharla handed them a couple
spoons. "These are on me," she said. "Gary added
something extra to it this year, and I think it's one of the
reasons it's selling so fast. People can't get enough of it."

"It's mangoes, isn't it?" Tyler said. "He added
mangoes, didn't he?"

Sharla shook her head. "I can't believe it." She
leaned in and whispered. "If anyone finds out, they'll
just go out and make it themselves."

"Good thing I'm an expert at keeping secrets,"
he said.

"All right then. Let's make sure it stays that way."

"Yes, ma'am."

"Sharla," Ellie asked. "Is Jimmy Joe Claude still working with you?"

"You bet your biscuits he is. I was telling Gary just yesterday that other than Carlos, Jimmy is one of the best employees we've had in years. He shows up on time, gets his work done properly, and stays late if we need him to. I know he had a lot of trouble with the law there for a while, but it looks like he may have really turned himself around."

Ellie was half impressed. Jimmy Joe Claude had been in and out of prison much of his adult life. A couple months ago he had offered up a couple key leads for Ellie's investigation into the local drug trade which brought about several arrests and the breakdown of a large drug organization.

"He's a hard worker," Sharla continued. "In that way he reminds me of myself when I was younger. Did you know that before Gary and I moved here we owned a cattle ranch up in Montana?"

"You're kidding me. How did I not know that?"

"I'm sure your father did. I know Warren does. Anyway, it was awful. All the cattle got diseased, and they had to get put down. We ended up going bankrupt. The man who owned the plantation that is now The Groovy Grove actually lived just a few miles from us, and he didn't know anything about growing mangoes properly, nor, apparently, did the folks he put in charge down here. Gary and I, we didn't know either, but we were willing to learn. So we bought the place from him and came on down. Watching Jimmy ask a million questions about mangoes and working hard at it reminded me, I guess, of myself all those years ago. Gary too, of course." Sharla took a five dollar bill from a customer and handed him a cup of ice cream. "Did you hear there's a decent hurricane brewing in the Atlantic? I sure hope it stays away. I really don't want a mess on my hands."

"I guess you've been through a couple of those," Tyler noted.

"We have. Every time, we lose trees and most of the fruit ends up ripped off. We lose an entire season."

A crowd of teenagers gathered to the booth. "We'll let you take care of them," Ellie said.

"Good to see you both," Sharla said, and waved a quick goodbye as they turned to leave.

Ellie and Tyler kept on down the pier until they came to the last table and turned back. Halfway back up the pier a voice came from behind them. "You kids being good?" It was Major. They turned around.

"For now," Tyler said. "We're going to egg The Salty Mangrove later tonight." He looked down at Ellie. "Was it okay to tell him that?"

"What are you doing out here?" Ellie asked Major. "The bar's hopping, isn't it?"

Sweat was glistening off his forehead. "The temp help is doing great. I had to run a couple bags of ice up to Henry Salvers' tent. He called me and said he was running out and couldn't get away." He rolled his eyes lightheartedly. "The Mangrove, as you know, has the only ice machine out here." He put a hand into a pocket. "I passed Reticle's table, Tyler, and picked up a keychain." He brought his hand out. A blue one. "These are terrific. You know, you should have gotten some koozies too. I'm sure they would have been a big hit." He laughed.

Tyler's eyes moved to half mast. He looked at Ellie. "You told him?"

"Of course I told him. I couldn't keep something like that to myself."

"Tyler," Major said, "you really should consider renaming your whole enterprise. Reticle. It's just not as memorable as say...Teticle."

Tyler sighed. "Good grief. I'm not going to live this down, am I?"

"Not a chance," Ellie laughed.

"I've got to run, kids," Major said. "Be good." He picked up his pace and hurried back toward the bar.

The live music at The Salty Mangrove grew louder as they drew nearer; the low pitched rhythm of the buleador, deep notes of the guitar, and the earthy, resonant timbre of the marimba together formed a distinct genre that had a magical ability to work its way into your muscles and relax them. "You want a drink?" Tyler asked.

"Sure. A longneck is fine." As she mindlessly scanned the crowds down the boardwalk and looked over the sea of tents, tables, and festival goers, she thought she saw someone she knew. Someone from her past. He wore a gray ball cap pulled down low over his eyes. She quickly shrugged it off as an overactive imagination. But then she paused on instinct.

"Give me a minute. I'll catch up to you in a little bit," she told Tyler, and looked back over the crowd.

"Umm...okay. Everything good?"

Her eyes were fixed over the sea of people. "Yeah. Yeah, it's fine. Give me a few minutes. I'll find you." She walked off, her face set hard toward the point in the crowd where she had seen Virgil disappear.

CHAPTER NINETEEN

He had intended for her to see him, to subtly catch her eye. Coincidences happened. What did not happen was one of the best spooks in the world randomly showing up in your small hometown on the busiest weekend of the year. As she brushed through the crowds, Ellie's mind raced, trying to conceive why he would be here. During their six years as a team, no one had known each other's real names. Toward the end, when she and Voltaire had begun a clandestine relationship, she had learned his—Brian Carter—but that was it. Virgil being here meant that he knew her and knew something that had led him to search her out and find her. She quickly negotiated baby strollers and loud groups of young men who had already consumed a little too much to drink. She passed The Salty Mangrove and walked toward the marina. The crowds thinned out as she drew closer to the marina. She passed the empty slips—most of the boats were out on the water for the day—and approached the marina's dry dock. She stepped inside, looked around, and walked past a row of steel racks and several boats. A thin metallic click carried across the building. It came from the back, from behind the farthest row of boats. The only door back there led to a storage room used to keep fishing equipment in the off season. Ellie walked down an aisle, passing a rack of skiffs and bowriders, her sneakers silently padding along the concrete floor.

She opened the door and stepped inside the storage area with heightened senses. There he was. Standing at the end of the room, on her left, his back toward her, handling a fishing pole that he had pulled back from the wall. "Ellie. How are you?"

It had been almost four years since TEAM 99 had been disbanded, but hearing Virgil's strong voice— seeing him—brought back a flood of emotions, nostalgia the most prominent.

Ellie didn't answer him. Hearing him say her real name was unnatural. She had only ever heard him address her as Pascal. Virgil set the tip of the fishing rod back against the wall and turned around. He looked nearly the same: thick, muscular upper body, legs as stout as tree trunks. The spaces beneath his eyes had started to hollow, but his complexion was still as smooth as butter; he still had that plump baby face.

Inquiry overruled a certain happiness she felt in seeing him again. She offered only a partial smile. "What are you doing here?"

"Sorry to interrupt your fun. You look good."

Again, no reply.

He came closer and looked at the door, making sure it was shut, and brought his eyes back to his old teammate. "I'm in some trouble."

"Okay..." Her tone was intentionally cautious.

He let out a deep breath. "I think I'm being framed for something. I think...well, I think we all are."

"What? What are you talking about? Who's 'we'?"

"Everyone from the team."

"Framed? Virgil, for what?" Her heart started pounding.

"I'm not sure yet. You don't know anything about this?"

"Of course not. Why would I? I got out." She motioned outwardly. "I'm down *here*."

"Yeah. All right. Sorry."

"So...what?" she prompted.

"Did you...did you ever feel at any point like maybe we weren't always fed the right information?"

"How so?" She had, of course. But she wasn't prepared to tell him about Saint Petersburg, about the night she received a secondary envelope containing details contradicting the dossier she had initially been given by Mortimer. "The briefings always seemed tight to me. Why?"

He didn't answer. Instead, he changed course. "Has anyone from the Agency been in contact with you since you made your exit?"

The answer, of course, was yes. Ryan Wilcox had come down to Pine Island just last month and left her with an uninterpreted picture of her father. Risking an honest moment, she nodded, and then asked, "Why?"

"You mind if I ask who?"

"Virgil, I—"

He put up a hand. "I get it. I'm sorry. I know this is weird, showing up like this." He ran a hand across the back of his neck, grimaced. "Was it Ryan Wilcox? He was your head in Kabul, right?"

Ellie's eyes thinned into slits, and her tone hardened. "How do you know that, Virgil? You need to cut it with the tip-toeing around whatever's on your mind. Have you been talking with Ryan?"

"That's the thing, Ellie." He looked unsurely at the floor and then back at her. "Ryan. He's dead."

CHAPTER TWENTY

A NAKED BULB HUNG ABOVE THE WORK TABLE AND cast a dingy glow across the inky room.

He had picked out the wrapping paper himself. Something he had never done in his life. It had taken a trip to Hobby Lobby to get it, something else he had never done before. Why any man would go into Hobby Lobby of his own accord he didn't know. Next time, if there was a next time, and he knew there wouldn't be, he would go to Wally World and get it.

While he cut off a section of paper, he hummed the melody to Pink Floyd's "Money," and it occurred to him just how much he could relate to the lyrics. Like, maybe, had he been born a generation prior and Roger Waters had actually known him, it could have been biographical. He thought of this because he had, in fact, been snagging cash with both hands, even stashing a good bit away. If he kept this up, he figured he'd even be able to afford a Learjet one day in the not too distant future.

He set the scissors aside and placed the package in the center of the blank side of the paper, started folding the wrapping up the little box. It crinkled, and he pressed it over the top, trying to fit a piece of Scotch Tape across the seam.

Three minutes later he stepped back and took a look at his handiwork. He shrugged. It wasn't flat or even. If fact, it looked more bulbous than square and a bit like it had been rolling around for some time at the bottom of a trash can.

But, well, that was all right. All right indeedy, he thought. What mattered wasn't the skill of the wrapping, but the contents of the gift itself. Even more, the heart behind the gift. That is what they said, isn't it?

A gift that would go to a delightful woman, someone who probably didn't get enough presents as it was. And shouldn't everyone get a little care package outside of their birthday and Christmas from time to time?

He picked it up and walked happily back to the main house.

Yes, a delightful lady indeedy.

CHAPTER TWENTY-ONE

"DEAD?" ELLIE'S THOUGHTS WERE SUDDENLY slogging through a mental swamp. "When?"

"Last week. He was in Moscow."

"An accident?"

"No," he huffed. "Definitely not an accident. But they made it out to be."

"Who? Who made it out to be?"

He paused. "I don't know. Ryan came to see me a few weeks ago asking me questions about a mission I had gone on while I was with the team. I didn't give him anything. I had never worked with Ryan before, and up until then I'd never even heard of him. I spent some time digging around, checking him out, and finally had a sit down with him two weeks ago. He was killed six days later."

Ellie looked away and stared at a stack of boxes labeled "scuba." Ryan Wilcox was one of the most capable men Ellie had ever had the privilege of working with. And now he was dead? He hadn't even reached fifty. Question upon question crashed through her mind.

She started with the obvious. "What did he want to know?"

Virgil slid his palms down a weary face. "Ok, so here it is. Faraday and I had been sent on a brief assignment that took us to Australia. Perth. It was labeled 'Bonsai.' The directive was to upload encrypted content onto a laptop left in a hotel room. Faraday planted the information while I took lookout. We got in, we got out— *semper idem.*"

Semper idem. It was a phrase Ellie had not heard in a long time. *Always the same.* Each mission was different, but what remained the same was a commitment to get in and get out. That never changed. But now an unholy entropy was beginning to taint everything Ellie looked back on; everything, it seemed, *was* changing.

"I was the only contact Ryan had for that mission," Virgil said. "Obviously, he couldn't ask Faraday." His voice trailed off. He was right. Faraday had been killed two years before the team broke apart. While on assignment, she had been hit in the neck by a sniper round after making a hasty exit from a building in Mogadishu. It had been the first and only fatality their team would experience.

Virgil continued. "And predictably no one knows where Mortimer is. You probably know that when we all left Brussels he retired from civil service altogether. But now it seems that no one can find him either."

Ellie had known that Mortimer retired. She hadn't, however, realized that he had ghosted. "What makes you think that you—we—are being framed?"

"Because whatever we put on that laptop in Perth evidently had information that detailed our complicity in not only all the missions we ever went on but, get this, each mission for the next fifteen months thereafter."

"How's that possible? Unless…" she stopped talking. There was a picture trying to form in her mind, and it was coming together rapidly. "Unless the wizard behind the curtain knew what levers he was going to pull well in advance." When her eyes came back to Virgil's, she knew she wasn't wrong. "Oh God," she said.

"Yeah," he said soberly. "I know I'm breaking all kinds of old protocol telling you all this, but, Ellie, I'm scared. One day I'm chartering a boat down in Panama, and the next my entire perspective of the last decade of my life is turned upside down." He looked at her with worried eyes. "Ellie." Their eyes met. "What did we do?"

She tore her gaze away and chewed nervously on her bottom lip. *I don't know*, she thought. The nightmare borne of her previous suspicions was true. There really was a monster under the bed. "What you are going to do?" she asked.

"I'm not sure. I can hide as well as anyone. But my concern isn't falling into the shadows as much as it is never being able to come back out of them."

"What all did Ryan tell you? Did he leave you with anything else to go on?"

"No. That was the only window he opened, but he hinted that well trusted people within the Agency are behind it. I think he was trying to put all the pieces together, someone found out, and," Virgil snapped his fingers, "lights out. Right now I'm trying to get in touch with everyone from the team and seeing if I can create a picture of my own. You're the first one I've reached out to."

"What about Bri—Voltaire," she corrected.

"You know his name?"

"Yes. That's...a different conversation. Do you know where he is?"

"No. He's vapor. Can't find him anywhere. Cicero's in Arizona. I'm going there next."

They couldn't stand here talking much longer, but Ellie still had one more question. She couldn't let him leave without knowing. A dread pressed heavily on her chest. She didn't want to ask because she didn't want to hear what she already knew would be his response. "Did Ryan happen to say anything about my father?"

"Your father? Why would he do that?"

Disappointment came easily. "Nevermind."

"Listen, I'll be in touch. I'm going to find out what's really going on. But you need to watch your six. I don't know what kind of purgatory we've just fallen into."

"Thank you for letting me know, Virgil."

He shook his head. "I'm not Virgil anymore. Haven't been in years." He extended a large hand. "Ethan. Ethan Bradford."

She shook it. "I always had you pegged for a Sam or a Barry."

He shrugged. Then with a final nod, Virgil opened the door and stepped out. When it clicked shut behind him, Ellie was left alone with only anxious thoughts and fresh concerns. She closed her eyes and rubbed her forehead with her fingertips. Ryan was *dead*. An adept man who had given his entire life to serve this country. She tried not to let it get to her that the one link she had to the mystery of her father was now gone and she had no other leads. But it was getting to her. By way of a tangled ball of anxiety whirling behind her sternum.

Who had killed Ryan? Why? Where was her father? Who was her father? Who was framing them? For how long, and why? She had no answers to these questions; neither, it seemed, did Virgil. He had come here and verified a suspicion that Ellie'd had for the last four years: that TEAM 99 had been complicit in illicit action and may have, in some part, acted as the muscle for the political version of a mobster. After all, isn't that what some politicians were? Mobsters with pretty smiles, corny comb overs, and firm handshakes? She had served her country with honor. They all had. If Virgil was right, then whoever was set against them wasn't going to get away with it. They had picked the wrong group of people to incriminate.

Ellie opened the door of the storage room and flipped the light switch off as she stepped out. She negotiated her way out of the dry dock and back to the boardwalk. Tyler was standing at The Salty Mangrove, holding a beer and watching a baseball game on the flat screen set above the bar. She didn't try to mask her concerned eyes, her taut face. "Hey," she said softly.

Tyler looked over and his smile evaporated. "Are you okay? Geez, Ellie, you look like you've seen a ghost."

She forced a smile. "I have."

CHAPTER TWENTY-TWO

THIS TIME, CÉSAR SOLORZANO HAD DEFERRED TO Ringo for the location of their meeting. For the last decade, like clockwork, the two men met once each year somewhere off the U.S. mainland, generally on the coast of a neighboring country—Cuba, Jamaica, Grand Bahama. The meetings were to discuss business: changes in the marketplace, new technologies, strategic alliances, the most recent government policies and directives— U.S., Mexican, and South American. With Ringo's policy of not speaking over the phone, it also afforded them an opportunity to ensure their relationship remained healthy and intact. It had been eight years since Ringo had agreed that Ángeles Negros, the fierce cartel that César represented, would be his one and only supplier. And for the better part of those eight years, the arrangement had worked well on both sides. The cartel gained another trusting and discerning associate in the U.S., one who continued to purchase larger quantities over time, and for Ringo it meant the cartel would not be selling to local competitors, few as they were now. For nearly a decade now, that relationship had held solid, and a genuinely mutual respect had been established between both parties. Up until recently, that is, when César had become more and more intent on getting Ringo to expand his portfolio of interests and products.

El Toto was Ángeles Negros' harsh and pitiless leader, and for the last fifteen years César, a childhood friend of El Toto, had risen through the top layers of the cartel's ranks to become one of only four men in their leader's small and trusted inner circle. But, as Ringo had come to see of late, the years of undisputed power and success had begun to make César forget that business, even illicit business, was built and maintained by a mutual respect and trust. Ringo was not a low-life. He was not an expendable border donkey or a boat runner speeding across the Gulf at ninety knots, hoping to evade detection.

No, he was the cartel's most valuable contact in Southwest Florida, and one who, every couple of quarters, increased the value of his orders. César had begun as a shrewd and discerning man of enterprise—one could even say a friend of sorts—but over the years he had cloaked himself with a hubris which spawned an incessant need to have his own way, even if he did maintain a charming and hospitable disposition.

Ringo had always been clear: one meeting a year, and up until this year César had respected that. Ringo had no desire to get caught with his hand in the cocaine jar. So, the less they spoke, the less they met, the easier it was for Ringo to lay low and stay off the radar of agencies intent on finding men like him. Today would be Ringo's third meeting with César over a span of ten months. Adding folly to folly, César had, of recent, begun prodding Ringo to sell heroin and guns in addition to cocaine. Ringo wasn't interested. Not in the least, and César knew it. Ringo's stance, even before his relationship with the cartel, was that he was only and ever interested in selling cocaine. Nothing else. New kinds of drugs, weapons—these required new networks, new allegiances and alliances, greatly increasing the chances that someone, somewhere, would slip and Ringo would be caught up in the net when it fell.

So now, here he was, waiting with Chewy and Andrés for César to arrive. Ringo had selected the Barracuda Cay Resort in Crown Haven, located on Little Abaco, one of the Bahamas' most northerly islands. He had been here before, this exact spot, a couple years ago, all by himself, after he received the news that his best friend had died in an automobile accident in Cape Coral. He had holed up here for two weeks, thinking that it might help him heal. The ocean had a way of doing that, its expansive waters and open horizons allowing you to pour your pain and confusion into it, absorbing it all like a faithful friend and carrying it far, far away.

But two years ago, when he was grieving the loss of Frank O'Conner, it hadn't worked. He sat here, here in this very bungalow, and cried, mourned, and drank far too many bottles of local rum that still couldn't—didn't —burn or cloud away the cradle of sorrow that had opened up within him. And it was then, toward the end of his stay, after he had set the impotent rum aside, after he had cried his last, that he discovered a hard kernel of apathy wedged inside him like a malignant stone. Maybe it had been there all along. Smaller for sure, much smaller, and he thought that maybe it had started to form that day when he found Norma Jean's body bobbing in the ocean like a fallen buoy. That day that she and Gunny were murdered. Maybe that's when it started to grow in him. A subsurface indignation that burned hot and, as the months and years went on, cooled and left a hard and dispassionate place within; a cavern in his heart that would never feel again.

Still though, he felt for so much.

Now, he stood with the toes of his Birkenstocks hanging off the edge of the bungalow's deck, looking out at the horizon, allowing his thoughts to return to the present and to the conversation he was about to have. The bungalow was an overwater style, mounted on hidden pilings and sitting only a few short feet above the calm, bright cerulean waters that flanked the island. The quarters featured glass floors in the master bedroom, outdoor showers, its roof and indoor ceiling made of dried palm fronds, and interior curtains that took the place of walls and doors. It sat two hundred yards off a private beach, positioned like an island of its own in the middle of the shallow, transparent waters.

Ringo walked to the back deck, found some shade, and laid down on a bamboo lounge chair. He closed his eyes and finally lost track of how much time elapsed before Chewy appeared from around the corner. Chewy had set his earbuds aside for the soothing sound of the water lapping beneath the bungalow. He sat down in a matching chair next to Ringo and adjusted the back support so that he was in a sitting position.

Ringo, shades on, looked over at him. Chewy was still wearing his trench coat. A delightfully sunny summer day in the northern Caribbean and Chewy was still cold. Ringo was stocky for a man his height, but not what one might call fat. If he put on that trench coat he would pass out in three minutes, maybe two. Chewy, on the other hand, appeared as content as an eskimo ice fishing in the North Pole.

Chewy said, "I just heard from one of César's men. His Viking docked a half hour ago. They should be here any minute." He looked like he was going to say something else but didn't.

"What's on your mind, Chewy?" Ringo thought he might hear a concern about the conversation they were about to have with César. Instead, Chewy said, "I think I would like to live here one day. In a place like this. My grandmother always talked about living in the Caribbean. She never did make it. Never had the money. I think this could be my most favorite spot I have visited with you yet, Ringo."

"You should buy it one day," Ringo said. "Make it your own."

"You pay me well, Ringo. I don't have the money for a place like this. It's not even for sale."

"All good things in time, Chewy, my friend. You deserve a place like this. Everything is for sale."

Andrés stepped into view. "He's here."

Ringo nodded at Chewy. They stood and Ringo tugged down on the bottom of his Hawaiian shirt, a white background graced with small images of palms and conch shells. Ringo then walked around the perimeter of the structure and turned down the short boardwalk that led to a docking slip. Three men had just stepped out of a skiff and were coming toward him. One wore cream-colored linen pants and a white dress shirt that was open four buttons down, revealing an ample carpet of chest hair and two gold chains that glistened in the bright sun. His dark black hair was slicked back with a high shine, and a brilliant silver watch adorned his left wrist. César Solorzano. Two large men followed behind him wearing navy blue shorts, white polos, and shoulder holsters. His bodyguards. Ringo met César halfway to the bungalow, and they exchanged a brief hug, a kiss on each cheek. The azure waters lapped beneath their feet and cast the entire panorama in a field of bright and stunning display.

"A beautiful location," César said.

"Come, let's have a drink."

They walked back into the bungalow. César acknowledged Andrés and Chewy with a nod. They entered a spacious room whose blue curtains were pulled back to an exterior wall and opened the view over the northern waters of the Atlantic. A calm breeze ran through the room, stirring the curtains. Ringo motioned for his guest to sit in a cushioned bamboo chair. When he did Ringo took the seat across from him. One of César's guards remained in the doorway, the other a few feet behind his boss. Chewy approached César with a glass of golden rum. "Two cubes, just as you like it."

César's teeth were perfect, large and white. They shone brightly, maybe too bright, as he smiled his thanks. "You remember well. Thank you, Chewy." He turned his attention to Ringo. "Well," he said, and gestured with his glass, "we have much to discuss, old friend. Many changes are happening, and I want to make sure you are a part of all that we are doing."

Ringo said nothing. He had come to listen, nothing more. César had wanted a meeting, so he had given him one.

But he was about to give him something else, too.

CHAPTER TWENTY-THREE

Jᴇᴀɴ Oɢʟᴇsʙʏ ꜰʟɪᴄᴋᴇᴅ ʜᴇʀ ᴘᴀɪɴᴛʙʀᴜsʜ ᴀᴄʀᴏss ᴛʜᴇ canvas and finished the flounder's tail to her satisfaction. She paused, scanned the canvas, then lightly jabbed the bristles at the image a few more times before smiling. It was perfect. She tossed the brush in a jar filled with murky water, and it clinked against the edge of the glass before sinking down into the water.

Now that all the planning and execution of Mango Mania was behind her, she was afforded more time doing what she really loved: letting her imagination dance on a canvas. Over the last few years, as her renown had grown, more time had to be dedicated to running the business, working at it more than on it. The image before her was the first original she had painted in over a month.

The doorbell rang across the house: the sound of seagulls followed by a foghorn. "Just a minute!" she called out. She stepped from her easel and worked her way down the hallway. She pulled the heavy door open, and her smile faded into a frown. No one was there. She took a step off the threshold and looked out, down the long steps, left and right. "Hello?" Nothing. She shrugged to herself and started to turn back into the house when her foot bumped something sitting on the mat. She looked down. A small package sat at her feet. She reached down, picked it up, and looked it over. It was wrapped with a blue and silver metallic paper. The wrapping was crumpled and looked as though a toddler had put it on unsupervised. Delightful, she thought. A small red bow was perched on top, and a tag hung off a nylon string. It read, in clean handwritten print: "To Ronnie's mother, Jean." She went back inside and shut the door behind her, walked back into the kitchen. She set the gift on the countertop, and the wrapping crinkled as she tore it back. The white cardboard box wasn't more than five inches square. She smiled. Her friends knew how distraught she was over her boy. Someone had thought of her and wanted her to know they cared. Oh, how she just loved this little community of hers.

Jean pulled back the top flaps and peered inside.

She gasped. Then she screamed. Her vision blurred and then spun, stirred by an unseen spoon. She grabbed the counter.

Peering up at her, like something behind the glass at a butcher's counter, was a severed thumb.

CHAPTER TWENTY-FOUR

RINGO HELD BACK A YAWN WHILE HE LISTENED TO HIS Mexican associate wax long on the virtues of extended distribution and product diversification. "When El Toto came to power," César was saying, "he was strictly involved in marijuana and cocaine. His business acumen in dealing with the latter has now put him above the success of Escobar and El Chapo. He is the most feared and successful leader in my country, more than even President Nieto himself."

"He has done especially well this last decade," Ringo agreed.

"And now he is running guns, heroin, methamphetamines. He is like your Walmart, our Superama, the most choices at the best prices." He chuckled to himself. "Now, that is El Toto. But let's talk about you. Ringo, you know that we have much product running into and through Miami. It has the largest ports with the most international cargo. But it does have its problems. With the appointment of your new Attorney General, your government has become more aggressive, resulting in more seizures. Very large seizures that are even making headlines in your newspapers and bringing swift promotions to your Coast Guard and DEA officers."

"I am aware."

"You have been slow and steady over these many years we have worked together. Like a turtle, I think is your expression. Our shipments get through a large percentage of the time, and you have continued to accept larger and larger hauls." César's ice clinked against the edge of his glass as he took another sip. "So, I must insist that you take on more than you are now. Our production is higher than ever, and we need to get it out of our hands. The two thousand mile border at our two countries, between Arizona and Texas, has forty-seven official border crossings. We control two thirds of those and will have three or four more by the end of the year. The preferred areas for tunnels and river crossings are overworked. That brings us to Florida. Most especially Southwest Florida, as a most effective entry point." He smiled confidently and took another sip. Then he took a brief glance into the glass and frowned at his hand. He blinked, seeming to shake off something that had started to bother him. He looked at Ringo. "What do you say?"

Ringo looked out toward the horizon, was slow to answer. "I can take another five hundred kilos each month. I understand that's nothing in your estimation, but I have increased my buy year after year by over fifty percent. Depending on how we decided to help you bring it on, that's one to two more drops each month."

César's expression revealed genuine disappointment. "I was hoping you would take on much more than that.

I need you, Ringo. El Toto has warehouses of product just waiting to be consumed by wealthy Americans."

Ringo kept listening, allowing him to speak, allowing him to believe that he was still in charge.

"You would continue to select the drop-off points. I do not want you getting caught, my friend. You are important to me."

"Why?"

César tilted his head. "I'm sorry?"

"Why am I important to you?"

César glanced curiously over at Chewy, who was standing against a wall, and then back at Ringo. "You are dependable. Very hard to find in this business."

Ringo sighed. "You have asked me to get into heroin. What was my answer?"

"You said no. At the time."

"You have asked me to get into guns. What was my answer?"

"Again, you said no, but I thought—"

Ringo held up a hand and sat up in his seat. He leaned in, took off his sunglasses, and looked at César directly in the eyes. "You and your fancy clothes and your women and your pride. You are dissolute, César. We all have our personal vices, but I have a real problem when those affect business. César," he said emphatically, "your vices have affected my business."

César waved him off. Just as he had for the last couple of years. He smiled, but it vanished on Ringo's next words. It would be the last smile of his life.

"What I have discovered these last couple of months, since our last visit in Cuba, was that El Toto's feelings are akin to mine on this matter. When it comes to you, that is. He has told me that you dishonor many other of your partners as well and are beginning to make more trouble for the cartel than you're worth."

César frowned. He looked down at his hands again, appearing confused, his voice now sounding as if it had imbibed a chill. "What is it you are saying?" he asked. "You expect me to believe—what was in that rum you gave me?" He blinked hard, and his breathing hastened. He tried to focus. "You expect me to believe that...you have spoken with El Toto?"

If this was a game of gin rummy, Ringo had the Joker. If it was Texas hold 'em, he had cowboys—pocket kings—and César had no aces. Ringo knew this because he had been the one to deal this particular deck, and he had taken the aces out. This was where he laid his cards down.

"This little thing you and I have. I'm putting the kibosh on this," he waved his hand, "whole thing." Ringo nodded to Andrés who stepped up and laid a cell phone into his boss's hand. Ringo pressed a few buttons, and the phone rang on speaker.

"*Bueno,* Ringo."

César's eyes grew into saucers, black pools of intense confusion. "What is this?" he growled. Now he was looking down at his legs, bewildered. "El Toto?"

"Ah, César. You are meeting with our American friend, yes?"

"*Sí.* What is the meaning of this?"

"Ah, I will allow Ringo to tell you. I must go. My helicopter is waiting."

César's stomach clenched. His boss had never been so short with him, so trite. And what was he doing speaking with Ringo behind his back?

Ringo gave the phone back to Andrés and stared

blankly at César, who could detect neither pleasure nor anger in Ringo's eyes. Boredom, perhaps, but not anger.

"What is this?" he asked again. Ringo didn't have to answer. He already knew what *this* was. He'd seen El Toto do this before. Many times. In fact, César had done it many times himself. He was being cut off, cut out. He tried to bring his hand up and scratch nervously at his throat, but he found that his hand came up only several inches off the arm rest before flopping back down. He tried again. Same result. He tried his other arm. That one would not even move.

"You asked what was in the rum. Excellent question. It is, as I understand it, called cardanerol." Ringo laughed. "And the funny thing is that I can't remember if it's derived from a fish or a frog. Either way, it has begun to enter your skeletal muscles, so at this point you won't be going anywhere."

César's larynx bobbed as he swallowed hard. That muscle still worked. For now.

"Tell me, César...I know that we would both say that El Toto, that he's the king. But would you consider yourself a king or a prince?"

"When you...put it like that, I would say that I am...a prince."

"Yes, I was hoping you would say such. Now, I agree with you. I believe that you are a prince. Perhaps I am one myself." He smiled. "You remember how, last time we met on your boat in Cuba, I said I didn't want to replace the king?"

"Of course."

"I spoke the truth," Ringo said. "But there was one thing I did not tell you."

"And…" It was getting harder to breathe now. "…what would that be?"

"It has been, for some time now, every intention of mine to replace princes."

César pushed past the dread in his chest and said, "You can do no such thing."

Ringo ignored him. "Your mother graced you with a name that means 'king.' But," he rendered a Davidic Psalm, "you will die like one of the princes."

"I…"

But Ringo interrupted him.

"For someone whose name means 'king,' you are a poor leader. Ambition is good, but your ambition tramples the honor of those you work with. You are irritating, and the way you flaunt your wealth as though it defines you makes you a pitiful man. El Toto is worth tens of billions. But the difference between you and him is that he is the same with or without his money. It's how he came to be who he is. Do you know what defines me, César? It's not what I do or even my success. It's love. Yes, *love*. But you—you amass boats and suits and shoes and houses as if without them you are nothing. Because, you know what? Without them you truly are nothing. El Toto is weary of your folly. And so am I."

A shadow moved behind César.

"You know that I try to be creative when I remove someone from this dimension. While you're not worth exercising much creativity over, I did think to double up. The poison, you see, is just to paralyze you. Nothing more. By now you are feeling an incredible amount of fear. And so you should."

And then Ringo smiled. A smile that sent an icy chill down the length of César's arms and would have turned them into gooseflesh had the poison not interfered with his nervous system. A garrote wire whisked around his neck. It tightened, and as César jerked against it his eyes registered a combination of horror and disbelief. El Toto had commissioned him to be taken out. But why? He had been good to El Toto all these years.

As if divining his mind Ringo said, "No doubt you are wondering why it has come to this. And that is the problem. You don't even know. What a shame."

César's face turned a deep reddish purple as he tried in vain to struggle against the wire. Blood oozed from under the wire and tracked down his neck. He sank into the chair back and attempted to use his feet to leverage up, but the back of his head was forced against the rear edge of the chair.

"Look, César. It is your own man doing this. Not mine."

Chewy moved in front of César and held out a small mirror. César's wide eyes registered the view of his own bodyguard standing behind him, strangling him. He tried to twist his head and, in a final effort of physical exertion, turned to face Ringo. Fifteen seconds later his body sagged in the chair, his pristine white shirt collar stained a bright crimson, the wire still buried in the soft folds of his neck.

Ringo stood and stepped up to César's limp body. His dead eyes were staring up into the corner of the ceiling: wide, black, and fearful, as though some haunting, unseen by anyone else, had visited him as he was making his exit from this world. His jaw was slack, and tiny beads of sweat still glistened on his forehead. Ringo reached down and patted the dead man's cheek. "What a shame. You had such beautiful teeth."

CHAPTER TWENTY-FIVE

It took Ellie ten minutes to arrive at Jean's house, half the usual twenty minute drive from her house in Saint James City. Three police cruisers were in the driveway, huddled together beneath high, massive oaks. Jean had called her in a complete panic, and it took a full minute for Ellie to calm her down and get her coherent enough to understand her. As it turned out, Jean had apparently been gifted a thumb currently separated from its owner, and it was sitting on her kitchen counter. Jean said Ronnie wasn't answering his cell and she didn't have Warren's home phone in her contacts. Ellie told her to call the Sheriff and then jumped into her El Camino and sped out, calling Ronnie on Major's land line on the way. He answered, said he was enjoying a 'drinky-drink' and reruns of M*A*S*H. She didn't tell him about his mother's present. She hung up with him, called Jean, and told her that her son was all right.

Ellie darted up the stairs and went through the front door without knocking. Sheriff Donald Gaines met her halfway down the front hall. He was in his early fifties, balding beneath his Stetson hat, standing slightly shorter than Ellie. "Hey, Ellie. Jean said she called you."

"Did someone really send her a thumb?" she asked quietly. There was a joke there somewhere. Perhaps one that had to do with a hitchhiker.

Don's eyebrows went up on an exasperated face. "Yeah." He walked her into the kitchen. "And that's not all. Take a look at this." He took a gloved hand and pulled back the flaps. "I've called in Crime Scene. I didn't want to disturb anything, but after throwing up in the kitchen sink—in a manly kind of way—I spent enough time looking in there to make out two thumbs and what looks like a couple big toes.

Ellie looked at the box. "No..." she said, peering in. The inside of the box was lined with cellophane which was poking out of the top. She squinted and saw a nail with dried, congealed blood covering most of it. The thumb had been severed all the way down where it should have been connected to the hand. Another thumb was topsy-turvy, lying just below it. Don twisted the box and Ellie saw the toes. Two very large toes, the limp, sallow skin sagging down around the severed edges.

Her stomach soured but didn't bring nausea. "Dear Lord." It was like a game of This Little Piggy gone bad.

"Jean told me you've been working on helping Ronnie out of a jam? I hope these aren't his. She said you were reaching out to him?"

"I called him on my way up here. He's good. Other than high BAC levels I'm sure he's fine. And not driving," she added. "He's at Major's house."

"Any ideas who did this?"

Ellie had a fair guess, but she had decided on the

drive up here to play the only legitimate angle she could. "Possibly. Don, Ronnie's trying to keep on the straight and narrow, and some people he knows aren't super thrilled about him doing that." Don knew Ellie was working with the DEA, so she said, "He's a source in an investigation we're running right now, and we're trying to keep it low key."

Don looked at the box. "I don't think it's low key anymore."

"Yeah," she sighed.

"Ellie, you know I have to bring my investigator in on this too. I can't have severed phalanges being gifted to my residents and have no answers for my constituents. This is going to freak people out. Hell, it's freaking me out."

"I know, Don. I'll have my boss connect with you so you both can figure out how to handle this across departments."

"That's fine. We're going to dust for prints—" He caught the pun and clarified. "The box, of course. We'll dust the box for prints and see if anything shows up."

Ellie looked across the kitchen. "Where's Jean?"

"Out on the back deck. I've got a deputy out there with her trying to keep her calm. She have any medication addictions that you know of?"

"I have no idea. Why?"

"If she has any painkillers left from her foot surgery, now might be a good time for her to take one. Don't tell anyone I said that, but hot fried bacon, Ellie, she's a mess. Has every right to be too, as far as I'm concerned."

Ellie opened the back door and stepped out on the deck. Jean was sitting in an Adirondack chair looking out over the water. Billy Under, a young deputy, was standing beside her. When he noticed Ellie coming over, he nodded a greeting at her and went back inside. Ellie stepped in front of her friend and got down on a knee. Jean's bright red eyeshadow had been smeared across her eyelids and left tracks down her face where the tears had dried.

"Hey, Jean."

Jean didn't move, just kept her stunned eyes on the water below. When she finally spoke it was in a soft, dazed tone. "My God, Ellie. Who would do something like that? Is it those people you thought might be looking for Ronnie?"

"I don't know, Jean. But you know we'll find whoever did this. Don is bringing in Crime Scene. They'll get the box to the lab. Did you see anyone when it was dropped off?"

"No. I was telling Don that. I opened the door, and no was around. I didn't even see the present until I was coming back in." Her voice started quivering. "It's so awful, Ellie." She threw her head into a hand and started crying again.

Ellie put a comforting hand on her shoulder. "Hey, it's all right. Ronnie's okay and we're going to find whoever did this and why. I'm so sorry."

Ellie had seen a lot in her days, but this? This was a first. And it hadn't happened to a detainee at Guantanamo, or to a prisoner in some darkened CIA safe house halfway around the world. No, it had occurred in her backyard, to a man whose choices could never have justified such treatment. It didn't matter who you were. This was unacceptable. Ellie had never met Dawson Montgomery, but she knew one thing, no one should be ever be treated in such a way. She felt a bitter outrage begin to rise up within her, a fiery angst to find Dawson and bring him to safety, assuming he was even still alive.

It took a couple minutes for Jean to gather herself. She wiped at her eyes, smearing the red even more. She looked down on her red fingertips but didn't seem to care. "Thank you for coming so quickly. Ruth is out of town, and I couldn't get a hold of Linda."

"Of course." Ellie pulled a deck chair close to Jean's and sat down, held Jean's hand. "I'll wait here with you until they're done inside."

CHAPTER TWENTY-SIX

ELLIE PARKED IN MAJOR'S DRIVEWAY AND WALKED IN through the side door that led into the kitchen. She locked it behind her and called out as she came in.

"Ronnie! It's Ellie."

His head swiveled from the other side of the couch. "Hey, Ellie. What's the word?" He was watching a rerun of M*A*S*H. Hawkeye Pierce was speaking to Major Burns from behind a surgical mask while they worked on a patient. A half-empty bottle of vodka sat between Ronnie's legs. Ellie took a seat on the couch next to him. She picked up the remote and turned off the television. She plucked up the bottle and placed it on the coffee table.

"Hey! What's that about?" His eyes moved slowly, the liquor showing its effects, his words slow but not yet slurred.

"Ronnie, we need to talk." Her tone was firm, and in spite of being in a state of mild inebriation Ronnie sat up and gave her his attention.

"Somethin' wrong?"

"You could say that. Someone paid your mother a visit a little while ago and left her a little present."

He nodded, like that was a good thing. "What kind of present?"

"Two fingers and two toes."

"What?"

"Two fingers and two toes," she repeated. "In a little wrapped box."

"Real ones?"

"I don't think they got them at Sears."

Ronnie's face darkened. "Oh my God...oh my God. You're joking, right?"

"I am not."

"Oh my God." He stood up and then, not knowing what else to do, sat back down. "Is Mama okay?"

"She's shaken up pretty bad. And worried about you. Are you and I on the same page here as to who might be missing a couple thumbprints?"

"Oh man. Well, Dawson, of course. It's gotta be Dawson. But why would they have sent them to my mother? They're trying to scare me," he said, answering his own question.

"You think Oswald is the kind of person that would do this kind of thing?"

"Oh, sure," he said quickly. "Maybe it's like a calling card of his. I guess that's what you might call it. But he's only talked about it before. He's never actually done it, not that I know of anyway. I heard him talk about this place in some old book, the Bible maybe, that talks about someone gettin' his thumbs and toes cut off. Oswald sometimes talked about how brilliant that was because the prisoner couldn't run away out of the camp or town without his big toes. If he did he wouldn't move very fast. And his thumbs, well, he couldn't weld a sword with no thumbs."

Ellie was fairly certain Ronnie mean to say *wield*, but she let it pass.

Ronnie started nervously rubbing the tops of his thighs. "You sure they were real?" he asked again.

"They're real, Ronnie. I won't hear back from the Sheriff's Office until later today or tomorrow as to who they belong to, if they even have the prints in the system. In the meantime, let's assume it is Dawson and they did this to send you a message. Do you think he's still alive or would they have killed him?"

"Man, I don't know. I don't know what Oswald's capable of anymore. I never would have thought he would have actually done this."

"You're still fine here for now. Only your mother, Major, myself, and the Sheriff know you're here. The Sheriff will probably be stopping by, if not asking you to go in to the station for some questions. Make sure it's really him before you open the door. Also, this is going to bring in the FBI. They'll have questions of their own."

"Okay."

"Right now, we have no leads on where any of your old buddies are, but we're still digging and have issued a BOLO for Curtis's Mustang. We'll find Dawson. I promise." Ellie noticed two hardbound books sitting in the middle of the coffee table. She leaned over and picked them up, set them on her lap.

"Major put these here for you to read?" she grinned, trying to lighten the mood.

"Yeah, but I'm just not a real big reader, you know. Other than Harlan's book, of course."

Ellie picked up the first one, flipped through it. All of Major's books were scarred with pen where he had underlined sentences, circled phrases, and scribbled tiny notes in the margins. This one, a biography on Maximilien Robespierre, written by J. M. Thompson, was no exception. Ellie could remember reading her own copy of this very book during her early training with TEAM 99, training that included hundreds of hours of classroom time, one class which was designated "Power and the Politik" and brought her face to face with ruthless political leaders such as Robespierre, Queen Mary I, Mao Zedong, and Slobodan Milosevic. They studied corruption in the business world including numerous Russian oligarchs, the pervasive political fraud in Nigeria, and rampant corruption that had begun to stunt India's development efforts. The class had been architected to give each person on the team an education on power: its influence and effects, and both good and bad exercises of it. Ellie had come away with a reformed view of power. Yes, absolute power corrupts, and absolute power corrupts absolutely, but what they quickly learned was that the powerful generally swam well below the surface, out of sight, exercising influence in subtle and unseen ways. And some of them posed a threat to the United States and needed to be taken out.

Virgil's haunting words echoed: *I think I'm being framed for something. I think...well, I think we all are.* She was going to have to face what that might mean, was going to have to peel back the layers of the last decade, the very thought of which forced her to fight back a settling nausea just thinking about it.

"Ellie?"

She shook out of it and glanced at the other title on

her lap—a lighter, albeit no less intriguing read—*The Letters of Hemingway*. She returned the books to the table.

"Just didn't really seem like my types of books...so, you know," Ronnie said.

"I think M*A*S*H is just fine. So Ronnie, after the Sheriff's Office talks with you, dollars to doughnuts, the FBI will be right behind them."

"Sure. I understand. I just hope they can find Dawson. Hope it's not too late."

"Me too. Listen, you cannot leave this place. Okay? Stay away from the windows and keep the doors locked. You'll be safe here, so don't go do anything stupid like going on a walk or getting a ride to go see your mother. Are we on the same page there?"

"Yeah. Same page."

"Listen, I would stay and wait with you, but I have to head to the airport. Call your mother and do what you can to ease her mind. That delivery really messed her up."

"Okay. I will."

When she left through the side door, Hawkeye was commenting to Radar about a visiting doctor's bosom.

CHAPTER TWENTY-SEVEN

THE FORT MYERS AIRPORT, SOUTHWEST FLORIDA International, came in just behind the San Diego International Airport as the busiest single-runway airport in the country. Its service area reached as far north as Bonita Springs and south all the way to Naples and the Glades. In an average year, nearly nine million passengers passed through its three terminals.

Today though, for Ellie, there were just two.

Four years had passed since she had seen her sister and her niece, since she had come home in-between assignments on an eight week furlough. Chloe had been only two years old at the time. Now she was heading toward her sixth birthday.

Ellie stood at the baggage claim, waiting for them to appear. Katie had texted five minutes ago to say that their Delta flight had landed and was making its way toward the gate. Ellie thought of the years missed, how life rarely conformed to the dreams you had when you were young. But today, the bitter years that had taken so much were starting to give back. The dry branches of a withered tree were beginning to bear sweet fruit.

Ellie watched as an older man stepped up to the baggage carousel and waited for it to turn on. He was tall enough, a couple inches off six feet, his slender build much like her father's. He wore a gray herring-bone fedora and had a windbreaker draped over an arm. Now, Frank O'Conner was the only missing piece.

A crowd of people emerged from around the concourse wall that blocked off the baggage claim from the terminal access. A few dozen people spilled into the baggage claim and gathered at various points around the carousel, waiting for it to jump to life so they could grab their luggage and be off. Ellie searched the crowd for a familiar face.

She saw it. Her sister's brown hair bobbing amongst the thinning crowd. Their eyes met, and they smiled at the same time. Katie looked down, and Ellie followed her gaze to a young girl, brown curls encircling her neck, a small backpack behind her. When they approached, the little girl looked up at Ellie with the widest hazel eyes Ellie had ever seen. Ellie squatted down and placed a hand on the girl's shoulder. "Hey, Boo. How was your flight, sweetie?"

She laughed and threw herself into Ellie's arms. "It was good, Aunt Ellie!"

Ellie wrapped her arms around her niece and grit her teeth to keep from losing it in the baggage claim. Tears pooled and she blinked them away. Ellie pulled back and took another look at the young girl. "Chloe! You're so big now. Look at you!" Chloe beamed under the compliment. Ellie put a knee on the floor and brought something out of her pocket. "I got this just for you." She handed it to Chloe.

"It's mine?"

"Yep. All yours."

Chloe giggled as she surveyed the pelican shaped lollipop.

Ellie stood. "Welcome home, Sister." She stepped in and gave Katie a hug that was years overdue. Katie held her tightly and started to cry. "I'm sorry," she said.

"Stop it," Ellie whispered. "You're here now. That's what matters. We're together." Katie nodded into her shoulder.

"Mommy, that's my bag," Chloe yelled, and pointed to a small pink suitcase moving behind them. Ellie leaned down and picked Chloe up. She kissed her on the cheek. "Come on, let's go get it."

THE DRIVE back to Saint James City would take nearly an hour. Katie ran her hand across the El Camino's dash. "I'm glad you took this," she said. "You always liked it more than I did."

"What's there not to like? A car and a truck in one. It's the perfect vehicular marriage."

"How is Major these days? I've talked with him a couple times these last few months, but he's not real good at talking on the phone. I think he tries, it's just not his thing."

"He's good. He still alternates his time between here and his other marina, but when he's up here we go fishing or grill out at least once a week."

"How's he doing with Dad being gone? They were like brothers."

Ellie pushed back the image of her father huddled in a subway. She hadn't told her sister yet. The truth was, she didn't know what to say. *I think Dad faked his own death. He's somewhere where it's cold, and I have no clue what he's doing. And, oh, my old boss who let me in on that has been murdered.* No, she would say nothing until she had answers, until the truth ascended and shed light on what was currently full of shadow.

She shrugged as she exited Interstate 75 and turned west onto State Road 884. "That's the one thing he never talks about. He's a closed lid when it comes to Dad. If I had my guess it still hurts too much for him to talk about. Dad was the only friend he had left from the old days." Ellie turned the A/C up and switched lanes. She glanced in the rearview and saw Chloe leaning against the door, her hands tucked beneath her cheek, her eyes closed. "How was Seattle?"

"Exciting at first, but, Ellie, it's like rainy and cloudy almost every day. I couldn't have gotten wetter had I just jumped in the ocean. But I needed that time away. I needed to get out of here and figure out how to grieve Dad. I couldn't do it wrapped in a blanket of memories. I met some good people out there, and Chloe had a couple friends from daycare. But the weather…" They laughed together, and Ellie glanced at her sister. Katie took after their father when she smiled. The corners of her eyes squinted, and her chin rose. Of the two of them, Katie resembled him the most. The higher forehead, the green eyes, and that laugh.

"Do you have a job lined up yet?" Ellie asked.

"I'm going to freelance. I made a few connections with some startups while I was up there, and they want me to do some software design work for them. How about you? You still grabbing up bad guys?"

"Trying to. It's been a change of pace, that's for sure."

"We're still on for Major's birthday party, right?"

"Yep. The night after next. It will be nice, just the four of us. I've got a painting from Jean Oglesby for him. It can be from both of us."

"Oh, I love her. Are you sure about the painting?"

"Of course."

"Thanks. Have you been by the house yet?"

"I swung by yesterday. It's all ready for you. The cleaning crew did a good job cleaning up after the tenant." Ellie pulled off the road and under the canopy of a gas station. "One minute," she said, "I need to fill up."

CHAPTER TWENTY-EIGHT

THE HEAVY SPIKED GATE SLID SLOWLY TO THE LEFT, and once it was mostly open he drove his Camry into the compound. There was no driveway to speak of, so he parked in the hard-packed dirt next to a white panel van. As he got out, the front door opened, and a man walked out to greet him.

"Aldrich, my man, my man. How are you?"

"Fine, Eli." He walked over to the trunk, opened it with the key fob, and reached inside. He withdrew a brown canvas bag and shut the lid again.

"Come on in," Oswald said.

They entered the dark, narrow hallway and took a step down into the carpeted living room where a couple men in cutoff t-shirts were sitting on the floor cleaning a couple rifles. Oswald extended a genial hand. "Have a sit, Jimmy Jangle. You want a beer, a whiskey?"

"I'm fine." They sat and Aldrich, looking down at the bag, said, "Thank you for keeping this for me."

"Sure, man. It's no problem. No problem at all. When will you be back to get it?"

"My buyer will be in town next week. No later than six or seven days. Where will you keep it?"

Oswald shrugged, like he hadn't considered. "Don't know. Does it matter?"

Aldrich glanced at the other men sitting on the floor. He looked back at Oswald. Oswald flapped a hand, and the men slowly stood up and left the room. When they were gone Aldrich said, "It's very important. I know you trust your men, but I need to know that you'll be able to keep this in a place they don't know of. I would prefer no one else knows at all. Is that going to be a problem?"

"Oh, no. No problem at all, Jimmy Jangle." Oswald stood up and walked over to the bag. He squatted down, unzipped it, and whistled. He zipped it back and returned to his chair. "Ringo know about what's in there? I thought he wasn't keen on stuff like that? Wouldn't that fall into the weapons category?"

"Let's just say that Ringo doesn't know about this," he lied.

Oswald chuckled. "I'm telling you, my brotha, Ringo's all messed up in the head. He doesn't see the value of diversification."

"What of Dawson?" Aldrich asked. "Is he here?"

"No, man. He ain't here. No sir, no way. What's it to you?"

"Let's say that people are looking for him. If they trace him back to you, then our relationship with you could be exposed. And Oswald, it's very important to me and Ringo that our relationship with you is not compromised."

"Chill out, brother. You are the only person who knows we're out here. This place isn't in my name. They won't find me unless I know about it first. The whole thing with Dawson will die down."

"I doubt that."

Oswald reminded Aldrich of a used car salesman who dressed like he'd intended on going hunting or joining a motorcycle gang but whose closet light had burnt out and forced him to get dressed in the dark. The oily, slicked-back hair curved up into a big wave and made him think of a bad Elvis hairdo, or a good Ace Ventura one. Bright, smiling eyes that seduced the naive into trusting him and his leather pants and leather vest and his thick mat of chest hair and the silver chain hanging off his neck all reminded Aldrich of someone from the Village People. Doing business with someone whose dress could let them double as a male hooker in the darker hours of the night gave Aldrich the willies. E Street Band, that would be better. Even the Heartbreakers or The Black Eyed Peas. But dear Lord, not the Village People.

He looked at the bag, asked again, "Where will you keep this?"

Oswald sucked on a tooth, thinking. He stood up. "Got just the place, Jimmy Jangle. Just the place." He yelled down the hall. "Jesse! Buffer! Go out back and finish the inventory."

A scuffle come from the back of the house, then a tired, "Okay." Aldrich watched as the two men who had been in the living room came back down the hall and drifted out the back door.

Oswald jerked his head toward the kitchen. "Come on, my man. We're gonna get you taken care of. Yes sir indeedy." Aldrich picked up the bag, followed him, and stopped with his host near the refrigerator. Oswald got down and opened the door to the lower cabinet. He dipped his head and looked in. "In there. Take a look."

Aldrich leaned down and squinted.

"It's a false back. A couple feet. I put it in myself. No one else knows about it. Just some cash in there right now. That work for you?"

Aldrich nodded.

"Good. Don't you worry about a thing now, Jimmy Jangle. You're my man and Ringo's my man, and I take care of my people, you better believe I do."

Aldrich motioned toward the hidden nook. "You mind if I do it?"

"Sure. Sure, brother. Just hang on a Montana minute." Oswald got down on his knees, reached into the dark cabinet, and fidgeted around for a few seconds before saying, "Got it," and a muted pop sound came out. He brought a thin, stained oak panel out of the opening, set it to the side, then reached back in and pulled out a small box wrapped in duct tape. He stood back up and swung a hand out. "All yours, Jimmy Jangle." As he watched Aldrich get down and wedge the canvas bag into the cubby, he asked, "Where'd you get this stuff, anyway?"

"You and I both know you can come onto anything these days for the right price." Aldrich stood back up and brushed off his knees. "I've got a monitor in the bag. In the event that it's moved or tampered with, if the contents are disturbed in any way, I'll get notified. Oswald, I don't want to get notified."

"I got you, brother. I'm the only one who knows, and I ain't going to mess with it. It's yours. I'll keep it for a week. I don't want that stuff hanging around indefinitely unless I can keep it way out from the house, out in the storage building or something. Seeing as you don't want it out there, I'm good for seven turns of this fine planet."

"That's plenty."

Oswald put up a crooked grin. "What's it for?"

"I didn't ask you about the .50 cals you have out here."

Oswald's eyes narrowed, he lifted his chin. "How you know about those?"

"I know things too. How your delivery was missing a final two .50 cals that your customer ordered."

"I refunded him for that."

"You know, it's not my business. I'm just making a point."

"Taken, brother."

FIVE MINUTES LATER, as Aldrich drove away, he wondered what had possessed Ringo to do business with Eli Oswald in the first place. The man could lead a crew, that was for certain. He could move cocaine like nobody's business, and Aldrich knew that underneath that strange and aberrant exterior there was a manifold intelligence that lived within. The eccentric facade was surely intended to get people to underestimate him, giving him the upper hand.

But in this particular case, Eli Oswald did not have the upper hand. He had crossed a line. He had broken one of Ringo's rules. And no one broke one of Ringo's rules.

Oswald had been informed that Aldrich needed a place to store a few pounds of C-4. Aldrich had it on good authority that Eli Oswald knew nothing about explosives, and what Oswald had not been told was that there was not C-4 in that bag. It was its close cousin, Semtex, and more importantly, it was packed and wired with a trigger device. A trigger device that could be set off via a wireless signal.

It had been less than a pound of Semtex that had been molded into a Toshiba tape recorder back in 1988 and used to bring down Pan Am flight 103 over Locker-bie, Scotland.

It would be two pounds of the same substance that Ringo would use to soap, scrub, and rinse himself of Eli Oswald.

CHAPTER TWENTY-NINE

ELLIE PARKED THE EL CAMINO BEHIND MAJOR'S JEEP Wrangler and stepped out into a humid evening. A dry rustling issued from a cluster of palms at the end of the driveway, and the air sighed above her as a pelican flew by. The front door of her childhood home was open. She pulled back the screen door and called out as she walked in. It was a bricked one story, its sides wrapped in lap siding, and it sat on a lot in Pineland that saw palms, pines, and oleanders spread generously across a half acre.

"In here," Major called out.

Little footsteps pattered down the hallway, and Chloe turned the corner and ran to her aunt, her arms open. Ellie leaned down and gave her a long hug. "Hey Boo, how are you?"

Chloe was beaming, "Very good. Happy birthday!"

"It's not my birthday, silly. It's Major's."

"I know," she giggled, and ran into the kitchen.

Ellie followed her. Major was sitting at the table nursing a beer. "Hey, kiddo. Beer is in the fridge."

Katie opened the refrigerator door and grabbed a Corona. She popped the top with a bottle opener and handed it to her sister.

"Thanks," Ellie said.

"Katie was just telling me about the job she had in Seattle," Major said. "Programming smartphone applications. Did I get that right?"

"Well done," Katie said.

"You need some furniture around here," Ellie noted.

"Don't I know," she said. "Major brought that couch in the living room over this morning. I think I'll get Chloe a bed with the card the Potters gave me."

Last night Ellie had taken Katie and Chloe down to The Salty Mangrove to see a couple dozen locals who had come out to welcome them back. Gloria and Fu had given Katie a homemade gift certificate to babysit Chloe when needed, and Sharla and Gary Potter brought Katie a gift card to a furniture store in Fort Myers. Other gifts had included more gift cards, a bottle of wine, a fishing pole for Chloe, and beach towels.

Katie took a seat at the table and tilted her head when she noticed the leather-strapped Fossil watch on her uncle's wrist. "Hey, where's your gold watch?" she asked.

"Weird, isn't it?" Ellie said. "It's like seeing Tom Selleck without a mustache."

"Ah, it broke on me. Ellie sent it over to Haskell's to get it fixed. I thought I would've had it back by now, but Fred had to order the glass special."

"Speaking of that," Ellie said. "What in the world happened to it? The glass was shattered pretty badly. Looked like you took it to the driving range and set it on a tee."

He smiled. "Don't worry about it. It was...stupid is all. Fred will get it looking right as rain. So there's a pretty big hurricane about to slam into the Virgin Islands. If it doesn't change course, they have it heading up our way in the next few days."

"Great." Katie rolled her eyes. "Seattle might have all the rain but hurricanes they do not."

Chloe jumped into Major's lap and rested her head on his shoulder. "You made me a happy man, Katie, bringing this little thing back to me."

From her spot at the table, Ellie could see into the living room. "You know, Major, you didn't buy me any furniture when I got back."

"You didn't need me to."

"But Katie got all that money from Dad after he died." She knew that Katie had set it all aside for Chloe's education.

"Uh, oh," Katie said. "Now you've pulled out the big guns. You know that money is for—"

"I know, I know," Ellie laughed. "I'm just messing with the big guy."

Major's brows lowered. "The big guy?"

Katie eyed his midsection. "I mean, she kind of has a point."

"Incredible," he said. "You both wait. All the burgers and beer with catch up to you too one day."

"Not a chance," Katie said. "Just look at us." She did have a point. Both ladies, taller than average and slim, were fit.

"Just you wait," Major said again.

Katie got up, walked over to the pantry, and returned with a wrapped package. She handed it to Major.

"What's this?" he said. "I said no presents."

"Whatever," Katie said. "Open it."

He slipped a finger underneath a seam, and as the paper tore away it revealed a large box featuring the young faces of The Beatles. "A Hard Day's Night," he read out loud.

"It's a collector's edition," Katie said. "It has deleted scenes from the movie."

"Thank you," he said. "This is great."

"Is it a fun movie?" Chloe asked.

"I think it is," Major said.

"About what?"

"It's my favorite band, The Beatles."

"Eww, a movie about beetles?"

"No," Major chuckled. "It's a music band called The Beatles." He looked at Katie, slightly incredulous. "How does she not know who The Beatles are?"

"Hey, she's spent the last year in Seattle. You're lucky she doesn't have Nirvana and Soundgarden memorized."

Ellie slid her chair back and left the room, walked down the hall, and returned holding a wrapped gift of her own.

"What is *that?*" Chloe asked.

"You'll see." She handed it to Major. "It's from all us girls," Ellie said.

Katie looked at her sister and smiled.

Chloe wiggled off Major's knee and stood beside him. "You want to help me with this?" he asked her.

"Yay!"

He lowered his voice. "What do you think it is?"

"I don't know. Open it!"

"Do you think it's a folding table?"

She tilted her head and looked at him sternly and placed her hands on her hips like an exasperated mother. "Open it, Major!"

Everyone laughed, and he and Chloe started in on the paper, pulling it away in sheets. "Careful now," Ellie said.

The back of the frame was facing away from him. Once all the wrapping paper was on the floor, he picked it up and turned it around. He cocked his head back as he took in the image of the pier he loved so much. He stared at it for a long time.

"Wow..." Chloe said softly.

Major looked up, his eyes misting. "Thank you," he said. "This...this is wonderful." He looked at the bottom corner. "Jean did this?"

Ellie nodded.

"I haven't seen this one before."

"It's new," Ellie said. "Fresh out of the box. Or, off the easel, rather."

"This is really great," he said. He stood up and then walked over to the front door, placing the picture up on its side so the bottom of the frame rested on the carpet. He came back in the kitchen and returned to his seat, picked up his beer.

"Chloe, honey," Katie said, "go ahead into the living room and watch some Llama Llama if you want to."

"Okay, Mommy!" She gave Major a quick peck on the cheek and was gone, sitting on the couch, remote in hand, ten seconds later.

"She's so glad to be here," Katie said. "I hate that I missed the last year."

Major shook his head. "Now don't start that. You

needed that time away. You're here now. That's all that matters."

"Yeah," Katie said, and then looked at her sister. "Has there been any progress looking for Ronnie's friend?"

No, there hadn't been, and Ellie was beginning to feel more and more unease over it. She, Mark, and several others in their office had spent the last two days poring over everything they had on each member of Ronnie's old group of friends. Ronnie had produced a few more names he thought might be helpful, names of those no longer in Harlan Tucker's old group but who Ronnie thought might be able to fill in some missing pieces. They hadn't been. No one knew anything at all. The FBI was conducting their investigation and coming up short as well. Each additional day that passed, the chances went down that they would find Dawson alive, if at all. In answer to her sister's question, she shook her head and said, "I'd rather table that for a couple hours if it's all the same."

"Sure. I get that." After Katie took a pull on her beer, she said, "Major, tell us a story about you and Dad."

The dark look in his eyes said that he was taken off guard at the request. He recovered quickly and tried to smile.

"I'm sorry," she said. "I know it's hard. I'm just missing him. It's so good to be back, but the memories didn't leave. Part of me still believes I'm going to see him somewhere. Even these last couple days, walking through the house and turning into the kitchen, half-expecting him to be sitting right where you are, sipping a cup of coffee and listening to All Things Considered on NPR." After Katie had graduated from the University of South Florida in Tampa, she had come back home to Pine Island and couldn't find a good reason to live anywhere else on the island. Their father had liked the idea of her coming back home, admitting that living in a house alone wasn't exactly the catch of the day.

"It's all right," he said. "We all miss him. It's hard either way you swing at it." He stared at the table top and sighed. "What do you want to know?"

Ellie slid off her sandals, brought up her feet, and pressed her toes into the front edge of her chair. "How about a golden oldie?" she said. "One from back before the Civil War?"

"Watch it now…"

"Yes," Katie chimed. "How about the one from when you both arrived at the Pacific with Lewis and Clark?" Katie looked across the table and shared a smile with her sister.

"You both keep being wise asses and see how much of a story you get. You can't go ganging up on me."

"We're sorry," Katie said.

"Yes, we're sorry, old man," Ellie said. "Now cough one up."

"First my weight, then my age. You two…" The back door was open, allowing a gentle breeze to come in. He looked out into the backyard and smiled as a memory surfaced. "You know, your dad and I used to go down to the Keys on the weekends and have a go at it. We loved it down at the lower latitudes. We had this shared passion for being troublesome back then, especially your father. He had this crazy way of getting me to do almost anything."

"Dad?" Katie laughed. "He was always so serious."

"No, no. Not always. Truth is, your mother's death mellowed him out. A lot of who he was died with her." He shrugged. "A lot of me died with him."

Ellie said nothing.

"Anyway," Major continued, "there was a watering hole on Big Pine Key called the Crazy Coconut that we liked to frequent. We didn't get down there much. Eight, nine times a year if memory serves. But this one time the four of us—Norma Jean and Gunny too—all stuffed into your father's little Datsun extended cab and drove the five hours down to the Keys. The ride alone was always good enough reason to go. We'd have the windows down, blasting The Grateful Dead and Billy Joel from the 8-track, and a couple of us may have enjoyed a few beers along the way. Anyhow, this particular weekend we get down to the Crazy Coconut and find that it's closed for a few weeks. A kitchen fire ripped through half the joint, and they were down for repairs. So it being a Friday and us having spent the last five hours rolling over the pavement, we immediately went searching for a different bar. Well, your dad found one." Major shook his head as he sat up and dusted off old memories. "It was, shall we say, not our typical kind of place. I couldn't tell if there were more Vikings or bikers there."

"Vikings?" Ellie said.

"I don't know what they were, but they were big, blonde, and broad. Everyone, even the women, had fire hydrants for necks. They all had leather vests and collectively had more tattoos than the bar had suds. Back then the Middle Keys were a little rougher than they are today. And as it turns out this particular joint had turtle races on Friday nights. Catch was you had to bring your own turtle. Well, we didn't exactly have a turtle of our own. And that's where your father gets this bright idea," Major chuckled. "He sees this monster of a man who had two turtles that he kept in a little cat carrier. Supposedly, this guy would bring two turtles, and once he got there he would decide which one to race for the night. That left one behind. Frank convinced Gunny and Norma Jean to go stand up on the stage with the band and start making out. They weren't dating, but Norma Jean was a lightweight. Get three beers in her and you could get her to...well, nevermind that." He paused and took another pull on his beer, set the bottle back down. "So the whole room starts cheering for them. Frank gets down low and starts walking across the room like a hobbit navigating a room full of orcs. He gets over where the registration table is and signs up this turtle."

"He won, didn't he?" Katie said, grinning.

"Hold on now, I'm not quite there. The race ends up being the best of..I think three rounds, and Frank and this turtle get to the last round. Trouble was, so did the guy whose turtle he was borrowing. It's four turtles on this narrow-framed table about ten feet long. And yes, as it turns out, your father's turtle won. By about half a shell. And when you win they ring this bell, make you throw down a double shot of local rum, and then hand you your envelope of five hundred dollars cash. When the end came, I saw it all happen in slow motion: the biker, who had fat arms, a gray handlebar mustache, and had a couple hundred pounds on each of us, his eyes zone in on this turtle still sitting on the table. He frowns, pushes through the crowd and back to his turtle carrier, and when he saw it was empty, he pushes back through the crowd again looking pissed and walks up to the turtle still sitting on the table for a closer inspection. When he looks up, he pretty much looks like an angry wolverine, and he starts stomping over toward your father."

"Now, by this time your father is up on the stage, has rung the bell—the room is going crazy cheering for him —and had just downed the rum and was reaching out for the cash when I put a couple fingers in my teeth and whistled hard from the back of the room. So Frank turns and looks at me from across the room, and I frantically point to the monster coming at him. He turns to look, but not before the big guy's fist lands square into his jaw. Frank flips around, and I see his eyes roll back and his face disappear and drop down past the sea of shoulders and heads."

Katie put her hand over her mouth.

"Norma Jean and Gunny are off to the side, and I hear her scream. The crowd goes nuts. No one knew why the winner of the turtle race just got knuckled by one of their own, but they loved it. They just ate it up, man. More cheering and now laughing. The big guy walks over to the guy with the cash and points to the turtle table then jabs his finger into his own chest. The guy with the money shrugs and hands him the envelope. The crowd cheers again. And then..." Major laughed to himself.

"What already?" Ellie pressed.

"And then I see Frank stand up, swaying like he has sea legs. He holds onto a microphone stand for balance, and then he's gone and I can't see him. Next thing I know, that envelope isn't in the big guy's fingers anymore, and I see the top of Frank's head bobbing up and down the side of the room, heading toward the front door. Norma Jean saw it too, so the three of us got out into the street just before he did. He's screaming and laughing as he bolts out of there followed by a whole herd of angry thicknecks."

"I don't think any of us ever ran as hard as we did that night. Norma Jean ended up flicking her sandals off. I did too. We booked it back to that Datsun and got it cranked up just as the herd got to us. As we drove away, your father sticks a hand out the window holding the envelope and waves it at them. Norma Jean was giving them the bird with both hands."

"They didn't chase you guys down?" Katie asked, laughing with him.

"We shot it over the Seven Mile Bridge and hid the truck in some overhanging mangroves behind a motel in Marathon. We ended up staying there for the night. I think it might have been Hemingway who said not to go on trips with anyone you don't love. He was right, you know. Those, I think, were the best days of my life."

Major looked into the living room, looked at Chloe watching the television. He looked at Katie and Ellie, sitting here with him. "This is right, all of us being together," Major said.

Katie smiled softly. "It's just missing Dad."

"Yeah," he said. "He and I could have gone out back and taken you both in horseshoes." He lifted a cigar from his shirt pocket. "I'll be on the front porch if anyone wants to join me."

"You go ahead," Katie said. "It's going to take me and Ellie the next hour to put the candles on your cake."

"There you go again."

Ellie stared out the open back door, at the old

wooden playset her father had built all those years ago, at the grass growing up the sides of the narrow horse-shoe stakes.

They were right. Frank O'Conner wasn't here.

But he was somewhere.

CHAPTER THIRTY

OFF-DUTY FLORIDA STATE TROOPER ROBERT BARNES was just finishing up his Philly Cheesesteak omelet at the Immokalee Denny's when the ruckus started.

For the last sixteen years, during which time this particular Denny's had gone through two remodels and countless managers, he came here every Thursday night for dinner. Trooper Barnes had kept the same spot too. All this time and it never changed: the booth at the far rear corner opposite the bathrooms. It wasn't that Thursdays were something special or held some kind of nostalgia or sentimental value. Trooper Barnes just happened to be a creature of habit, and somewhere in the yellowing pages of his past, he had made a habit of coming here on Thursday nights. Thursday night, Denny's, Philly Cheesesteak omelet, two cups of decaf, black, and then home to read thirty pages of Louis L'Amour, shower, and lights out by ten forty-five.

He stood up and wiped his lips with his napkin. After tossing said napkin onto his plate, he made his way toward the front. Martha Sue was standing near the register sobbing into her hands, so he put a hand on her shoulder and asked her what happened. She lifted her head to reveal two tear-streaked jowls, and then she pointed an arthritic finger toward the parking lot and told him that the man had just cursed at her for seating him at a table with crumbs still on it. "I didn't see the crumbs," she told him, "really I didn't." He patted her shoulder and stepped toward the front door, reached for the handle.

But then he paused. It was the color, that very bright color, that gave him such pause. That shiny and terribly obnoxious orange. He didn't see many of those out this way. But here it was. A bright orange Ford Mustang with a plate number of...he squinted through the glass at the bumper: 24X-994A. And, "That's a bingo!" as his brother Gerald would say. Martha Sue was still crying behind him, now retelling the event to an assemblage of co-workers, but Trooper Barnes surprised himself to find that he was nearly smiling. Well, and why shouldn't he be? This was only the second time he had gotten a BOLO himself. The first one occured when he was a young buck, back when it took him four whole days to grow a decent five-o'clock shadow and he didn't know his gun from his holster, way back when he had just started up with the Miami PD and back when they still called it an APB. As it happened some goof in Fort Lauderdale had hopscotched right over his probation and then thought it wise to rob a record store, leaving with eighty-two dollars in cash, but not before he gave the manager two slugs for eyes and left his body strewn out amongst second hand vinyls of Fleetwood Mac and Charles Ray. Stephen Fleming, as Trooper Barnes recalled his name to be, saw his luck run out when he and an off-duty Officer Barnes shared the same laun-dromat one Sunday afternoon. Officer Barnes was not but a few moments away from being fully hypnotized by watching his underwear go round, and round, and round, and round in the coin-operated dryer when Fleming walked in with a plastic bag full of clothes.

So that must be the secret, he told himself now. Off-duty. And he allowed himself a full smile at that.

He slid his wallet from his back pocket and pinched out two twentys, turned and handed them to Martha Sue, told her to keep the change and that he hoped she felt better and that he'd see her same time next week. She smiled weakly and thanked him with genuine grati-tude at the generous tip, and then went back to drying her tears.

He stepped across the threshold and walked down the three steps to the parking lot. Three spaces to his left the Mustang's engine revved up and the driver worked the pedal so the engine belched out a magnificent rattling drone. Trooper Barnes went two spaces to the right and got into his 1998 F-150. He started it up.

The Mustang revved up again, sounding like an adolescent boy roaring for attention. The man who was rude to Martha Sue threw it in reverse and, when he was clear of the parking space, left a thin layer of rubber on the asphalt as he peeled out and turned onto U.S. Route 29, heading south.

Trooper Barnes kept back a fair distance and followed the orange Mustang for three miles, passing through Harker and finally turning east onto Oil Well Road.

Then he slipped his phone from his shirt pocket and called it in.

CHAPTER THIRTY-ONE

THERE WERE THIRTY-TWO PEOPLE IN THE CONFERENCE room; fourteen at the polished walnut table, two sitting in the corners, the rest standing along the wall, everyone in possession of a folder. Special Agent Tim "Jet" Jahner had spent the last hour and a half briefing everyone on the raid scheduled for this afternoon. Six of those present were from other agencies; two with Alcohol, Tobacco, Firearms, and Explosives, three with the FBI, and one with Homeland Security.

Last night, as Ellie was driving back home from Major's party, Garrett had called her in. Much to every-one's relief, Curtis Smith's orange Mustang had been identified. He had led the off-duty State Trooper right to the location of Eli Oswald's compound. Ellie had gotten to the office at just after eleven and didn't slip into bed until five hours later. They had spent the early hours of the morning coordinating with other agencies, Garrett fighting to keep the raid under his control, and waiting for retasked satellites to bring back images of the compound. Garrett was losing his battle to the FBI until, at just after two-thirty, surveillance showed two white panel vans enter the compound and, after being unloaded, leave and end up at a particular dock at Port-Miami, a dock with a history of receiving shipments of drugs from Cuba.

The package that had been left at Jean Oglesby's home had yielded no leads, but finding Dawson Montgomery remained everyone's top priority. The FBI allowed Garrett to take the lead with the understanding that a couple of their agents tag along. Because of Ronnie's testimony that Eli Oswald had also been moving illegal firearms, ATF was sending someone along as well.

Two Special Response Teams divided into three groups would be in full gear and would enter from the front, with the exception that three agents would break off and cut through the rear chain link fence and hold that perimeter. Glitch and his team would be in a surveillance van a quarter mile out, relaying real-time drone footage of the area. Ellie would be set up in the woods; sniper backup in the event that someone fled unnoticed and made it as far as the compound wall. Eric Cardoza had nearly escaped when they raided the Ridgeside property last month. Garrett couldn't afford to chance such a slip-up this time around.

Jet wrapped up the briefing and thanked everyone for their participation, reminding them all why they had signed up for this kind of thing, and then dismissed them.

Mark, Garrett, and Ellie stayed back with Jet. After everyone cleared the room and the glass door had shut, Garrett said, "Listen, we need to get this right. I don't want another agency getting credit for this. Ellie, you got us where we are and we need to make sure we finish this right. Stay smart out there today."

Mark glanced down at the folder in his hand and then back at Jet. "I didn't see what role I have in this. Ellie's my partner. She's up in a tree with a rifle. What am I doing?"

Ellie said, "Didn't I see something in here about you staying back in a cruiser and playing Angry Birds or something?"

Mark rolled his eyes. "I'm serious."

Garrett said, "You didn't get anything on paper because it's all being shared with the other agencies. I want you to keep an eye on the agents that are not with us."

"Keep an eye on?" Mark repeated.

"Yeah, you know, babysit," Ellie said.

"Oh, come on…"

"I was trying to be a little more polite, Ellie," Garrett said. "But yes. Mark, I need you to babysit. They make a call, I want you to hear it. They talk to someone in cuffs, I want you to shut them down. This is our raid, not theirs. They'll get their chance to talk with anyone we bring in. Just not before we do. Either way, I want you on them."

Ellie detected a hint of disappointment in Mark's body language, but he maintained his professionalism. "All right, Garrett."

Forty-five minutes later, much to Citrus's great joy, Ellie took her Bayliner out on the water and spent the next hour mentally preparing herself for the raid, thinking through possible scenarios, outcomes, and the individuals involved.

She and Mark had started this investigation looking

into Oswald's connection to cocaine. But now, at least in her mind, that had all taken a back seat to finding Dawson Montgomery. This afternoon, if they were lucky, Dawson would be at the compound, and they could get him to safety and lock up the crazies that had wounded him.

By the time Ellie brought her boat back up the canal, she was ready to go.

CHAPTER THIRTY-TWO

OSWALD'S COMPOUND WAS EXACTLY THAT. AN EIGHT-foot-high cinder block wall that ran for half a football field across the front of the property and then down the east and west sides. The rear of the property had a standard chain link fence with three-wire barb at the top against which sat tall mounds of dirt, an acting backstop for their shooting range. Access was granted at the front through a sliding chain-driven steel gate, spiked at the top. The compound was the only place within a mile, and other than a couple stragglers at the front of the property the compound had no trees to speak of. They had all been cleared away.

Ellie sat in a thick pine tree a hundred and thirty yards from the compound's southern perimeter. This gave her a view of the entire property. With her depth of experience, this range might as well be point-blank. But setting up further out was unnecessary; just over one hundred yards gave her adequate coverage in the woods without too many trees blocking her field of vision.

From her perch she could see the entire length of the wall and over it into the compound.

She had shimmied up the tree twenty minutes ago, attached her tree seat, and sighted in the rifle, letting it rest against a sturdy branch. Modern sniper doctrine did not see a tree as a preferable sniper's perch as it limited the sniper's ability to "shoot and scoot." However, in a non-battle environment such as this, a quick and sound-less exfiltration was unnecessary. The Florida terrain was flat, and Ellie needed a higher elevation from which to observe the inside of the compound and its perimeter.

Ellie peered through the scope and waited for the raid to begin. DEA policy would not allow her to use any personal rifle which had not first been certified with the agency, so she had been provided with an M110 chambered in a 7.62 NATO caliber. It had a 20" chrome plated barrel with an accompanying 14" suppressor that brought down the sound of the bullet's explosion and discharge to only twenty-eight decibels. An XM151 3.5 - 10x variable power scope was mounted to the rail. It was an excellent weapons system, and, while most certainly an overstatement for such a close range engagement, Ellie found that she was nearly excited for the opportunity to handle it.

Her directive was simple: to provide any necessary coverage for their teams on the ground and to prevent anyone from escaping from the perimeter. She would be the final means of detainment, should it be needed.

The compound had three buildings. Besides the main, one-story house there was a large building thirty yards to the east, framed in corrugated steel. It appeared to be a storage facility. The third structure was a small storage shed that sat at the rear of the property. Early this morning, a Dodge Ram had driven in through the front gate, and Eli Oswald had gotten out and gone inside. No one had come out since. Two hours ago four men had spent a half hour on the compound's makeshift shooting range, discharging rounds from both handguns and semi-automatic rifles. Surveillance over the last fifteen hours put nine people on the property, and no one was discounting the possibility that more could be on the compound that surveillance hadn't picked up yet.

The mood throughout the teams was now grave. This wouldn't be a raid on a stash house where half the occupants might have a few handguns lying around. Today's raid would be against a group that appeared to be dealing in drugs and possibly illegal weapons and had no issues with kidnapping and torturing those who tried to rat them out.

A rush of controlled adrenaline warmed Ellie as she heard Jet's voice through her earpiece.

"All teams report."

"Alpha One, ready." Alpha would come in the front door.

"Bravo Two, ready." Bravo would snake around the rear of the home.

"Charlie Three, ready." Charlie would break off and inspect the two standalone buildings.

"Standby," Jet replied. Only the occasional breath could be heard.

Glitch was in a surveillance van down the road, parked on a dirt trail used only by seasonal hunters. The teams waited for the order to move, waited for Glitch to finishing hacking into the wireless connection to the front gate. Finally, when the gate shuddered and slid a few feet back along its track, Jet said, "Go, go," his voice quiet but urgent.

Ellie watched as Jet silently led the way in, trailed by a team of twelve other officers clad in muted woodland SWAT gear. They silently snaked their way to the edge of the inside wall and moved stealthily toward the main house. Arriving there they tucked in behind the Dodge Ram, the Mustang, and a brown van. Jet gave the thumbs up, pointed two fingers at the front door, and he and his team left the cover of the vehicles. They crept up to the front porch, and Jet stepped back. One of his men sent a battering ram crashing into the door lock. It cracked and splintered under the force.

Barking loud commands, the team swarmed inside.

CHAPTER THIRTY-THREE

He had come out of the rear of the steel building, running like the wind toward the compound wall. Ellie spoke into her microphone. "Charlie, tango approaching south perimeter. Be advised."

"Copy. Engage at—" He was cut off by bursts of handgun fire.

The man on the loose kept coming. He disappeared from her view as he arrived at the wall's perimeter. Peering through her scope she saw a few fingers appear at the top of the wall and quickly disappear. The wall was high. The fingers appeared again, stayed a little longer now as they struggled to maintain a grip. They vanished again and quickly reappeared.

This time, they didn't fall away.

A tangled mess of dirty blonde hair peeked up above the top edge of the cinder blocks. The man was giving it his all, and as his face began to appear Ellie could see that it was flushed red as the man held his breath and struggled to pull himself up. She slid her finger off the trigger guard and aimed just to his left. She slowly squeezed the trigger.

Snap.

Concrete exploded from the wall as Ellie's round tore into the cinder block and exited the other side.

The surprised man slid back but surprisingly didn't let go. His head reappeared, and he struggled up again. He threw an arm over the top and heaved himself up, his chest now leaning on the top of the wall.

She could picture his feet struggling like a frantic mouse on the other side of the wall as they raced to find purchase. Using his arms, he pulled more and came up another few inches. Another half a foot and he would be able to straddle the wall and drop to the other side. He hadn't heeded her warning shot.

That left Ellie only one choice.

She heard Jet's voice advising the teams that they had secured the house. Shots in the steel building had ceased.

Ellie put the man in her reticle and spoke into her mic. "Medic. Make your way to the inside southeast quadrant of perimeter wall. Man down." She slowly breathed out.

Then she fired.

CHAPTER THIRTY-FOUR

THE ROUND HAD PUNCHED THROUGH HIS RIGHT HAND. She had aimed just below his fingertips on the hand that was extended the furthest from his body. She could hear him howling from the ground on the other side.

She waited and watched. No one else manifested. Three minutes later Jet called the all clear, and now that he had agents freed up he stationed one near each inside corner of the compound, directing them to watch the perimeter.

Ellie shuffled down the tree. She saddled her gear and jogged through the woods toward the front entrance to the compound. She trotted past the gate and into the compound that was now swarming with department vehicles. A Kevlar vest sat heavily across her chest, hidden beneath a wooded polo, and it rubbed against the soft flesh of her neck as she moved. She looked toward her left, toward the back end of the property, and saw three agents huddled over the man she had wounded. Mark was a couple cruisers over, speaking with the FBI. Garrett was standing near his Expedition, wearing an agency ball cap and sunglasses. He had his fingers at his ear, listening. He nodded at what he was hearing and then noticed Ellie. "Hey, good job."

Ellie motioned in the direction of the man she had shot. "What's the damage?" she asked.

"He may not be able to give anyone the bird anymore, but he'll be fine."

"Did we get them?" she asked.

"No. Jet said Oswald and Smith are still unaccounted for."

"Dawson?" she asked expectantly.

"No. I'm going in the house. Come with me." An agent came out the front door. Garrett gestured toward Ellie. "Bruce, take Ms. O'Conner's gear, please, and secure it."

"Yes, sir."

Ellie unslung her rifle. She cleared the chamber and removed the magazine, returning it to her waist pack. She handed off her tree seat, rifle, and utility belt to the officer who walked her belongings over to an agency truck.

The interior was dark. Dirty, cream-colored linoleum floors lined the front entrance into the kitchen, and dark wood-paneled walls formed the interior. They walked into the kitchen where seven people—five men and two women—were sitting on the floor next to the table, their hands cuffed behind their backs, a steel cable wrapped through their arms until they were to be escorted off the premises. She surveyed faces that were impassive, stoic. One of the men was even grinning against a nose that was bleeding and appeared broken. None of the faces belonged to their leader.

Jet materialized behind her. He pointed to the man

with the broken nose. "That's the gentleman who opened fire on team Charlie."

"Everyone all right?" she asked.

"Yeah. Lucky for them he seems to have been one of the few people around here who didn't spend enough time at their practice range."

Garrett, addressing Jet, said, "Tear this compound up. I didn't storm in here today to not come away with Oswald. He's here somewhere. Find out where."

"Yes, sir."

Garrett brought out his handgun and started down the main hallway. Ellie unholstered her Glock 23 and drew the slide back, making it hot.

She followed Garrett through the house. They had reviewed old blueprints of the home earlier in the day. Now, as they assessed it in person, they took special notice of where someone could hide. The attic had been cleared. There was no basement. The house was built on a concrete slab and had no crawl space. Together, Ellie and Garrett worked through the master bedroom, tapping the walls, tugging and prodding at the carpet, double-checking the closets. They moved into the master bath, the guest bath, and two more bedrooms before entering what had been set up as a leisure room of sorts.

Ellie touched her mic. "Glitch. Run back tapes from earlier when we saw Oswald and Smith enter the compound. Confirm again they didn't exit. We don't have them."

"You got it."

A green felted pool table sat in the middle of the floor, and a couch sat against the far wall facing a flat screen TV. A refrigerator in the corner hummed loudly like it was about to give out. A bedroll in one corner, beer cans on the floor. Cardboard boxes up to the ceiling in another corner. She slid the boxes around and peered behind them. Nothing. She examined the contents of the boxes. They were filled with Magpul 30 round magazines and military MREs. There was no sign of anyone hiding in the room.

"Glitch," she said into her mic. "You still have a drone on the house?"

"Affirmative."

"Anyone on the roofs? Any irregularities?"

"Negative."

She paused and thought. There were only two options before them. Either Oswald and Smith were hiding somewhere or they had managed to get away. The former was the strongest possibility. They had drones in the air during the entire operation, and the feeds had been closely monitored prior to the raid. Last they had seen, Oswald entered this house from the front door and hadn't left. He hadn't even gone out onto another area of the property. Which meant that he was still here or somehow he had slipped out unnoticed. "We're sure the attic is secure?" she asked. She knew the answer. They wouldn't have sounded the all clear unless it was.

"Yes," Jet replied. "And we're not getting anything out of these morons in the kitchen."

Garrett said, "Let's find them, people. We're not leaving without them."

Attics, closets, under beds, and behind furniture. Ellie walked across the room to the window and checked the lock. It was closed, locked. She moved to the side of the room and slowly checked the paneling and the carpet for seams. She stepped around the hutch that held the television and continued her track forward. She came to the couch and then, with a hard push, sent it away from the wall. Nothing seemed out of place. She pushed the couch back and, as she did so, the tip of her right boot felt a give. She slid the couch back again, pushing harder this time and moving it completely out of the spot where it had been sitting. She pressed her foot into the carpet again and it gave more than it should have. She holstered her gun, got on her knees, and pressed down with both hands. The carpet depressed like a tiny trampoline. Ellie came back to her feet and stepped up to the wall.

Garrett came over. "What are you seeing?"

A tiny strand of carpet stood out from beneath the grimy baseboard. She bent down, grabbed it, and pulled. It lifted a few inches, and after gaining a tighter grip she pulled harder. The carpet came back, and Ellie immediately felt the temperature around her turn cooler. Garrett groaned. She looked down and shook her head. "Well done, Oswald. Well done."

CHAPTER THIRTY-FIVE

ELI OSWALD GAVE A FINAL PUSH UPWARDS, AND THE severed tree stump gave way and light poured down into the tunnel, temporarily blinding him. He heaved it aside and scurried up the last few rungs before falling into a dry carpet of pine needles and scattered leaves. Curtis Smith huffed as he pulled his large frame up behind Oswald and then slid the stump back over the hole. They took a minute to catch their breath. Oswald looked in the direction of the compound, but he couldn't see it. It was only sixty yards away, but from where he was sitting the trees and the unkept growth on the forest floor blocked a clear view.

"What now?" Smith said angrily. "I'm so pissed. We were on such a good roll."

Oswald rubbed the loose dirt off his forearms. "It's Dawson, man. That's how they got to us. No other way I can think of. I should've been more resolute in getting Ronnie. They would have never known it was us if Ronnie didn't talk." He spit then set his jaw hard.

"We're gonna regroup, that's what. First we've got to lay low. Now they're onto us. It won't be like it was before."

"Dammit. We were doing so good too."

Oswald came up into a crouch. "We've gotta go. They'll find the tunnel soon enough, and I don't want to be within a Montana mile of near here, my man."

"Where're we goin'?"

"*We* aren't going anywhere. We're splittin' up. Lay low and don't get caught."

"How will I find you?"

"I'll reach out when it's time, my man. Might be a Montana minute. You should go up to Tennessee and visit Janey. They don't know about her."

"Good idea."

He clapped a hand on Smith's shoulder. "Be careful, my man. Once everything dies down, me and you will come back right as rain, yes siree." Then Eli Oswald stood up and disappeared into the woods.

———

ELLIE HELD HER HAND OUT. "I need your light." Garrett unsnapped his small flashlight and handed it to her. She clicked it on, got on her stomach, and peered down the hole. A makeshift ladder assembled with two-by-fours ran through the home's foundation and into the soil beneath. "It terminates...ten feet down," she said. "And tunnels north." She examined the ladder for anything other than wood or nail heads: wires, a metal or plastic box, switches. Seeing nothing, she squinted down at the end of the ladder and saw boot prints in the dirt. She stood back up.

Garrett had already notified Glitch to reposition the drones over the woods and further down each end of the road. Then he had told Jet to send his men north into the woods and begin a search.

To Ellie's surprise, Mark entered the room. "What are you doing here?" she asked.

"I conscripted him for the search," Garrett said. "That's a priority over keeping the other agencies in line."

"I think they're good," Mark said. "They're hanging back waiting for us to give them the go ahead."

"They'll be waiting a while."

"Is that what I think it—?" Mark asked.

"Escape hole," Garrett interjected.

Mark stepped toward it and peered down, let out a low whistle.

Ellie slid to the edge of the opening and dangled her feet inside.

"What are you doing?" Garrett asked. "You're not going down there, Ellie. Let Jet's guys do it. It could be rigged."

"Do you want to find Dawson or not?" Ellie said.

"Ellie—"

"Look," she interrupted. "We don't have a bomb squad on site. I don't see anything on the ladder. The soil at the bottom isn't freshly turned, so the odds are against it being rigged. Might as well be me." Still, Garrett could be right, so Ellie intended to bypass the ladder altogether and hope for the best. Mark stepped back when she grabbed the edge and started to lower herself down.

"Okay," Garrett said, albeit reluctantly.

Ellie brought her body down into the narrow cavity until her arms were straight and she was holding on by just her fingertips. She let go and landed on her feet. Nothing happened. She ducked down and shined her light down what was a narrow tunnel with no light source. Wood supports ran across the ceiling and down the sides every five or six feet, clearly intended to prevent a cave-in.

"Mark, you coming?" she called up.

Mark looked at his boss. Reluctantly, Garrett nodded at him.

Mark, who felt more comfortable in an office than in some crazy man's escape hole, sighed. "Coming." He maneuvered his legs into the hole.

Ellie told him to bypass the ladder and then crouched into the tunnel and moved out of Mark's drop zone.

Ten seconds later he was in, holding his elbow and grimacing.

"You all right?"

"Yeah. Fine. Just scraped it on the foundation coming down."

"More respectful than a paper cut, I guess."

"Shut it. Let's go."

She took the lead and spoke into her mic, "It's heading due north, Garrett. As far as the light shows, I don't see any turns yet."

"Copy."

The tunnel was narrow, less than five feet high in some places. The smell of damp earth filled the space, and trees and plant roots poked out where they had been partially severed, or not at all. She paused briefly every few yards to listen and inspect for trip wires, but she saw nothing alarming and heard no sound from the other end. Ellie estimated that they had gone roughly fifty yards when Mark said, "This tunnel was not a small feat. They were serious about not getting caught."

Ellie now knew where the dirt backstop to their shooting range had come from.

They continued on, and the further they advanced the greater the certitude Ellie had that they would not find them. You didn't put this kind of effort into an escape route and not do everything not to get caught. They went another fifty feet when the flashlight caught something. Two-by-fours set three feet apart reached upward. "Here it is." They came to the bottom of the next makeshift ladder and looked up. It was seven rungs to the top and terminated at a large tree stump whose largest roots had been severed. Smaller roots dangled off like thick worms with clods of hard packed earth wedged in between. Ellie examined each rung, checking again for anything that would tell her it was connected to an explosive. Again, she saw nothing. Half holding her breath, she climbed up a few rungs and checked again. Then she examined the circumference of the stump's bottom. Still, nothing ominous. She had two choices at this point. She could wait for an agent at the top to locate the stump and examine it from above or she could go now.

She looked down. "Step back. I'm moving this."

"Wait. What if—"

She heaved upwards and shouldered the heavy stump off the opening and onto the forest floor.

"...it's rigged," she heard Mark finish sheepishly.

Ellie brought out her Glock, scanned the immediate area, and exited the hole. She notified Garrett and Jet of their distance and direction from the compound and then called down to her partner. "It's clear. Come on up. Watch your elbow."

CHAPTER THIRTY-SIX

GARRETT STOOD OVER THE HOLE'S MOUTH, PEERING down. The muted sounds of Ellie and Mark shuffling down the tunnel finally turned faint and then disappeared altogether. He turned around and examined the room. The hole had been well hidden and had it not been for Ellie's thoroughness they may not have discovered it until much later.

Something caught his eye on the wall near the window.

He walked toward it. The wood paneling was bulging. Not a large bulge—it could possibly pass for being warped. Garrett decided to look closer. He ran his fingers up the seam where it joined the panel next to it. He tapped on it with his fingertips.

It was hollow. He walked to the next panel, one that wasn't bulging, and tapped. The vibrations were muted. There was insulation behind it. Just as it should be. Walking back to the first panel he pulled out his pocket knife and wedged the blade into the seam, and the makeshift level pressed the thin wood outward. It popped and he slid the knife down further, repeated the motion, popped another brad nail.

Garrett closed the blade and returned the knife to his pocket. He grabbed the panel, and successive pops rattled through the room as he tore it away from the wall. He pulled one more time, and the entire piece gave way. He stepped back, and as he let the panel fall to the floor he stared at the opening it left behind. In the wall, sitting along the cross studs, was the beginning of a veritable armory. The insulation had been removed to make room for the weapons. Fragmentation grenades, handguns, and two rifles, one being the Barrett M107 anti-materiel rifle and the other a Heckler and Koch G3 battle rifle, the grandson of the German 'Storm Rifle' that had been ubiquitous on so many World War II battlefields.

Garrett spoke into his ear mic. "Eight and nine, I need you back here with me."

"We're the only two watching the detainees, sir."

"Jet," Garrett said, "can you replace them?"

Silence, and then, "I have no one freed up right now."

"Eight and nine, they're cuffed and strung together. They aren't going anywhere. I'll switch with you. I need you to document this."

"Yes, sir."

Seconds later two men clad in full gear entered the room. Their eyes bulged as they looked at the weaponry. "Holy Toledo," one of them said.

"Pull all the paneling," Garrett said. "Make sure not to touch anything. I guess I need to get Greg from ATF in here."

"Yes, sir."

And that was the moment when the house was violently shaken by the explosive force of two pounds of Semtex discharging at 8500 meters per second, when everything in the kitchen—the refrigerator, twenty-three linear feet of upper and lower cabinets, a table, five chairs, a sink, a coffee maker, and seven people who had recently been read their Mirandas—disappeared into vapor.

CHAPTER THIRTY-SEVEN

THE AIR SHOOK AROUND THEM, PULSING WITH sonic fury.

Mark froze. "*What* was that?"

Ellie turned wide-eyed toward the compound. "An explosion."

"Oh, no."

They had spent the last two minutes searching the woods around the tunnel opening and found little. Mark had discovered a single boot print. That was it. Ellie had found nothing.

"Let's go," she said.

At that moment three agents appeared from the trees and called in Ellie and Mark's location. Ellie drew up. "What happened?" she asked.

"We don't know."

Ellie pointed back to the stump. "There's the opening. See what you can find. And expand your search perimeter," she yelled as she and Mark ran back toward the compound. They came out of the woods near the road and rounded the wall of the compound, entering through the front gate. A light gray cloud was dissipating high in the sky. Agents were scrambling furiously like terrified ants, and someone was screaming like a banshee in the medic van. Ellie pulled up at the south end of the house where the kitchen had been. The foundation lay bare in a ten foot radius, a large hole in the center of the concrete. The roof in that area was gone, and what was left of an exterior wall lay sagging into the rubble, propped up only by the other end. Ellie could see right into the living room and down the hall, rubble and debris littered everywhere.

Mark muttered something unintelligible, and he followed Ellie around to the rear of the home where they found Garrett sitting on the ground, thirty feet off the rubble, his head drooping between his legs, his arms lanced with tiny cuts, and flecks of wood lay strewn through his disheveled, dusty hair.

Ellie raced up to him, kneeled down. "Garrett. Are you all right?"

He looked up slowly. "Yeah." A long cut was bleeding under his eye.

"What happened?" Mark said.

"They rigged the place. The blast came from...from the kitchen."

Jet ran up and, after silently assessing Garrett, said, "Sir, we just loaded Agent Riggs into a medic van. They're heading out now. Emergency services has been called in." His face was grave.

"How is he?" Garrett asked warily.

"A long piece of timber got him underneath his vest, and it's lodged in deep. It's pretty bad."

Garrett nodded and looked back at the ground. He

put his hands in the dirt, shifted his weight, and grimaced as he stood up.

"You sure you're okay?" Ellie asked.

"Yeah. Fine. Anyone else?" he asked Jet.

Jet touched his ear mic, listening. "Team leaders just reported in. Other than Agent Riggs, we've got one with severe burns on his forearm and neck and another with a broken tibia. We're lucky that, besides you three at the other end of the house, the rest of the team was out searching the area. What about the detainees?" Jet asked.

Garrett shook his head, pointed his chin toward where the kitchen had been. "What do you think?" He pointed to a spot at the other end of the house. The bottom half of a leg, a mangled tennis shoe still attached, lay red and skinless. "We'll only find pieces," he said.

Jet removed his helmet, ran a frustrated hand through his short white hair, and cursed. He threw his helmet down, and it skittered across the hard-packed dirt. "I need everyone to move away from the structures and back toward the vehicles," he yelled across the yard. "We'll need to bring in Bomb Squad and have them search."

They all gave the smoldering rubble a wide berth and followed Jet back to the front.

CHAPTER THIRTY-EIGHT

ANDRÉS PULLED THE INCONSPICUOUS MALIBU INTO the circular drive and waited. He didn't honk. He had learned that lesson the very first week he came to work for Ringo. Honking was disrespectful, in Ringo's opinion. You pulled up, you waited. You waited no matter how long it took.

In this instance Andrés waited less than five minutes, and while he did he turned on his Spotify playlist and sent it via Bluetooth through the car's speakers. The artist of choice was Eminem. Andrés leaned his head against the headrest. He closed his eyes. His cousin Francisco had loved this song, "Not Afraid." It had been his theme song, and he, like the song, said he would break out of the cage one day. The cage that was Ciudad Juárez. That one day when he made enough of his own money, he would get out. But now that day would never come for Francisco. Not after he'd gotten gunned down in the street, murdered by a rival cartel, the individual names of the murderers never to be found out.

Andrés missed his family. His missed his madre.

The door opened, and Andrés sat up and quickly turned off the music. Ringo got in and shut the door. "Andrés. Thank you for picking me up."

"Of course, *Jefe*." He pulled away from the house, down the driveway, and out onto the main road running through the community of mansions. He pulled an envelope from the visor above his head, handed it to Ringo.

Ringo took it and rested his hand on his knee. "He got away?" Ringo finally said.

"Yes," Andrés replied.

"How?"

"A tunnel from what I understand."

"You tell Aldrich I want to meet with him. Yesterday. He has a lot of explaining to do. The wrong people could have gotten hurt. Or worse. It's unacceptable."

"I will tell him when we speak next," Andrés said. "He said he was going dark for the next several days. He also said that he was having problems with the detonator and had intended to do it the day before but that the timing worked out better anyway, at least in his opinion."

Ringo clenched his teeth, and a muscle stood out along his jawline.

"It was foolish, *Jefe*. The timing."

"Yes." He changed the topic. "What is Yolanda reporting?"

"Only good things. Mr. Armstrong has become...what is the word?" It came to him. "Amenable. I am not sure if it had anything to do with the picture we gave him of his children getting on the school bus, but he has not been griping as much."

Ringo adjusted his fedora. "He's a smart man and has built a good business for himself. In time he may come to see that we have done a good thing for him. He's going to make it a long way in the distillery business."

Ten minutes later Andrés pulled up to a small brick building occupied by separate organizations. On the right was the local chapter of the American Heart Association and on the left was the Harry Miles Cancer Research Center.

"After this, do you want to get some shrimp for lunch?" Ringo asked.

"Sure, *Jefe*. You know I am always good for shrimp."

Ringo stepped into the warm, humid afternoon air, cooled slightly by a breeze blowing across the massive Caloosahatchee River just beyond. Ringo took the door on the left and was greeted warmly before he made it to the receptionist's desk.

"Well, there he is. It's always so good to see you." The plump lady had a sweet face and graying hair that curled naturally at the ends. She wore pearls and a shade of lipstick that complemented her complexion. She was classy. Ringo liked classy.

He offered up a charming grin. "That's because I help pay your salary. Hello, Margaret."

"You should pay for my dinner one of these days."

He handed her the envelope.

She took it and stared at it for a while before looking up at him. "You don't know how many lives you're changing," she said softly. "How many you've changed already."

"And I don't need to."

"You need to take it easy," she said. "With all these

businesses you have running, you need to take time for a rest. Don't overdo it."

"You keep on sounding like my mother and you'll have to wait a long time for that dinner." He winked down on her.

"Don't tease me now," she blushed.

He looked at the envelope. "There's a little extra in there this time."

"More? How...can—I'm sorry," she said quickly. "It's not my business. You just do so much."

He couldn't tell her the truth, so he said, "I've cashed out of some investments that came due."

"Molly isn't here. I'm sure she would want to thank you in person, as always."

"No need. Maybe next time. Give her my hellos."

"Of course."

"And as usual—"

"We keep your name out of it all."

He smiled. "You found it under the doormat."

"You should come see me someday when you don't have anything to drop off."

"One day I will. That's a promise."

"Don't break my heart now," she smiled.

"I'll see you again in a couple weeks, Margaret. You're getting away from this storm, right?"

"Leaving in an hour."

He nodded approvingly. "Be good." He walked back out to the car and, as Andrés pulled away, said, "You and Chewy both need to get out of here and head north. That storm is getting bigger. I know you don't get a lot of hurricanes in Juárez, so I'll tell you that they're nothing to mess around with." He turned and looked out the window, looking past the tint but not really looking at anything.

"We will." Andrés could see that Ringo was more contemplative than before he had gone in to drop off the gift. He always was when he came out of there. Andrés knew what he had done, what he had given them. Andrés had gotten the cashier's check himself. He kept his eyes on the road and turned south onto McGregor Boulevard. "You are a good man, Ringo. There are no men in Mexico who work in drugs and then go do what you do. Not unless they are seeking more power. It is honorable."

Ringo didn't answer, just continued staring thoughtfully out the window, an uneasiness crawling through him. One he couldn't quite pin down.

CHAPTER THIRTY-NINE

ELLIE HATED PAPERWORK MORE THAN ANYTHING. SHE couldn't think of what might be worse. Cleaning Porta Potties perhaps, but right now she was thinking that even that wouldn't be so bad.

The raid had ended with one suspect getting two of his fingers blasted off by a close range shot from Ellie's rifle. Forensics had later shown that the man had been high on mushrooms when the raid occurred, and after the medics got him back to the van to care for his hand he started bellowing about the ostrich that was munching on his hands and kept letting off horrific screams as though someone were eating him alive. But the reason forensics had been brought in for this particular individual was that, as he was screaming and as the medics were trying to hold him down, he had managed to unholster one of their sidearms and blew his brains out.

And then there was the explosion that left seven dead, and with Eli and Curtis escaping there was no one to question, no one to put pressure on. So the pressure was coming from inside. She had spent all morning in the conference room with a team from the DEA's Inspection Division, answering questions about the raid and her decision making process. It was standard procedure, but the team from Virginia may as well have told Ellie that they thought she had set the bomb herself. They were just doing their jobs, being objective, but that didn't mean she had to like the way they went about it. In addition, it all meant hours of reports, thousands of words.

By everyone's standards the raid had been fully unsuccessful. They ended up with three wounded agents, one still in critical condition, seven prisoners that had been ripped tooth to toenail, and another who had executed himself with an agency-issued firearm, because of, you know, the ostriches. The explosive used in the blast had been identified as Semtex, a hard to acquire explosive that was still available on some parts of the black market. Early on, Muammar Gaddafi, the deposed leader of Libya, had kept storehouses of Semtex and then in the late 1970s sold tons of it to the Irish Republican Army, among other worldwide factions. After his death the remainder was broken up and pressed into the unpredictable hands of the black market. It appeared that Oswald and Smith had not only escaped but had literally cleared the bases, setting the explosives in an attempt to ensure that no one was left to squeal on them. They had gotten lucky. Eli Oswald had just batted a thousand.

And yet, those reasons weren't the biggest failure of all, in Ellie's opinion. Letting Oswald and his buddy escape was bad all right, but it didn't touch the fact that they hadn't located Dawson Montgomery, and no one remained to tell them where he was, whether he was still alive. That fact alone, accompanied by the image of that open box on Jean Oglesby's counter, had left Ellie with very little sleep last night.

Ellie's desk phone rang. She typed out a few more words and grabbed up the receiver. "Hey, Garrett."

"Ellie, can you put a pause on what you're doing for a minute? Come see me in my office." His voice was strained.

"Sure. Give me a minute." She returned the phone to its cradle and clicked away at the keyboard, finishing her paragraph. She saved the internal document, shut the lid to her laptop, and walked across the room.

Before she could knock on Garrett's glass office door, he motioned for her to come in. "Have a seat." His face was taut. A tiny butterfly bandage clung to his upper cheek where he had gotten nicked in the blast the day before.

"What's up?" she asked. "You don't look so good."

"Ah, I'll be all right. Listen, we need to have a hard chat."

Ellie shifted in her chair. "Okay. Let's have it."

"You've done a hell of a job since you've come on my team. It's been what, nearly three months?"

"Something like that."

"I invited you over here on a whim because I was frustrated that we weren't getting the right people locked up. But as you also know I haven't been given much of a budget to do that. Then I ended up pulling Mark off his primary directive and putting him with you."

"What are you trying to say, Garrett?"

He tried to smile, failed, and then said. "I've got to let you go. For now," he added quickly.

His words scraped against her. "Like, leave the agency?"

"Yes."

"What for?"

"Honestly? Ellie, the casualties have mounted so high I can't talk my way around them."

"But this is the line of work we're in, Garrett. I haven't stepped out of line. Not once."

"I know you haven't. But think about it. We've got two dead Mexicans and five wounded from when you were escorting Victor Calderon back to prison. Then we've got Special Agent Sanchez getting shot in the arm when we raided the stash house over at Ridgeside. And then," he tossed out his hands.

"The compound."

He nodded.

"But why me?" Ellie asked. "The raid was executed properly. By everyone involved. We couldn't have known about the Semtex. Bringing dogs in on a raid like that isn't standard. To search for drugs, sure, but not explosives. Who would have known that Oswald would be the kind of guy willing to nuke his own people? On top of that, the shootout at the barn and the raids on the stash house and the compound were all because of what I brought to the table."

He threw his hands out. "You're preaching to the choir, old friend. But you're the one who shot those men at the barn, and," he paused briefly, "that makes you an easy target. There's just too much politics involved right now. You know as well as I do that raiding a stash house here and there gives up enough kilos to hold up in front of the camera. That looks good for the higher ups. All these deaths? Not so much. I have to answer for them, and my superiors have to answer for them. You know as well as I do that it gets really hard to explain away almost ten deaths in three months. Had we actually come away with someone we could lock up and question, that might be one thing. But Oswald's gone, Smith is gone, and," he tossed his hands out, "who even knows about the Montgomery guy? He's not even part of our MO anyway."

"Unbelievable," Ellie said. She knew how these things went. Someone had to take the fall. Why not her? Administratively, she was on the fringes; part time, a contractor. She sighed. "Okay. When?" She already knew the answer.

Garrett folded his arms. "As soon as you're done with your reports," he said flatly.

"That will be this afternoon."

He stared at her blankly, sighed.

"Garrett. I've been around the block enough to know that it's politics that drowns out good people and good decisions. You know that all we've done these last few months will be for nothing unless we can go the final push. If we don't, the wrong people will just surge into the hole we made and fill the vacuum."

"I know."

"What about Mark? Will you keep him on it?"

"Where I can, yes. He'll need to wrap up loose ends."

The office door opened, and a lady in a gray pantsuit entered, clutching a leather notepad holder, her black hair pulled back into a tight ponytail, her face impassive. Sheila Davis with the Inspection Division. Sheila and her team had flown down from Virginia before the sun came up this morning, and Ellie had spent half the morning with her all the while feeling a little like a lamb to the slaughter.

Garrett motioned for Sheila to take a chair. She shook her head. "Miss O'Conner, thank you for your time earlier this morning. I'm sure we'll have additional questions for you, so please leave a good phone number with SAIC Cage here."

Without replying, Ellie asked, "Do you know the FBI's plan? I brought this case forward. Can you at least give me that?"

"Of course," Sheila said. "From what I understand they have a local team working on it and are bringing in support personnel after this hurricane passes. It's set to make landfall here late tomorrow night, so there isn't much they can do for putting feet on the ground until it passes."

"After the storm passes? You're kidding, right?" She came to her feet. "This isn't just a missing person. He's going to be in awful shape. Please tell me they're not dragging their feet trying to locate him."

"I don't think they are dragging their feet at all. As I said, they're flying in a team to help."

"In *two* days," she snapped.

"Ellie," Garrett said, "you've got to let Quantico do this their way."

Sheila scribbled a few notes on her pad, tore the page off, and handed it to Garrett. "Ms. O'Conner," she said curtly, and left the office.

"What a jewel," Ellie said, and then asked the question still weighing on her the most.

"What about Ringo? He's out there somewhere."

"Ellie...I just don't have any answers right now. What

I do have is a conference room full of Sheilas who won't be getting off my tail anytime soon."

Ellie walked over to the window. From here she could see the north part of the city: strip malls, George H. Walker Elementary School, Scott's Scuba Shop, Putt-Putt Palace. This community was so full of life. She thought back to her initial reluctance to jump on board with Garrett's offer to come work for the DEA. Now, she wished she would have started sooner. "I'm glad you brought me on," she said, still staring out the glass. This was all surreal. It would pass, she knew, but for now this entire conversation felt like some kind of warped dream. "We got some things accomplished."

"Me too, Ellie. I'm still hopeful that I can get a role like yours back on the budget come early next year. You'll be the first person I come to when that happens." He stood up, and Ellie turned around. She stepped in and gave her old friend a hug.

"If it's all right, I'll go get everything sorted out on my desk and computer. There's still a few mental loose ends I'd like to tie up before I shut this down."

"Sure thing. I'll have Sandra stop by your desk with your exit paperwork. I may need you to come back in over the next week or so to answer a few more questions from team FUN in the conference room. Turn in your laptop to Glitch when you're done and drop your badge off with security on your way out."

"Okay."

"Ellie."

She looked over at him.

"I'm sorry. I really am."

She tried to smile. "No worries."

When Ellie got back to her desk, she slumped back in her chair and closed her eyes, replaying the conversation over and over. It didn't really matter where you were— CIA, DEA, Washington, Wall Street—politics and bureaucracy were sure to follow. It was the way of the world. So that wasn't what was really bothering her. What was making her fidget with her pen, what was causing her to gnaw hard on her bottom lip, was that she was leaving here with so much left undone. Where had Eli Oswald and Curtis Smith run off to? Who had been supplying their drugs? Who exactly was Ringo? And currently the most pressing, where was Dawson Montgomery?

She had not yet found Adam Stark's killer. With everything she had accomplished up to this point, she had still come up empty on that. She'd be damned if she was going to let Dawson Montgomery elude her too.

CHAPTER FORTY

"I can't believe I came back a week before a major hurricane," Katie grumbled. She zipped up the suitcase and slid it against the wall. "We just finished unpacking these. Chloe! You about ready?"

"Just a minute, Mommy!" Chloe called from her room down the hall.

Ellie had come over to see her family off. Katie was meeting Sharla and Gary Potter in North Fort Myers where she would park her car further away from the effects of a possible storm surge. From there she and Chloe would ride with the Potters to a vacation home they kept up in Jacksonville.

Hurricane Josephine was now a Category 4 storm, with sustained winds hovering at one hundred and thirty-two miles an hour and was set to start bludgeoning the Keys within the next few hours. A second U.S. landfall had been forecasted for Lee County less than twenty-four hours from now.

"I probably don't need to tell you this," Ellie said,

out don't expect Major to join you. I know he said he would, but he'll be securing boats until the last second."

"I know. I hate that he does that. That's what insurance is for." Katie set a hand on Ellie's shoulder. "Are you all right?"

"Yeah. Why?"

"I don't know." An ice chest sat on the kitchen table. She turned around and started organizing the food inside it. "This whole thing about the DEA letting you go. It's ridiculous."

"There's nothing I can do about it."

"What about Garrett? He can't work some magic or something?"

"He already did that just bringing me on. I'm not going to worry about it. It is what it is, as Major likes to say."

Katie shut the lid and looked around the kitchen, making sure they weren't forgetting something. "Well, speaking of Major, I'm going to be helping out at The Salty Mangrove, if it's even there after this storm."

"So you're mad that I'm out of a job, and you're going to take the last one I have?" Ellie laughed.

"Hey, he's paying me. I need it. He told me he's offered to pay you a hundred times and you won't have it."

"He has. And I won't."

Chloe came down the hall, struggling with a suitcase she was dragging behind her. She ended her fight in the kitchen. She clutched her aunt by the leg and squeezed. "Are you coming with us, Aunt Ellie?"

"No, Boo. I hope not to be too far behind. Do you have your teddy?"

"She's in my bag." She looked around the room. "It's dark in here. I thought it was the morning still."

Major had boarded up the southern-facing windows two days ago, before all the stores sold out of plywood. Ellie and Tyler had boarded her own windows up yesterday and filled sandbags, placing them around her back porch.

"There's no light coming in from those windows," her mother replied. "And the clouds are getting darker."

Ellie noted the time on the microwave's digital clock. "I've got to get going," she said.

Katie reached out and gave her older sister a long hug. "Be careful, all right? I don't like that you aren't leaving with us. Don't get stuck here."

"I won't. I just have a few things I need to finish up."

CHAPTER FORTY-ONE

MARK PALFREY KNOCKED ON ELLIE'S FRONT DOOR, and the growing winds whipped at him as he waited. The door opened, and a Jack Russell terrier jumped up off all fours, reaching all the way up to his belt line before returning back to earth. It barked in sheer pleasure, either at Mark's arrival, his existence, or the sub sandwiches he carried in a paper bag. Mark pulled back, and Ellie called out to the dog.

"Citrus! Citrus, get down." She looked up at Mark. "Sorry. My uncle says he's got more energy than a gassed-up speed boat." Citrus bolted away, jumped across the couch, then ran three circles in the small kitchen before darting back to his owner's feet. "Come on in. Thanks for bringing lunch."

"Of course. Here." He handed her the bag of sandwiches. "I have to get a box out of the my car."

Citrus followed Ellie to the kitchen table. She set the bag out and, digging into it, brought out two wrapped sandwiches. She looked down at the dog. His head was set to vibrate, and his tail was fanning the floor. "No. You're not getting any." He whined. She raised her brows, and his head lowered. He looked out the back door, and his ears perked. He looked back at Ellie. "No. You can't go for a swim. There's a big storm coming, and I don't want you getting ripped down the canal."

Citrus tilted his head like he didn't understand—because he didn't understand. Ellie pulled a box from the pantry and tossed him a dried pig's ear, and he tore off down the hallway. Mark returned with a cardboard file box. He shut the door with his foot and came into the kitchen. "Here, just set it on the table," Ellie said. He plopped it down and then took a seat.

"I think this will get you started," he said. He sat down and looked at her. "Ellie?" His tone was somber. She knew what he would say. "I could get fired for this. Please, be careful with it."

"I know. I will. Thank you for doing this."

"Yeah, well, I'm as upset as you are that they let you go. It's like, what are we doing, you know?" He looked at the sandwiches. "Here, this one's yours. Your nasty Reuben."

"Nasty?"

"Sauerkraut? Yuck. And then you put it on a sandwich?"

"I spent some time in Europe. It grows on you."

They ate their sandwiches in relative quiet. Ellie finished, rolled up her wrapper, and sent it sailing into the trash can. "Where are you going to get out of the storm?" she asked.

"Kissimmee," he said. "If I can even get there. From what I see on the news, all the roads going north are gridlocked. But I'm going to try. I'm not getting stuck around here." He tossed his balled-up wrapper toward the trash can. It hit the side and bounced to the floor.

"Guess I should keep my day job," he said, and then glanced at Ellie as he stood up to retrieve it. "Sorry. Poor choice of words."

"It's fine. I don't worry about what I can't change," she said, and then looked over at the box sitting on her table. "So I move on to what I can do."

Mark took the cover off the box. He reached in and removed a short stack of papers. "It's not very organized," he said. "I don't know what you think you're going to find. We went through most of this a couple weeks ago." Mark slid the stack over to Ellie. "Here's what I have on Oswald," he said. He reached in again and removed another handful. "And this is Smith. The rest of it is stuff on their associates who were killed in the blast." He shook his head. "I was at the office until one o'clock this morning printing all this off. Had to change the ink cartridge halfway through. I told them I wanted to work through it while I was out of town these next few days so I could focus on something else when I got back." Ellie didn't need to thank him. He was as bought in on this investigation as she was. Garrett's office was under undue media scrutiny for how the operation was run and why they hadn't known that hot explosives were on site at the time of the raid. Yesterday, the Department of Justice, the parent agency of the DEA, had officially relegated the case over to the FBI. The explosion at the compound had made national news, and finding Oswald and Smith was now priority. But after the storm, it seemed.

What was clearly missing from the conversation was any kind of zeal to find Dawson Montgomery. The man had no family to speak of, so no one to grease the wheel and step up for him. Oswald had blown his own people to bits, and the media outlets had vilified him. And so they should. But that meant that simply catching Oswald seemed to be the thing that would quench everyone's thirst. Ellie did want him to be caught. And she wanted him to pay. But more than anything she wanted to find Ronnie's friend, and the two escapees were the only trail to him.

After being released by the DEA yesterday, Ellie had driven to The Salty Mangrove, poured a beer into a plastic cup, and walked down the Norma Jean pier to process what had just transpired.

The beer had relaxed her. But it was the breeze, the tangy scent of salt water infused with the cool air from the coming storm, that whipped the confused clouds from her mind and allowed clarity to descend. And so it came to her, snapping in her mind like a mainsail that finds a fresh wind on open water.

She had finished her beer and called Mark, asked for a face-to-face. They met later that evening at The Rocky Road, and over a couple cones of ice cream and after Mark spent the first ten minutes venting his anger over why Ellie had been let go, Ellie proposed that she and Mark find the fugitives before anyone else. It had been, after all, their investigation, and the explosion was not due to any incompetence on their part. It was just sheer bad luck.

It had taken her several minutes of patient massaging to convince him to keep going hard after Oswald, even if priority had been given to another agency, and to let her do it with him, behind the scenes.

Now, they both combed through small stacks of

paperwork, trying to find a breadcrumb, a tiny scent that would lead them closer to the man who was prone to remove small appendages and blow up his own crew.

Citrus's nails clicked back down the hallway, and he returned with a pleading whine.

"No. One is enough," she said.

His ears perked, and he tilted his head again.

"I said no. Now go lay down." She pointed to his cushion. His head fell, and he obeyed.

Mark laughed. "You run a tight ship."

Ellie returned back to the paperwork, and for the next ten minutes they worked through the information until Mark's phone buzzed. He looked at a text. "Ah, I have to go. I'm riding with a friend up to Kissimmee. He's leaving in a half hour." Self-admittedly, Mark possessed a visceral fear of hurricanes and didn't plan on being anywhere around Lee County for the next couple days. "If you find anything, you'll wait until I get back to move on it, right?"

She stared blankly at him. She didn't want to lie.

"Ellie! Come on. There is a massive storm heading this way. The outer bands are nearly on us. Don't go all cowgirl on me now. Wait until I get back if you find anything. It's just a couple days."

"I probably won't find anything," she deflected.

"Just look through what you can and secure it in your safe. But you have to get out of the area. It will all be..." He started to say that it would be here when they got back, but as the words came out he realized that, depending on what the storm did, it might not be. "Forget the safe. When you leave can you lock the paperwork in your truck's toolbox or something like that?"

She smiled. "Of course. Don't worry. I know how to handle sensitive information. This won't come back to you."

"God, it better not. I'm putting my entire career on the line here, giving you all this."

Ellie walked him to the door. "Relax. I know what I'm doing. Probably won't find anything but this won't get back to you. I promise. I just want to try anything we can."

He sighed. "I know." He jabbed a finger toward her. "Don't stick around. You get out of the area."

After he left Ellie returned to the table. So far she had combed through Oswald's credit card and bank statements going back the last five years. Nothing stuck out that might indicate where he might be holing up.

It was a half hour later, after Citrus had turned a tennis ball into ribbons and ran a marathon around the living room, that Ellie's eye landed on something that turned on a circuit behind her eyes. A tiny fragment of information that connected with something Drew Oswald had said in passing when they spoke with him last week.

Ellie stood up and grabbed her truck keys from the kitchen counter and told Citrus to be good. She returned everything to Mark's box, grabbed it up, and headed toward the door.

She was going to get Eli Oswald.

CHAPTER FORTY-TWO

When he opened the door and stepped out onto the concrete breezeway, an unorganized flock of seagulls were cutting across the sky, no doubt fleeing from the meteorological wrath to come. He pulled out a pack of Pall Malls from the inside of his leather vest, selected a stick, and lit up. He leaned into the rail as he breathed out and set his right foot on the bottom rung. Purple paint was peeling off the scabbed metal rail, revealing a gray primer undercoat that had been sloshed on some twenty years prior. Eli Oswald loosened his neck and bobbed his head to the tune of Pink Floyd's "Comfortably Numb." He really was, he supposed, comfortably numb himself. The feds had gotten to him; he had underestimated the combined effects of presenting Dawson's extensions to Ronnie's mother. That, he knew now, was a bad move. And yet it wasn't all bad. That explosion did what he might have ended up doing himself. Starting over was an adventure, and like those gulls that had just passed on by, the entire orb of the sky was his to fly in.

But the feds were not the only people he had underestimated.

Ringo.

The name made his stomach curl, made him salivate just thinking of the day when he would get his revenge. Aldrich had dropped off those explosives, claiming that he needed a place to keep them out of his boss's eyesight. But now it was clearer than a bottle of gin that Aldrich had in fact been representing Ringo with that little move, and that they had intended to blow him and his compadres higher than a weather balloon.

Oswald hocked a thick wad of spit over the railing. He watched it tumble and splash on the pavement below. He sucked on a tooth, thinking of how he would move ahead. He had worked for years to be given the helm when the Enlightened Cowboy, old man Tucker, kicked the bucket. He'd gotten it and for the last two years had whittled away at the organization until only a handful of faithful were left—those who needed Eli Oswald to believe in them and, when he did, would do exactly what he asked. He was a big brother of sorts, he liked to fancy, and now his siblings, everyone but Curtis, were dead. And Curtis would probably get picked up soon enough. Oswald would make sure of it. "Go up to Tennessee and see Janey," he had told Curtis. Well, he wasn't going to get very far. Oswald had lifted his wallet off of him as they were negotiating their way through the tunnel. Curtis always kept a lot of cash on him and, boy, did Oswald love him some cash.

The motel was basically empty. Hurricanes had a way of making people get outta Dodge: "Go north young man, go north." This storm had everyone scared out of their panties, and the parking lot and most all the rooms of the Purple Parrot Motel were vacant. A rusting Plymouth sat low on balding tires just outside the front office. A gray truck was parked in a bay of the Clean As A Whistle Car Wash across the street where a lady sat in the driver's seat pecking away at her cell phone. And that was it.

This is where he would ride out the storm. He wasn't going anywhere. He was an hour east of the coast as it was. He flicked what was left of his cigarette past the railing, and it sailed off and landed into an oily parking space below. When lady Josephine blazed on past, he would regroup, and the first thing he would do is find out who Ringo was and carry out a bit of good, old fashioned, straight out of the box revenge. Aldrich too.

He didn't really know anything personal about Aldrich either. Nothing a little digging around couldn't solve. Right now the FBI thought that Oswald had blown his own people halfway to Cuba. But he hadn't. It's not to say that he didn't have it in him or that the right scenario would not have shown itself in the future, a scenario in which Oswald would have done it himself. But the facts stood. This event had not been his doing. It was that slimeball Aldrich with his perfectly cut and combed hair. That's who had done it. And Aldrich and Ringo would both pay. Ol' Ronnie boy would too, just the way his little buddy Dawson had. He would start with their thumbs and take his time until there was nothing left. Not even their arms.

And then. Then he would begin recruiting for a new squad.

Other than bone fractures and thick, throbbing bruises, there was one thing he had gotten from his old man, the man who had donated his sperm to endow him with life. It was the ability to make people feel like the star of the show when you wanted to. He had learned it early, right around the time he'd hit grade school. It's how he had recruited Garber Hunt and Ben Victorino who, according to the papers a couple days ago and that short clip on Fox News, had been blown through the ceiling of his compound during the raid. People were people. Everywhere you went they were the same. Somewhere, deep within, they were empty, lonely, or hurting. And most of it could be, superficially, cured within two minutes. It would start with a compliment, "You look nice today," or "That cheeseburger was *deeeli-cous*...do you always make them that tasty?" And after seeing the giveaway glimmer of appreciation in their eyes, he would ask them how their day was going, which was when the proverbial lid popped and they would start down the path to spilling their guts:

"I'm doing all right."

"No, say, what's wrong?"

"Well, you see, my kid brother, he's run off again and my mother can't work because of her diabetes and this...well, this job doesn't help all that much."

It had to be the right person, of course. But that was just the thing. Eli Oswald could spot the right person the way an eagle could narrow in on a mouse in a grassy field from a half mile up.

And that's what kept Eli Oswald going like the Energizer bunny. The thrill of manipulating the heavy-hearted and weak-minded and the high-rolling, blood-spiking power that came with it.

He would start again after the dust settled. It would settle. It always did. Oswald would find another batch of down-and-outs and would make them his own. Then they would begin anew and would learn from the mistakes of the past.

A renewed surge of confidence shot through Eli Oswald, and he belted out a few lines from the song still running though his head. He bent his knees, snapped his fingers along with the rhythm, and made his way to the stairwell looking like someone practicing for a stage production of Grease. He needed to snag a fresh bottle of whiskey if he was going to be holed in for a couple days. Nothing like waiting out all the fury of Mother Nature with a hard buzz riding your veins.

He got into the Town Car, the one he had paid cash for yesterday, and pulled out into the road.

———

ELLIE SAT PARKED in a grimy bay of the Clean As A Whistle Car Wash for two hours before Eli Oswald stepped from his second floor room of the Purple Parrot Motel. She'd watched him lean into the railing, light up, and remain there for ten minutes, periodically swaying his head to an inaudible beat. His dark hair stood up in a swoop that curved to one side and made her think of Elvis.

Ellie had easily gotten the pimply-faced young man at the Purple Parrot's front counter to give up Oswald's room number, to confirm that he was here. It just took a wink and a drawling little "please," and, like someone had greased him in the right place, he opened right up.

The kid did not seem to know that one of his guests was currently on the FBI's most wanted list.

Waiting here in the car wash had given Ellie plenty

of time to think, time to consider the timing and nature of getting released from the DEA. On one hand it was infuriating. She was getting things done, and yet they thought it best to scapegoat her. But on the other hand she could do things her own way now. Her rule book was written in a different language than the one kept by the DEA's bureaucrats. She didn't blame Garrett for letting her go, and she hoped that he was right, that down the road she could come back.

Mark had asked her to wait before she did anything, if she did anything at all. The simplest course of action would be to call the FBI. It was their case now, and she had no formal authority to do anything but phone it in. She was just an ordinary citizen now. But the storm had slowed the FBI's efforts. Many agents at their local office had already gone upstate to get out of the way of the hurricane. Ellie wanted to get Oswald, but she wanted to find Dawson Montgomery more, and two days could make all the difference.

If she had learned anything from her time with the CIA, it was that lines were meant to be crossed. Sometimes they were meant to be torn down altogether or moved halfway down the field. Doing so, however, came with consequences that couldn't be avoided. But she had decided it was a line worth crossing. She would face the consequences on her own.

Oswald got into a black Town Car, started the vehicle, and pulled out onto the main road. He headed north.

Ellie followed him.

CHAPTER FORTY-THREE

OSWALD PULLED OFF FIVE MILES DOWN THE ROAD AND parked in front of the 7-Eleven. It was full of busy patrons who had decided at the last minute to try and stock up on chips and Gatorade, the bare necessities in hurricane preparedness. All of twelve gasoline pumps were in use with extra cars waiting in line at each pump. Oswald navigated the car to the side of the building and parked next to the open dumpster enclosure. Ellie drove her Silverado to the edge of the lot where the asphalt stopped and the forest began. Oswald parked his Town Car and stared down the backside of a lady as he walked into the store, still bobbing his head to some rhythm.

Ellie exited her truck and approached his Town Car, noting that the lock on the passenger door was still up, peeking over the glass. The door was unlocked.

She waited off near the dumpster until Oswald came out holding his keys and a brown paper bag. He opened the door to his car and plunged into the driver's seat. The door squealed on an ungreased hinge as he shut it and, before he had a chance to slip the key into the ignition, his passenger door opened and a hot blonde chick was in the seat next to him. He started to speak but didn't get very far. The hot lady slammed her door and sent her right fist crashing into his solar plexus. The brown paper bag hit the floorboard with a thud, and Oswald's eyes bugged out as he doubled over and wheezed. He turned his pained and confused face toward her. He grabbed the steering wheel and, while he wheezed, felt something cold on the skin of his wrist, followed by a series of clicks. He pulled back and saw his right hand cuffed to the steering wheel.

The words didn't come easily. "Wha...wha…"

"You'll want to know what this is all about. I get that," she said.

Ellie looked around and made sure that they hadn't caught anyone's attention. Oswald sucked in a deep breath, and his face gained a measure of color as oxygen reentered his bloodstream.

"Eli Oswald. So nice to finally meet you." She waited patiently until his breathing returned to normal. "You and I need to have a conversation."

He looked at her suspiciously. "Where, little lady, did you learn to punch a man like that?"

Ignoring him, she peered down at the paper bag at his feet. She asked, "What's in there?"

"Jim Beam. Cigs. Funyuns."

"Perfect. Reach down—slowly—and hand it to me." With his free hand he did what he was told. Ellie grabbed the bag and the keys off his lap. "Now, I'd rather not make a scene, so when I speak I want you to do exactly as I say. Got it?"

He narrowed his eyes, nodded.

Ellie got out and walked around to the driver's side. She handed him a carbon fiber handcuff key. It was a universal key, had a clip on the side, and looked more like a pen than a key. "Slowly remove the cuff off the steering wheel and step out."

He took the key and paused for a fraction of a second, a pause that told Ellie he was pondering his options. Ellie slapped an open hand into the side of his head. "Now. Let's go."

"Hey! Okay now, Julie Jangle. Say, no need to get aggressive." He did as instructed.

"Now turn around."

After cuffing both hands behind his back, she shut the door and shepherded him back to her truck, walking close behind him so as not to gain any attention from customers filling up their cars.

He retained his confident swagger as he walked. Ellie opened the passenger door. She frisked him, and besides his wallet she found a small pocket knife and a BIC lighter. She unlocked a cuff and said, "Get in." Again, he paused, and Ellie pushed him between his shoulder blades, impelling him into the truck.

"All the way to the driver's side." He muttered behind clenched teeth and complied. "Cuff yourself to the wheel. You're driving." He sighed and grabbed the loose cuff. He set it against the steering wheel, and it clicked in.

She saw what he did and smiled inside. There was only one way for her plan to work: Oswald had to feel out of control in her presence from the very start. Oswald would be assuming that he could easily take her and get out of this new and undesired situation. She had intentionally provided him a window to crawl through, to test him. He had tried to crawl through.

He wasted no time. He had indeed closed the cuff, but he had not attached it to the steering wheel as he had been instructed. Ellie got into the passenger seat, and, as she was shutting the door, Oswald shifted his weight and shot a hand out to grab her. What happened next he could have never accounted for.

With electric speed Ellie slapped his hand down and sent her right fist crashing directly into his nose. The muffled crunch of bone filled the cab, and Oswald screamed as his nose flared with the agonizing sensation of torn cartilage mixing with blood. His head hurled backward and thunked into the driver's side window.

Ellie relaxed back into her seat, put her hands on her lap, and stared at him.

Oswald touched his face with his hand and, seeing it come away bloody, stared at her in painful disbelief. "You...you *bromme noose*!"

"I did break your nose, Eli." She reached over and slipped the right cuff's cheek plate around the steering wheel. "Try anything else. You'll just get hurt again."

He sat there, his chest rising and falling as he came to grips with the pain. He stared out the windshield, smelling like acrid cigarette smoke and days-old sweat. Clearly, he had not taken advantage of the shower amenities at the Purple Parrot. She reached around and buckled herself in and then twisted the keys in the ignition. She opened the glove box and tossed the handcuff key inside. "Let's go."

"Where?" he mumbled.

"Head north. Drive until I tell you otherwise."

His fingers could barely grab the gearshift. He

pulled down on it, moved it into drive, and slowly accelerated.

THE FIRST THIRTY minutes of the drive was shrouded in silence. It was only now, as Ellie gave him directions, telling him where and when to turn, that Oswald began to sense that they were nearing their destination and started to speak.

"Where are we going?"

She said nothing.

"You know, you didn't actually arrest me back there and verbalize my rights. What you're doing right now ain't legit."

"I'm not government."

Oswald said nothing else. She motioned for him to turn right onto a sandy road.

Oswald knew he was in trouble; he just didn't know what kind. It was a favorite tactic of Ellie's. The more questions a captive asked, the more his chances went up that he would get some kind of an answer. Answers would make him feel some measure of control. It gave him something that he wanted. But when questions were ignored, when they were not returned, it created a sense of powerlessness and served as a reminder of who was really in control.

Ellie directed him to take one more turn and, after passing through scrub oaks and hickory for a half mile, they stopped at what looked like a rickety shack sitting back in the trees.

"What the hell is this?" Oswald said. "This some kind of a joke?"

Ellie retrieved the handcuff key from the glove box

and got out, walked around to Oswald's door, and opened it. Extending the key she said, "Uncuff yourself."

An amused grin crossed his face. He took the key, and the cuff fell from his wrist and hung off the steering wheel.

"Come on, get out. Try anything and I break something else. Got it?"

"Yep, yep." He dropped a foot into the sandy dirt and followed it with another. He stood up and looked into the sky. The clouds were a darker gray than they were an hour ago and hung lower and thicker in the sky. The wind had picked up considerably, and he squinted to keep the sand out of his eyes.

"Recognize this place?" Ellie asked.

He hocked a thick loogie, tinted with blood, at his feet. "Nope. Should I? This your place? You gonna cuff me to your bedpost? Cause I think I might like—"

"This is Ronnie's place, Oswald. Where your little pals tried to get the squeeze on him."

"Oh."

"Yeah. Oh." Oswald was looking at the shack, sizing it up, so he didn't see his captor palm her Beretta, nor did he see her swing it around with nearly the same speed that David's stone had left his sling. The butt of the gun slammed into the back of his head, and, before he could even let out a grunt, his lights went out.

CHAPTER FORTY-FOUR

SOMEONE WAS SITTING ON HIS HEAD. NO, SOMEONE had driven a car onto his head and parked it there.

The space between Oswald's ears pounded. He grimaced against the fierceness of the dull pain. He found that he was sitting up and his chin was sagging on his chest. He blinked hard and shook his head. Bad idea. The pain increased with the movement. Slowly, he brought his head up and looked around. When his vision cleared, he saw a couch to his right. On his left was a counter and a small sink. When he zoned in on what was in front of him, his most recent memories fired up through his consciousness. There she was, sitting five feet away on a table, her legs dangling off the side. She was smiling at him.

"Welcome back. Do you always take naps in the afternoon?"

He didn't answer at first. He could remember that he wasn't very fond of her, but he couldn't remember why or how he got here. Where was here?

"Take your time," she said. "It will come back. 7-Eleven. Funyuns. Does that help?"

It did help. It helped very much. This chick had kidnapped him and broken his nose. She had knocked him out. And now they were here at...whose place was it again? Oh yes. Ronnie's place.

She smiled pacifyingly, lazily swung her feet back and forth under the table.

"You knocked me out?" he asked indignantly. His lips curled, and she saw a threat coming. "Why, you're gonna wish you—"

"Oh stop, Eli. Don't threaten me, please. It's cliché. I just hate clichés. They're predictable, and that makes them boring. Let's talk about you. How are you feeling? You've got quite the bump on your head there."

That was the moment he realized that his ankles and hands were tied to the chair with a fair measure of jute twine. "What is this?" he demanded, looking back and forth at his bonds.

"The name Dawson Montgomery ring a bell?"

He stopped. Then the corners of his mouth curled up, and he replied with a crooked smile. "Why yes, Julie Jangle. What is ol' Dawson to you?"

"Well, last I checked he can't count to ten with two hands anymore."

"Yeah, that uh, that was most unfortunate. Hey, can I get some Advil or somethin'? My head, it's aching like, super bad."

"I don't think so." A wallet was sitting beside her. She picked it up. "What are you doing with Curtis Smith's wallet?"

His eyes moved into slits, and he looked her up and

down, sizing her up. "What are you? A bounty hunter or something?"

"No. Not a bounty hunter."

"Then...what, Nancy Drew?"

"Oswald, I have plans to head out before this storms gets much closer, so I'd rather this not take all afternoon. You injured three federal agents in that blast back at your place. To say nothing of your friends."

"Look, I didn't have anything to do with that. I didn't know the place was rigged. It was all Aldrich, man."

"Aldrich? You're trying to tell me that explosion wasn't your doing?"

"It wasn't. I swear."

"Right. Who is Aldrich?"

He shrugged. "Ringo's right-hand man, I guess."

Hearing Ringo's name gave her pause. "You know Ringo?"

"Ohh, well look at you, gettin' excited all of the sudden." He sighed. "But now, that...that is not your business."

"Oswald. Any questions that I ask are my business. You know Ringo? Who is he?"

"I couldn't rightly say. Never met the man. Curtis is under the impression that he owns a proper establishment on Pine Island. But who's to say?"

"Why would Ringo or one of his men want to terminate you and your buddies?"

He said nothing.

"Fine," she said. "Let's try a different angle. What happened between you and...what did Ronnie call him? The Enlightened Cowboy?"

Oswald's brows rose at that, and he smiled large. The blood that poured from his broken nose had smeared down his lips and chin, making him look a bit like a carrion bird who had been feasting on roadkill for the last hour. "Harlan was an old man who cared too much for this country. This country never did anything but get him screwed up over there in Nam and then turned him into a hobo."

"So picking yourself up and dusting yourself off doesn't count for anything? Writing a book about your convictions doesn't matter?"

"Not to me it doesn't," he said smugly. "Harlan had people. He had followers. When he died I was the natural choice to step up."

"And Dawson was a part of your new little black market enterprise?"

"Until he wasn't. That fool was a rat. I couldn't trust him anymore. Simple as that, Julie Jangle. Say, how 'bout a glass of water?"

"Why did you send that package to Ronnie's mother?"

"No water, huh?"

"Why did you send that package to Ronnie's mother?"

"Why do you think? Ronnie was a snitch same as Dawson. Ronnie just needed to know we had his number. Plus, I thought it was sort of creative. Biblical, you might say." He grinned. A large, sinister, mischievous kind of grin. Like the Cheshire Cat.

"Where's Dawson?"

"Wouldn't know. I'm not his mother, not his brother."

"Where is Dawson?"

"I *said* I don't know. If you dragged me all the way out here just to ask me that, you've wasted a lot of time. You know, we could be sharing that bottle of Jim Beam and cuddling on that there couch." He winked at her.

"Okay, you don't want to tell me where he is. Why don't you tell me why you tortured him."

"Torture...that's...kind of a strong word. But, for the sake of this little conversation here, we'll go with it. Dawson, he about crinkled my can, man. He about tore my little enterprise into kibbles and bits, and he would have if I wouldn't have gotten to him first. But I did get to him first, you see?"

"How did you do it?"

"Do what?"

"How did you do the...operation. Tell me about it."

He looked surprised by the request. But then he smiled, and his eyes filled with a kind of nostalgic pleasure. "Well, we snagged him and tied him up," he chuckled. "Kind of like I am now, I do suppose. I asked him some questions, and as he was answering I stuffed a cancer stick between his lips and then lit it for him myself like the worthy host that I tend to be. Ol' Dawson, he likes Kools—the menthol cigarette—and I get it. I really do get it. That menthol gives you an extra buzz laid over that nicotine the way icing is spread over a birthday cake. That got a little more info out of him. Then I offered him a glass of whiskey. Of course he couldn't grab it, but Curtis held it for him, and Dawson, he proceeded to apologetically tell me everything I needed to know, which I happened to know already, and then," he laughed, "well, then I got a little chop-happy, I suppose."

Ellie stood up. "See, that wasn't so hard. You want a smoke?"

"A smoke? Well, dear lady, I would *love* a smoke. Are you offering one?" His eyes found grace when they fell on the red box of Pall Malls that Ellie slid out from behind her. "Well, by my dear Lord, you *are* an angel sent from the mighty heights above, Julie Jangle." His eyes held onto the box with the feasting desire of a starving man. He looked her in the eyes and nodded politely, like they were old friends and she was toasting to their reunion.

Ellie removed a cigarette and took his lighter off the table where she had laid it earlier. She slid off the table and inserted the cigarette between his full lips. She held the lighter up and flicked the spark wheel. Oswald worked at it furiously, got the cigarette lit, and puffed hard and quickly. He closed his eyes as the nicotine hit his blood like an overdue freight train. His eyes popped open along with his hands. His body stiffened. "Now, *that*. That is juuuust fine. Just fine." The cigarette rode his lips as he spoke. "You...you're all right, Julie Jangle."

"So, you were saying," Ellie said. "About Dawson?"

"I was, wasn't I? Talking about Dawson."

"The way Ronnie says it, Dawson had no intention of ratting you to the feds. He said Dawson only wanted out."

"He's right. Certainly right. But see you don't just walk away from Eli Oswald. That's the funny thing. I mean, it's real funny, man, when you think about it. He just needed to learn a lesson. Needed to learn that you don't run from Eli Oswald. Besides, like I said, he would have squealed at some point, given enough time. Ronnie too."

Ellie walked back to the counter, opened the bottle of whiskey, and poured a fair amount into a red Solo cup. She walked back to him. "Whiskey? It's yours, after all."

"Well, by my dear Lord...yes. Yes indeedy. You and me, we're getting along just fine, aren't we? I can just feel it, sugar pie honey bunch."

Ellie removed the cigarette from his lips and held the cup to them. She tilted it, and he drank. She pulled it back. "That's enough."

He jutted his bottom lip out, feigning a toddler's pout. And that was when the lights turned on for Eli Oswald. That was the moment he made the connection. He had given Dawson a smoke. He had given Dawson a drink. He smiled nervously at her and chuckled the same.

Ellie set the cup down and walked over to the kitchen counter. She opened a drawer and removed something. He heard a click and a soft metallic grinding, like a bolt being turned. When she turned around she was holding a pair of vise-grips. She stepped up to him, squatted down, and grabbed his hand.

"Hey. Heyyyy, what are you doin'? Don't, don't do th —" The pliers snapped down and bit into the soft part of his hand just above his bottom thumb joint. "Ow! Damn, lady. What are you doing?" But he knew what she was doing.

He looked back down at the vise-grips, and a dreadful panic entered his chest. He swiveled his gaze toward her. "You wouldn't do that." But he said it with a false confidence. "You can't touch me, no sireee. You'll end up in the slammer same as me." His hand started throbbing from the pressure. He looked down. It was turning a hue of purple that was most unnatural. His wrist was secured to the side of the chair. He flopped his hand around, trying to rid himself of the powerful pliers. He couldn't shake them. It just made it hurt worse.

Ellie sat back on the tabletop, still calm, ankles swinging again. "Is Dawson alive?"

"Far as I know."

"And where is he?"

"See, you're not getting it, lady. That is not something I'm going to tell you. Acting like you're going to take my thumb, it's a cute game, but you and me know that isn't going to happen."

Oswald looked away and started whistling.

Ellie nodded to herself. She got off the table again, turned around, and picked something up. When she turned back, she was holding a Bowie knife.

When Oswald saw, the whistling ceased.

"Look   nowwww,   Julie   Jangle,   quit   playing games, now."

Ellie grabbed the vice-grips in one hand and set the edge of the blade to the meaty area where his thumb joined his hand. "I'm sure you know that the thumb bone goes all the way toward the wrist," she said. "So I'm going to cut at your lower knuckle, just above your metacarpal. That should do it. What do you think?" She winked at him.

Oswald jerked, nicking himself in the process. Frantic, he yelled, "No, man. Ho, now! Who put a bustle in your little hedgerow? What are you doing? What are you do—"

Blood squirted as the blade pierced the skin and

muscle. Oswald's scream reverberated around the thin walls of the cabin as his tendons were severed and the knife sliced into flesh.

There was no one around to hear.

CHAPTER FORTY-FIVE

HE WAS GOING TO HAVE TO SWEET TALK HIMSELF OVER the Matlacha Pass Bridge. According to the text message he had just received, they stopped letting anyone onto the island over four hours ago. He wasn't going out on the water. Not in this mess. Last he saw it, the Caloosahatchee River was starting to look like an angry pot of stew, and wind gusts were already coming in at sixty miles an hour in some areas. He'd been in worse before, out at deep sea. But that was over thirty years ago, and Pine Island Sound would be angrier than the river.

Ringo watched Andrés's Malibu disappear down to the next level of the parking garage. He got into his Jeep Wrangler, started up the engine, and descended.

He didn't feel right. Something was off. He didn't like the shrimp he had earlier, but it wasn't that. The feeling wasn't physical; it was further in, deeper. Something in his soul, an unspoken tremor. Maybe it was the chaos of the last few weeks.

Maybe it was Eli Oswald. He was out there somewhere, and he was a very long loose end. Eli was smart, and it was why Ringo had gone into business with him in the first place, a decision he now deeply regretted. Eli could run, but even the smartest ones eventually get caught. 'Whitey' Bulger was finally apprehended. So was Eichmann. Ringo didn't think that Eli Oswald could evade capture for a couple decades like those men had. They were in a different class altogether. The bomb at his compound was a good idea. The feds were under the impression that Oswald had killed his own people, and that was very good. But it also meant that they would go after him harder. This storm would dampen the investigation, but only temporarily. He was out there, and he would be caught. And then, as men like him always did, he would talk. When it came to his knowledge of Ringo, Eli Oswald had none. He knew the name, he knew who Andrés and Chewy represented, but he had no identity, no face, to give the FBI or the DEA. Still, Ringo didn't like it. He didn't like it because he didn't like loose strings. Loose strings had to be cut.

Still however, the feeling, that feeling that he couldn't quite pin down, gnawed at him like a termite in a treehouse.

The rain was coming down in sheets now, another storm band overhead. He sat up straight, turned the windshield wipers on full speed and squinted onto the road ahead.

He had to work up a plan to get over that bridge.

CHAPTER FORTY-SIX

TORTURE WAS ALWAYS UTILITARIAN. ONLY A PSYCHO like the man in front of her did it for its own sake; simply for the sake of doing it. Torture was intended to reveal information, information that would save lives or ensure future security. In this case it was the former.

When Eli Oswald came to, his head was pounding again, but someone had a blowtorch pointed on his hand. He tried jerking it back as he opened his eyes, and then he screamed from the fiery pain that shot through it. He looked down. There was no fire. No blowtorch. His hand was wrapped in gauze, the sterile white covered with a bright red flower where blood had seeped through. He heard a muted thud at his feet, and he swiveled his head to see something lying on the dirty floorboards in front of him. He squinted forward then looked back at his hand. Then he understood. A hot bolt of nervous dread shot through him. That was his thumb lying there at his feet. He looked up, and that lady that he used to think was hot was right where she was before, sitting on the edge of the table looking at him with her head tilted, a smirk on her lips.

"Welcome back."

Oswald snarled and, once again, jerked against his ropes and, once again, was reminded by a flash of fire up inside his wrist that he no longer had a thumb on his right hand. "Well, you little whore! I'm going to—"

"Again, I'm not so big on clichés. You're not going to do anything to me, and if you say anything else before I ask my next question, you, good sir, will never be able to grip a handgun again." Her unwavering eyes bored into his.

Oswald's breathing was rapid; tiny beads of sweat had popped on his forehead. He looked back down at his hand with wide, unbelieving eyes.

"Now. I'm going to ask you the same question I did earlier. It's a free country, so it's your choice if you want to try and stonewall me again. I do believe in free will."

He glared up at her.

"I need to know where Dawson Montgomery is."

What happened next Ellie had seen a dozen times. The moment when the interrogated makes the turn. The turn: when they finally concede defeat and start giving you the information you want. Oswald's shoulders slumped, his face went slack, the fight temporarily gone out of him, but the vitriol in his voice remained. "The Haitians offered to take him."

A weight dropped into Ellie's gut. "What does that mean exactly?"

"It means that some friends of mine across the water heard what I did and wanted to use him as an example to their people of what happens when you mess with the

Americans. They agreed to come get him. Simple as—guuhhh this hurts!"

Ellie's nostrils flared. "You haven't told me where he is."

He shrugged weakly. "I don't know if he's still there. They probably picked him up by now. Were supposed to grab him yesterday. We left him the night before the feds raided my compound. With this weather maybe they didn't get him yet."

"And where exactly did you leave him?"

He shoulders rose up again. "Now that, I cannot tell you. The Haitians aren't exactly the kind of people you forgo an agreement with. They want their people to be scared of us, I'm a little scared of them...works both ways, I suppose. My old elementary teacher used to talk about dotting your 'i's' and crossing your 't's'. You leave an 'i' undotted with these crazies and you lose your head."

"Head, huh? How about another thumb?"

He said nothing. Ellie sighed. "Oswald. I'll be honest with you. Looking at you doesn't give me the immediate impression that you have a lot of smarts about you. But somehow you managed to systematically dismantle what Harlan Tucker had created and rally a group of men dedicated to a new cause. So I'll give you credit. But for such a planner, you are being very nearsighted. I've already taken your thumb. I will take your other one." She looked down his wrapped hand. "And then I will keep going. What I have in mind might be worse than the Haitians. Are we...communicating, Oswald?"

His face was now pallid, clammy. "Who are you?"

She stood up. "Last chance."

He dropped his head. "Fine. We left him on Sanibel."

"Where on Sanibel?"

"Well, more like off Sanibel. He's in a raft in the wildlife refuge."

"You think he's still there?"

"Dunno. The Haitians aren't the most punctual of people. And with this storm...who knows. I'd bet he's gone though. If he ain't he's probably slipped on to the other side by now."

Ellie pulled out her phone and tapped the Maps app. Her reception only showed one bar. She typed Sanibel Island into the address bar, and the app loaded slowly. When the map came up, she zoomed into the general area Oswald had mentioned. She stood up, walked over to him, and set the phone in front of his face. His hands were tied, and she planned on keeping them that way. Holding an index finger near the glass, she said, "Show me where."

"Left of where you are now. Now north. Just a little more to the west. Yeah, right there."

Ellie zoomed in on it and took a screenshot. She looked at her prisoner. "You understand that you're mine until this is all over. So if you're lying to me, there will be a problem."

"I'm telling you straight."

"We'll see about that."

Wincing, Oswald said, "Can I get some pain killers or somethin'? It's killing me."

"Did you give Dawson painkillers?"

"Yeah. We gave him painkillers."

"Sure you did."

Ellie produced a pair of handcuffs and started

cutting at the twine holding his hands into place. "Let's go," she said.

———

ELLIE SPED down the dirt road that led away from Jean Oglesby's cabin. The wind was blowing hard, sending the tops of the trees dancing and whipping dirt off the road and scattering it into the unknown. A glance at the clouds told her that rain was imminent. Oswald was resting not too comfortably in the bed of her truck, hidden beneath the locked hard cover. Her Bowie knife she had wiped clean and locked safely in her glove box. Oswald's whiskey, his Funyuns, and Curtis's wallet she had tucked away into her center console.

Hurricane Josephine had plowed through the Keys seven hours ago and remained on course to make a direct hit in Lee County. The Sound would be indignant and wild, and only an insane person would go out on waters like that.

Today, Ellie happened to be insane.

If Dawson was out there, nothing could keep her from bringing him back.

She could call the Coast Guard. Not only did they have the right equipment, but their personnel were trained for exactly these kinds of conditions.

But she couldn't do that. Because then she would have to explain how she found the wanted man who was in the bed of her truck and how he had come to lose his thumb. She would have to explain all that, she knew, but at this very moment she had no idea how.

She turned onto U.S. Route 27 and went south. If she booked it, it would take an hour to get to the marina. She grabbed her phone and pulled up Tyler's name. He would be up at Reticle by now, having opted to wait the storm out there, the facilities capable of withstanding Category 5 winds. She tapped his name and put the phone to her ear.

———

SHE HAD GOTTEN LUCKY.

The bridge had a checkpoint set up and a police officer stationed at it. As Ellie had passed through east Matlacha and approached the bridge, the officer's plastic-covered Midway cap had been lifted from his head and blew across the street. There was just enough space for her to navigate around the orange and white striped traffic barriers, and before he noticed what she had done she was halfway over the bridge.

Now, as she approached Saint James City, Ellie pulled off on the grassy shoulder, got out, and unlocked the bed cover. The small hydraulic cylinders hissed as the cover rose, and Oswald moaned. He squinted against the storm-dimmed light and cursed. "Where'd you learn how to drive? I've been like a raggedy doll back here."

Ellie pulled back on the tailgate. "Come on. Get out." His hands were cuffed in front of him. With most of his thumb gone on one hand, Ellie had to make that particular cuff a little tighter than normal. Oswald awkwardly shimmied out of the truck, sliding his heels out in front and then moving his backside forward. He repeated this several times until his legs were dangling off the tailgate. Ellie pulled him off and led him around to the front passenger seat. "Please don't be stupid and try something." He simply nodded. Ellie shut his door and went back to the rear to close up the tailgate and the cover. Oswald was now in her cab because, in the highly unlikely event that someone was still sticking around at the southern tip of the island, she didn't want them to see her extracting someone from the bed of her truck. She brought the Silverado back onto Stringfellow Road, and three minutes later they were pulling into the crushed-shell parking area at the south end of Henley Canal. Ellie turned off the truck, slid the keys from the ignition, and reached behind Oswald's seat. She brought out a green windbreaker and carefully tucked it over his hands. He winced but said nothing. "Make sure this stays over your cuffs."

"Okay."

Ellie got out of the truck and opened his door. "Let's go. Hurry up."

He stepped out into the rain. "Where're we going?" he asked, somewhat guarded.

Ellie ignored the question. "Stay next to me and look normal." He was wearing a leather vest over nothing but skin, had a bloodied face and a tattoo of a purple parrot on his shoulder. Oswald looked anything but normal. They worked their way up the ramp, passed The Salty Mangrove, and headed for the marina beyond. The bar was shuttered, hunkered down against the upcoming onslaught from Mother Nature. If the storm hit the island dead on as a Category 4, the community would be unrecognizable for months, even years afterwards. The bar and the marina would be wiped out, homes on the canals in Saint James City, on the waterfront in Bokeelia, and all along the coast would be flooded, Ellie's home included. It was one of the very few concessions one had to make for the privilege of living in paradise. The outer bands were bringing hard, intermittent rains and now, looking out at the water off the marina, Ellie was staring at four to five foot swells.

The steel pedestrian door leading into the dry dock was open, and Ellie led Oswald through it. "Ellie." It was Tyler. He came out of the office wearing a black windbreaker and his red, sun-faded Hornady hat. Sizing up Oswald, he said, "This is him, huh?"

"It is."

"You're a real goober from what I hear," Tyler said.

Oswald smiled. "Hey now, Jimmy Jangle. Nice to meet you too."

"How did you get over the bridge?" she asked Tyler.

"Might have fibbed a smidgen." He pointed to a chair in the small office. "Have a seat in there," he said to Oswald.

Oswald looked at Ellie, as if asking permission. She let go of his arm and nodded to the chair. He did as instructed. Tyler walked Ellie several paces across the concrete and said quietly, "Ellie, you can't go out there. Not with the water the way it is. Just call the Coast Guard. That's what they're for. The eye of the storm will be here in five hours."

"Tyler, I can't."

"Why? You didn't do anything wrong. You found a wanted man. They'll probably give you a medal or something."

The windbreaker was covering Oswald's bad hand, and Tyler hadn't seen the bloody gauze. "I just can't. Not right now. Just trust me, okay? Did you get the boat ready?"

Reluctantly, he said, "I did. I found the battery and

depth finder in the back and installed them. Your uncle had everything labeled back in the storage room. It should be good to go. But Ellie, this is stupid." His tone wasn't condemning. It was nervous, full of concern.

"You're probably right, but if Dawson is still there he'll drown in this storm, raft or no raft. I'm not leaving him out there, Tyler." She looked back at Oswald who was sitting quietly where they had left him, staring at the floor. He reached up and scratched his cheek and as he did the windbreaker fell to the floor. "I have to figure out how to explain Oswald. I didn't exactly arrest him, you know."

"Whoa," Tyler said, "what happened to his hand? It looks nasty."

She stared blankly into his eyes.

He blinked. "Oh good Lord, Ellie. You didn't—"

"I know where Dawson is, okay? We can talk about this later."

"You actually—"

"I need to go," she interrupted. "Now."

Tyler blinked again and shook his head in disbelief. "Then I'm coming with you."

"What? No. No, you're not. You hate boats. This is the worst possible time to be out on the water."

"Ellie. You're not going out there with this guy alone on water like that. And what if you find Dawson and need help getting him on the boat? I'm coming with you."

He did have a point. "All right."

Tyler went back to Oswald, grabbed his upper arm. "Come on, Bozo."

CHAPTER FORTY-SEVEN

MAJOR'S 1978 BERTRAM 31 FLYBRIDGE CRUISER WAS a jewel at the marina, and other than a couple friends from his Rotary Club, Ellie was the only other person he would allow to get behind its helm. Four years ago Major had restored the vessel, adding a new teakwood deck to replace the glassed-over plywood, a reverse-cycle marine air conditioner to the cabin, and a transparent livewell at the transom. He had also repowered the vessel with Twin 315 Yanmar diesels. The Bertram had a remarkable design. Made of high-impact, multi-laminate fiberglass, its deep-v hull was what made the vessel unique, making it the perfect boat to navigate the choppy swells out in the Sound. The Bertram was still sitting in a slip at the marina. Major had run out of time to get it away from the island.

Early yesterday, after the storm's course had been updated by the National Weather Service, Major had recruited several friends to help him move some of the boats further north into Tampa Bay. They each ran a boat up to Tampa, moored them at a friend's commercial dock, and rode back to Saint James City in another friend's truck. A few of the boats were loaded onto trailers and taken away. Major's marina down at Marco Island was forty miles further south, and, because of its close proximity to the storm, nothing could be done about the fleet down there.

Major felt a personal responsibility for the boats at his marinas, and this time of year many of them belonged to snowbirds who were still away for the season and couldn't get down to Pine Island to move their boats themselves. The covered dry dock had forty-two dry slips and was built to withstand hurricane force winds. On any given month five or six slips were available to rent out. But when the update on Hurricane Josephine had come through, Major selected five boats from the dock and put them up on the racks. Ellie's Bayliner was the last one he made room for. Ellie didn't trust her boat lift not to snap or fall off into the canal. Most everyone else on the island, those who didn't have the time or the means to get their boats to a safe spot, had cross-tied them off in the canals using double mooring lines, securing them into eye rings on the other side. From a view above, the canals now looked liked a giant spider had crawled out of a Tolkien or Brothers Grimm story and seen fit to begin a new web through the canals, criss-crossing back and forth between the seawalls.

Fu and Gloria had, for the first time in years, unmoored their Gibson houseboat and hugged the coast until they got to Bradenton, where a friend had offered for them to moor at his private dock further inland. That houseboat was all the Wangs owned, and, while they weren't planning to stay on it during the storm, they didn't want to see it damaged.

It was during storms like this one, when hurricanes danced into coastal areas, that nearly half of all storm-related deaths could be attributed to boat owners trying to secure their boats at the last minute or deciding too late to leave the area in choppy or quickly rising water. Looking at the current state of the marina, it seemed that all preparations had been made in time. The boats that remained in their slips had been secured according to standard high-windage protocol. All movable equipment such as canvas, outriggers, sails, radios, cushions, deck boxes, and biminis had been removed and put into the rear storage room in the dry dock. Then the boats had all been carefully moored higher up on the pilings and, for whatever it might be worth, extra fenders hung.

Ellie, Tyler, and Oswald braced themselves against the lashing wind as they worked their way down the dock and stepped onto the Bertram. Ellie led Oswald through the narrow companionway and into the cabin. She cuffed him to the head's door handle and said, "Try to be good, all right?" He sketched her a weak salute with a couple fingers from his bad hand and slumped down to his backside with his back to the door, his cuffed hand hanging loosely above his head. After assisting Tyler with the mooring lines, Ellie gave him the handcuff key and went up to the flybridge and started the engines. She slowly brought the vessel out of the slip and took it out of the marina and into the Sound, her bearing set southwest toward Sanibel Island which lay just two nautilus miles across the water. Ellie estimated the wind was coming out of the southeast at just over forty knots, and she assessed the swells to be at four to five feet. Swells like these were never seen here, east of the barrier islands. The barriers—Sanibel, Cayo Costa, Captiva—generally took the menacing brunt of an angry ocean.

Ellie grabbed the wheel tightly as a sheet of spray rained down on her. The key to navigating these waters was to anticipate the next swell as it came toward them. Far ahead, to their port side, the Sanibel Island Lighthouse was faithfully keeping watch over troubled waters.

Tyler climbed up the leg ladder of the tuna tower and stood next to Ellie, keeping a firm grasp on the back of her seat for balance. Ellie took her eyes off the water long enough to steal a glance at him. He didn't look so well. Coming out on waters like this was sure to make him nauseous, especially swaying up on the bridge as they were. If he got sick he would be in no position to help. Nausea sucked energy straight from your innards and left you weak for hours afterwards. "You need to get below!" she yelled over the wind. "And keep your eyes on a fixed point ahead! Don't turn your head." He didn't answer. "If you're going to lose it—"

Tyler turned and scrambled back down the ladder, back to the deck. He staggered to the gunwale, then he yanked his hat from his head, leaned over, and emptied the contents of his stomach into the churning waters.

Ellie steadied her feet as the bridge pitched hard to starboard and more spray rained down on her.

She kept on.

CHAPTER FORTY-EIGHT

THE J. N. "DING" DARLING NATIONAL WILDLIFE Refuge was located on the north edge of Sanibel and consisted of over sixty-four hundred acres of cordgrass marshes, mangrove forests, submerged seagrass beds, and West Indian hardwood hammocks. The location Oswald had given her was tucked deep within the refuge, west of McIntyre Creek. The wind had begun to taper down just as the Bertram exited the sound and entered the thick coastal vegetation that made up the refuge. Behind them, the water was calming too.

Ellie turned and yelled down to Tyler. "I need Oswald up here!"

He nodded silently and struggled into the cabin. Oswald took one look at Tyler and whistled. "Hot diggity dog there, Jimmy Jangle. Looks like somebody done forgot to bring their sea legs with them."

"Shut up," Tyler said weakly. He handed him the key, and Oswald came to his feet. "Uncuff it from the door and then cuff your other hand. No funny business."

Oswald winked at him. "You got it, boss." After he did as instructed, Tyler grabbed the key and then his arm. "Come on." They exited the cabin, and Oswald went up the ladder and stood next to Ellie. "I think your boyfriend is allergic to the water, honey."

"He's not my boyfriend."

Tyler came up and stood next to Oswald, his face ashen, his eyes nearly swimming in their sockets as if he'd been poisoned. His stomach lurched, and his mouth opened like it was trying to rid him of some vile creature that had taken up residence within his guts. Nothing came out.

"Tyler, get down from here."

He nodded and, without any argument, slid back down.

"Now, where am I going, Oswald?"

"Hmmm...well, let me see if I can remember. It's been a few days now. Allow me to get my bearings." He licked his lips and looked Ellie up and down. His confidence had returned, his swagger, his apparent zest for conversation.

She reached over and grabbed his blood soaked bandage. She squeezed.

"Whyyyyy?" he howled, "...would you do thhhhhat?"

"Where am I going?" she repeated calmly.

Now he was breathing heavily against the pain. Looking out over the narrow, winding inlets, he jutted his chin. "Over there, to your right. What is that, Starbucks or something?"

"Starboard."

"That's the one."

Ellie brought the Bertram to the mouth of the small

inlet and moved into it. A half minute later Oswald told her to go left where a cluster of mangroves forked the water into separate directions. The inlet was getting more narrow. Ellie only had a couple feet on either side before she brushed up against the reaching branches of the thick vegetation.

Oswald squinted down on the water. "Now am I crazy or is the water going down just a tad bit?"

Ellie looked down and frowned. "You are crazy, but you're not wrong."

"Now I am not much of a seafaring person myself, but aren't we still a bit from slick tide, or slack tide? Whatever it's called. The voluminous waters should still be rising if my mental facilities continue to serve me well."

Oswald was right. Storm aside, the tide was still coming in and the water should be trending upward, not going down. The wind had nearly vanished altogether.

Oswald looked around, took in his surroundings. "Turn in there," he said. "It's kinda hard to see, but there's a grove out front that you'll have to get around to see the entry point." Ellie followed his directions and a minute later he raised his cuffed hands and pointed. "There. Right over there. Go around that cluster and cut a hard right."

They came out into a tiny cove. Then Ellie saw it. Forest camouflage netting flapping in the breeze, tethered against a cluster of mangroves. A dark brown, rigid-hull inflatable raft floated beneath it. Oswald had finally come through, and her heart rate quickened. Now she could only hope that Dawson Montgomery was still there and, if he was, that he was still alive.

Ellie idled the Bertram just past the raft and put the

engines into neutral. She pressed the power button to engage the windlass, and the anchor moved down into the water. Then she backed up the Bertram while still letting out more rode. When she stopped the windlass, the line tightened as the anchor hooked into the sandy bottom and held them true. The raft now sat hard on the Bertram's starboard. Ellie turned off the engines and told Oswald to get down to the deck. She followed him down. Tyler was sitting on an engine box with his head between his knees. He pushed himself up and came to unsteady feet. "Hang in there," Ellie said. "Can you cuff him to the tower leg?"

Tyler nodded weakly, and Ellie looked toward the raft now just a couple feet off the starboard. It was well hidden. The camouflage wasn't a perfect color match against the brighter greens of the mangroves, but it was probably unnecessary anyway. No one would find their way out here. Perhaps a straying kayaker exploring in detail, but no one would have been out here these last couple of days.

Ellie slid onto the gunwale and surveyed her drop point. The camouflage netting made it impossible to see what might be underneath. There was only one way to find out if Dawson was under there or not. She slid off from the Bertram and landed on the bulbous edge of the raft. She held onto it with her knees and brought out the butterfly knife that had been resting in the seam of her shorts. She grabbed the netting, opened the knife in a single motion, and slid the blade through the material, cutting it back to give her access underneath. Ellie pulled up, and, seeing nothing beneath, continued slicing. She moved along the length of the raft until she had cut through the entire length of camouflage. Once she had gotten to the end, she turned, grabbed the edge, and flung it back, exposing everything beneath.

What she saw next took away her breath.

Dawson Montgomery lay at the far end, curled up into the side, his back to her, wearing jeans, a white t-shirt, and tennis shoes. The shirt was stained with blood and torn in several places. Ellie stepped into the raft and made her way over to him. His wrists were bound behind him with black zip ties, and his ankles were under the same fate. She kneeled down and called out. "Dawson!"

Nothing.

"Dawson, I'm a friend and we're here to get you out of here!" Still nothing. She set her index and middle fingers on his neck and pressed firmly over his carotid artery, checking for a pulse. Still nothing. She positioned her fingers and pressed down more firmly.

A faint pulse.

She sliced through the plastic ties and slowly brought him up so his back was resting against the edge of the raft. His head swung loosely on his neck, and his chin came to rest on his chest. During their investigation Ellie had reviewed several photos of Dawson. What was in front of her resembled nothing of the likeness she had seen. His face was caked with dried blood that been wettened by the recent rains. His eyes were nearly invisible under puffy, purplish skin. An untreated, obviously broken nose had swelled and now leaned heavily toward one side. Dawson's hands were loosely bound in red-stained gauze that was starting to slip off his wrists. Ellie lips curled when she saw his shoes, the fabric panel above the toes also red. They had put his feet back into his dirty shoes.

Tyler called out from the boat. "Is he alive?"

"Barely." They had to get him to a hospital. The man had been severely wounded and then left here for the last three days with no water, no medical treatment. He had clearly lost a lot of blood.

Ellie reached down and hooked her hands under Dawson's armpits. She pivoted and pulled him across the raft. Tyler leaned over the gunwale and put his arms out, Ellie slid Dawson's weight over to Tyler, and he heaved the heavy, limp body into the boat. Ellie scoured the raft for anything else Oswald's people may have left behind. There was nothing. She got back on the Bertram and looked up. Dark, wispy clouds mixed with ominous greens were stirring overhead. The wind, oddly enough, was still down considerably from what it had been earlier.

"Hey, Ellie?" Tyler was leaning over Dawson. "We need to move fast and get him to a doctor."

"I know." She turned to go back to the bridge.

"Hey, Ellie?"

"What?"

"Is it just me or is the water going down?"

She looked off the port side and over at the vegetation for reference. She blinked. The water line had clearly dropped a foot from where it had been earlier, after Oswald had pointed it out. The upper roots, the trunks, and branches were dark with moisture from where the water line had been just a few minutes ago. The water shouldn't be receding. It should be rising with the onset of storm surge, not trending down. It was striking. The water line was clearly diminishing.

And then it hit her. "Oh, no," she whispered. "Oh, no, no."

"What?" Tyler asked. "What's wrong?"

"It's a reverse storm surge," she said.

"Reverse? What does that mean?"

"Sometimes a powerful storm like Josephine can temporarily suck water away from the coast. The closer the storm gets to us the more water it's going to take with it."

"I know I'm from the Texas desert, but I thought hurricanes brought rising water levels. You know, flooding."

"They do, but with the really big ones the winds closer to the eye displace so much water that the surrounding areas deplete and run out into the Gulf. If I'm remembering correctly, as the storm gets closer its winds will shift in relation to the drainage and bring it all back in quickly." She looked back up at the clouds. "But if it keeps up it may suck the sound and the canals dry." If they didn't move fast they would soon find themselves beached and, like Moses had almost four thousand years ago, standing on dry land.

Tyler rubbed at his temples. "So you're telling me I've got a crazy man cuffed over here, three-quarters of a dead man to get to safety, and we're about to not have enough water to get back to the marina?"

Ellie's jaw tightened. "Yes."

He groaned. "I'll get Dawson to a bunk and you get us out of here."

Ellie went to climb up the ladder to the bridge, but Oswald, cuffed to it, was standing in her way. The area around his nose was puffy, swollen like a swarm of bees had been working on him. Still though, he maintained that haughty air, that steadfast hubris that he thought was so cute and Ellie found so repulsive. She didn't ask him to move. Instead, while holding a fresh image of Dawson Montgomery in her mind she curled her right hand into a tight fist and sent it into his face.

Oswald howled like a wolf in mating season and swung off to the side. Ellie scrambled up the ladder, got behind the wheel, and when she started the engines the boat hummed beneath her. She bumped the boat into forward gear, the anchor line slacked, and she shifted to reverse. Being in such a small cove and so close to so much vegetation beneath the receding waterline, the last thing Ellie needed was to overstrain the windlass motor under the weight of the hull. She bumped back into forward gear again, and the final yards of the rode came out of the water, bringing the anchor with it. Relieved that the anchor didn't catch, she engaged the transmission a final time, maneuvered the boat around, and exited the route she had come through a few minutes earlier.

Behind her, Oswald was cursing.

The Bertram's draft—the distance between the waterline and the bottom of the v—was roughly three feet and determined the minimum depth of water that could be safely navigated. The props and rudders extended a foot beyond that, which meant that if the water got below four feet they would start dragging the bottom. And if the water went anything below that, they would beach. Most of the areas at the southern end of Pine Island Sound were generally at a nautical depth of six to twelve feet. The immediate problem was that, unlike someone like Major, Ellie didn't know where those areas where. She turned on the depth finder, and as she came out of McIntyre Creek and back into Pine Island Sound, it gave her a depth of five feet. The transducer was mounted a little higher up from the very bottom of the keelson, so Ellie guessed she had an extra six inches more than what her depth finder was telling her. In this phenomenon every single inch was going to count.

The contrast from their ride out here was almost chilling. The waters were relatively calm, and the wind had died down to around five knots. Ellie's adrenaline surged as, from her view up on the bridge, she witnessed random color shifts in the water.

The sandy bottom.

Oswald was now humming loudly behind her, as if this entire ordeal was somehow comical.

Ellie gave the boat more throttle and for the next mile navigated via the depth finder. Then, with no warning at all, as though the gods had ordained this the perfect time to play a joke on her, the depth finder blinked twice, flashed pink and blues lines against a white background, and cut off. Ellie turned it on and off again, slapped it, and received no response. The depth finder was not coming back. She sighed.

They were only halfway back to the marina. She was going to have to do this on her own. Taking a deep breath, she navigated the colors of the water, trying to stay in the darkest areas. Suddenly, the water moved to a deeper brown, and Ellie throttled back. Her stomach and shoulders tightened as she felt the running gear snag on the bottom before coming clear again. "Come on," she muttered, and turned the wheel, quickly moving into a darker area of water. Her head jerked forward as they hit bottom again, harder this time, shining the propellers. Ellie turned briefly and saw a cloud of silt stirring up behind the transom. Her heart was racing and her knuckles white as they gripped the wheel.

She could see the marina clearly now, and she kept her speed. They snagged the bottom again, but Ellie kept going, the boat now vibrating like it had a bad tire, droning like a tired animal. She grit her teeth. Ellie had grown up here, spent the first twenty years of her life on these waters, and yet she had never witnessed anything like this in person. It was like someone had yanked the plug out of the bathtub. "Come on," she muttered again.

The channel coming into the marina was deeper; Major had dredged it a couple years ago, and when Ellie turned her attention to the dock she again saw something she had never seen before. The remaining fishing boats were hanging suspended above the water by their mooring lines, like spiders in their webs. To her relief, the boat surged forward as it entered the deeper waters of the channel. She turned and yelled for Tyler. He staggered out of the cabin still looking weak, but better than he had earlier. "Drop the fenders," she called. "Tie off at starboard!" Then remembering that Tyler knew nothing of boats, she said, "Over here. Right side!"

He gave her a weak nod and started flipping fenders over the side. They might help against the pilings, but the dock was now five feet higher than it usually was. She idled in, and Tyler scrambled to the bow and pressed his hands into a piling to keep the boat from hitting it. Ellie cut the engines, left the helm, and went to the port side. She grabbed a mooring line and reached up and tied it around a cleat. She repeated it at the next piling, pulling the line tight, and wrapping it some more. A minute later the boat was as secure as it was going to get, given the circumstances. If Josephine was going to make landfall anywhere near the island, the Bertram wouldn't make it, no matter how well they tied it off. Someone might find it a week from now next to that old fishing boat on Mondongo Rocks, or stuffed into the fringes of a barrier island or, worse, a backyard in Fort Myers. Tyler brought Dawson out of the cabin and laid him gently on the deck while Ellie clambered up to the dock. He uncuffed a still-chuckling Eli Oswald and told him to get up to "get up there with Ellie." A minute later the four of them were on the dock: one passed out, two of them bloody, all of them soaking wet.

Tyler hooked his arms under Dawson's armpits and, after cuffing Oswald again, made him hold Dawson's feet. As they passed The Salty Mangrove, the side door leading into the covered patio swung open. Major stepped out and nearly ran straight into Oswald.

Ellie stopped, a puzzled look on her face. "Major? What are you doing here?"

CHAPTER FORTY-NINE

Major looked curiously at the motley crew before him. He blinked, and without taking his eyes off Oswald said, "I had forgotten to empty the vault under the bar." He looked at Ellie. "What's going on here?"

"We found Ronnie's friend, Dawson," she said, and then nodded toward Oswald. "And this is the guy who was looking for Ronnie."

The rain had started up again. Major opened the screen door and motioned for them to step inside the covered porch. He had the clear plastic weather flaps lowered so that, at least for now, the inside was dry. They all went in.

Major surveyed the odd looking man in handcuffs standing beside Ellie. "That's Ronnie's friend? The guy who sent those fingers to Jean?"

"Yes, it's him."

"Well, well, now," Oswald said, "I suppose my reputation doth precede me." He looked around the space. "Hey now, good sir, any chance for a local celebrity to gain a glass of water? I'm buyin'."

Major ignored him. "How did you find him?"

"Long story, I can fill you in later. I've got to get Dawson to a hospital."

"She kidnapped me, that's what," Oswald protested.

Major surveyed Dawson and shook his head. "The hospitals have evacuated, but their emergency rooms should still be operational."

He eyed Oswald. "Why don't you let me take this guy while you get Ronnie's friend here to the doctor?"

Ellie hesitated. Having Oswald would continue to complicate things. Ellie wasn't exactly in a position to just drop him off at the local precinct. If she locked him back in the bed of her truck, there was no guarantee he wouldn't start making noise or scream for help when they pulled up to the ER. She had kidnapped a fugitive wanted by the FBI, DEA, and ATF, tortured him in secret, and then forced him to come with her across hurricane infested waters to find one of his kidnap victims.

"He's a wanted man," she explained. "And to be honest, I'm going to get in some trouble for having him. I don't want to implicate you."

"You went off the reservation and got him on your own."

She just stared back at him.

"You know what?" Major said, "I think we can figure something out. You found Ronnie's friend here after all. But right now you need to get this man some help. "

She thought about it, unsettled by both options. Finally, "Okay. But please, be careful. He's dangerous. You sure you're good with him?"

"Go on. We'll be fine. We'll go somewhere safe and

away from prying eyes. If you still have service, call me when you're done at the hospital and we'll figure out a plan. Tyler, you take care of her, son."

"Of course."

Turning to Tyler she said, "I need two minutes to run by my place and get Citrus." There were a few other items as well. Specifically, the copper samovar Vida Murad had given her, the straw doll that little Khalida had made, and a couple items her father had left behind.

"Sure thing. Let's go."

Ellie took Dawson's ankles, and as Tyler walked backwards he bumped the screen door open with his backside. Ellie paused. "Major. Are you sure? Like I said, I'm not supposed to hav—"

"Go," he said. "I'm on your team, kiddo."

"Yeah," she nodded. "Okay."

"Go on now. Get that poor man some medical help."

The wind was picking up again and sent the window flaps jouncing. Major watched the party of three make their way down the ramp to Ellie's truck. He waited, and when he saw their taillights fade up the road, he crossed his arms, lifted his chin, and gave Eli Oswald a predatory grin.

Oswald chuckled nervously. "Why you lookin' at me like that?"

"So...you're the one who stole some of my cocaine and swapped it for guns?"

CHAPTER FIFTY

ELLIE SLOWED HER SPEED AS SHE APPROACHED THE Matlacha Pass Bridge. The rain and wind were coming down in hard, stinging sheets again. When she got to the other side, a police officer dressed in a neon yellow rain slicker waved her down with an orange signal light. Tyler was sitting behind her with Dawson propped next to him. "Can you reposition him so the officer can't see him? The last thing I need right now is to get a bunch of questions."

"Yeah. One sec." Ellie saw Dawson disappear from the rearview mirror. She heard a thunk and then a shuffling. "Okay. We're good back here."

Ellie rolled down her window. The officer yelled to keep his voice above the wind as he spoke. "Where are you headed?"

Citrus bounded into Ellie's lap and yapped at the officer, thrilled that someone else was willing to have a discussion with him. Ellie laid a hand on his back. "Shhh, boy." Citrus darted onto the passenger seat and set his two front paws on the dash. He looked out the window and barked at the rain.

Ellie had half expected the officer to say something about evading him when she snuck back onto the island earlier, but he said nothing. Maybe it was a new shift. "To a relative's house further inland," Ellie said. She wasn't going to tell him that she needed to take someone to the hospital. Naturally, as a public servant, he would want to get eyes on him and see how bad off he was, possibly call in an escort to help her get there safely. Dawson's face looked like ground meat, and one look at him would only prompt a series of sober questions from the officer.

"All right," he yelled. "But you'd better hurry up and get there. The bridge is closed to all incoming and won't open until after the storm passes. You should have left hours ago."

"Yes, sir."

"Be safe now!" He stepped back and waved her on.

"Captain Obvious, there," Tyler mumbled. Citrus barked, agreeing with him.

Ellie rolled up her window and slowly advanced. "How's he doing?"

"His breathing is more shallow since we got him in here."

Ellie scanned both sides of the road for any pedestrians crazy enough to be out in this weather. Seeing none, she punched the accelerator.

CHAPTER FIFTY-ONE

OSWALD EYED THE MAN STANDING BEFORE HIM. HE had grown weary of being carted around all day. In the last few hours he had been taken to that cabin, hurt real bad, forced to ride out to Sanibel, and now, this. When that Ellie lady handed him off to this guy, Eli Oswald had had enough. He was going to get rid of these people, find a way off this island before the storm came, and get out of the state—for good. That's what he had been thinking while he stared at the bar owner in front of him. But all that had changed with the man's last words.

"What're you talking about?" Oswald said, scowling.

Another smile broke across the man's face. A smile that sent a chill down Oswald's spine and into his thighs. "You can...call me Ringo."

Oswald grinned suspiciously. "You? *You're* Ringo?" He laughed to himself. "I don't think so, Jimmy Jan—"

"I've been intending to make your acquaintance, but I must say that I was a bit disappointed to hear that you escaped the raid on your compound as well as the little present that Aldrich left you."

Oswald stopped smiling.

"And now look at this. Fate has dropped you right in my lap. I think we have some talking to do, you and I." He looked down and noticed the wet bandage on Oswald's hand. "What happened there?"

"That Ellie girl. She cut off my thumb, man."

Ringo laughed. "You're joking. My, my. She's the brightest beam of sunshine in my life, but she'll burn the wrong person to toast if they aren't wearing sunscreen."

Oswald was beginning to feel a bit nervous. "She know about you? She a part of your little enterprise too? I thought she was with the good guys."

"She does not know about me, Eli Oswald, and I've been very careful to keep it that way." He placed a heavy hand on Oswald's shoulder. "Do you see the dilemma that puts me in with you? It puts me in a position where I have to trust you, Oswald. Do you think I'm prepared to trust you with something like that?"

Oswald swallowed nervously. "Oh, come on, man. I wouldn't say anything. You and me, we got common interests. We can help each other. You know what I'm sayin'?"

"Yes. I do think we can help each other," Ringo said, now rubbing his chin. "How about you and I go some-place we can chat?"

"Boy...now you're talkin'."

Ringo opened the door and led Oswald back out into the elements. A heavy gust of wind cut across the boardwalk like a bulldozer. The two men crouched down and steadied themselves against the onslaught.

Ringo grabbed Oswald and pushed him toward the ramp that led to his Jeep.

———

WHEN THEY DREW near to the hospital, Ellie followed the signs to the emergency room entrance. She pulled the Silverado underneath the carport, and she and Tyler jumped out. With speed and care, they drew Dawson out of the cab and entered through the sliding glass doors. Before they were halfway to the front desk, they caught the attention of a nurse who raced over. She called for a gurney, and Ellie quickly updated the nurse on his situation; what had been done to him, estimating for how long, and under what circumstance they had found him.

The nurse called for her team to assemble faster.

———

WARREN HALL'S house was a modest two story a couple miles north of The Salty Mangrove and sat close to Dobbs Preserve. Butting up against the east side of the island his was the last house on Sunburst Drive. He brought his Jeep Wrangler into the driveway and, after opening the passenger door, said, "Let's go."

Oswald complied. He stepped out into the gusting wind, ducking down to keep his footing, and followed Ringo through the side door of the home. They entered the kitchen, and Ringo pulled out a chair at the kitchen table. "Have a seat."

"Say, I am most thirsty. Can I get something to drink?"

"Like you gave that young man I just saw? Like you gave him something to drink?"

"Oh, come on, man. That was just business. We didn't mean nothin' by it."

Ringo leaned against the gray granite that formed the top of his kitchen island. He folded his arms and looked Eli square in the eye. He had already decided how to handle this. He had known right after Ellie had handed him off, before she and Tyler and Dawson were even halfway to her truck. Sometimes life gave you lemons. This particular lemon happened to be sweet, and today Ringo would be making lemonade. He wouldn't even need to add sugar.

"Eli, you broke one of my rules. You were to receive my product and move it. It's been, what, less than two months since I decided to start working with you?

"Are you gonna get me something to drink?"

Ringo ignored him. "But—forgive me if I'm assuming—you got greedy and so thought that I wouldn't mind if you packaged my product with your guns."

"I'm just out to make a buck. Same as anyone else."

"You know, Ronnie Oglesby has been staying here for the last couple weeks. Right here, in this house. He left yesterday with his mother and got off the island."

Oswald's expression changed from smug to disbelief.

Ringo nodded toward the fireplace. "That painting hanging over the mantel—the one of the shrimp trawler —was done by Ronnie's mother. She happens to be one of my favorite artists. Jean is a good friend of mine and keeping Ronnie here safely away from you was the least I could do." He stepped over to the refrigerator, reached in, and grabbed a can of Pepsi. He shut the door, and the aluminum top clicked as he popped the tab.

"Thank you," Oswald said sarcastically.

Ringo took a sip and set it on the counter. "When I decided to let you distribute my goods, I did so full well knowing that you are a radical and espouse certain philosophies that I view as crude and elementary. You're not half the man that Harlan Tucker was—and I didn't agree with his view on life either. But I decided to take a chance with you, Eli. To test you out and see how the first few runs went. Did I not make it clear before we even started working together that when you moved my product you were to move it and it only? Did I not make it clear that I did not want multiple government agencies looking for me?"

Oswald shrugged defeatedly.

"You start dealing illegal or unregistered arms then you get the ATF on your case. When you kidnap people of even minimal social worth, and do it sloppily, do it in a way that can easily be traced back to you, then you get the local police and the FBI involved. Those are agencies I want to stay off my trail, not be hot on it. I'm not worried about the DEA. Them I can handle. But once you got all these spotlights to shine right on you, you opened up a little portal for them to start snooping around and find a road to me. That's not difficult to understand, is it?"

"Suppose not."

"I've been doing this for a very long time, Eli. I am very good at what I do. I'm very good at it because I am smart. I'm smart and I am not greedy. Greedy people get caught every time because they make foolish decisions and stop doing the thinking that kept them safe in the first place."

"That Ellie girl really don't know that you're the guy she's after?"

Ringo took another sip of his Pepsi and smiled. He looked at Oswald's hand. "She really cut your thumb off?" It was more a statement than a question.

"Yeah. That little whore."

The word was hardly out of his mouth before Ringo's heavy fist connected to his jaw. His head snapped to the right and, with the displacement of his weight, his chair tumbled outward, and he crashed into the wall and onto the floor. His wounded hand slammed into the tile, and he howled as the pain radiated through his arm all over again. He lay there, dazed from the furious punch, trying to wish the fire in his hand away along with the throbbing in a broken nose that had been hit three times in as many hours.

"Get up," he heard over his shoulder. "Get. Up."

Oswald groaned and, slowly pushing off the kitchen floor with his good hand, stood up. He grabbed the edge of the table and steadied himself.

"Pick up the chair and sit back down."

He leaned down, grabbed up the chair, and set it upright. It felt like his jaw might be broken. He sat back down, cowering under the torrent of pain weaving through his body.

"You want to call my niece a whore again?"

"Your...niece?" It was barely a whisper spoken across a swelling tongue.

"It's not often that I regret doing business with people, Eli. I'm quite good at judging character.

Somehow I knew my relationship with you would come to this. I sensed it. But I was willing to take a risk, a risk which I now regret."

"I'm sorry, man. You're right. It was stupid."

"I didn't say stupid, did I? No, I said foolish. Stupid implies that you are lacking the capacity to make the proper decision. Foolish, now that is simply choosing the lesser; choosing the option that is clearly not the best. You, Eli Oswald, are a fool, and it is time for our relationship to end."

Oswald smiled weakly. "Yeah," he whispered. "I agree. Let's just go our separate ways and put all this behind us."

"Yes. Let's." Ringo opened a closet door off the kitchen and retrieved a rain jacket. He put it on. "Let's go for a walk."

Oswald demurred. "A walk? We don't need to do that. Let's just get off this island before that storm blows us away." Oswald's throat was as dry as a cotton ball.

Ringo stepped back into the kitchen and paused before a drawer. He opened it and produced a chromed .45 ACP. He lifted a false bottom from the drawer, reached in, and withdrew a suppressor.

When he saw the gun, when he heard the soft metallic scrape of the suppressor rounding the threads, Oswald made an attempt to protest but found then that his jaw was locked, as if the hinges had rusted out. He couldn't talk. He thought his bladder might give way.

When Ringo was finished, he shut the drawer, brought the gun across his chest, and racked the slide. The crisp sound of a round entering the chamber chilled Oswald's skin. Ringo held the gun down at his side, not bothering to point it at the terrified man sitting at his table. With his free hand Ringo graciously motioned toward the door they had entered earlier. Oswald reluctantly stood up and walked toward it, his breath halting.

CHAPTER FIFTY-TWO

WHILE THEY WAITED ON AN UPDATE ON DAWSON, Ellie and Tyler watched the Weather Channel on the waiting room television. It had been over an hour, and as yet there had been no word from the nurses. Ellie had gone out and checked on Citrus a half hour ago, who was not at all pleased that he was not allowed to go inside and play. She moved her Silverado into the parking garage to keep both truck and dog out of the way of flying debris.

According to the news, Hurricane Josephine was now cutting west out to sea, with the eye of the storm just leaving Naples, forty miles south of Saint James City. Tyler finally got tired of seeing weathermen standing in ninety-mile-an-hour winds, yelling into the microphone for people to go inside and seek shelter if they were still outside—how are they watching this if they are outside? he'd asked—and walked into the hallway and started pacing. Ellie followed behind him and caught up.

"I can't believe someone would do that kind of thing

to a man," he said. "I can't wait for him to rot in prison."

"Yeah," she said softly.

"You really took his thumb?"

She sighed. "Yes. Tyler, he wasn't going to t—"

"I don't need an explanation. I trust your judgment, Ellie. I just...wow. You're pretty amazing." He pointed down the corridor. "That man might live to see tomorrow because of you."

"Thanks."

He stopped and his eyes found hers. "I mean it, Ellie. You did good."

"Yeah?"

"Shoot yeah."

At the other end of the hall the double doors opened, and a gray-haired doctor wearing surgical scrubs approached them. He introduced himself as Dr. Flynn. "We have Mr. Montgomery stabilized now," he said. "We've sent his blood samples to the lab for group and crossmatching, but it will take another hour to get his blood type. In the meantime we've given him saline and O positive. He lost a lot of blood and is severely dehydrated. Once we have the infection under control and the swelling goes down, we can stitch him up." He flipped a page on his clipboard. "His feet will heal faster than his hands. You told the nurse he had been on a raft in the wildlife preserve?"

"Yes."

"It appears that some salt water made contact with his feet. His socks were heavy with it. The salt, while not preventing a serious infection, did mitigate against sepsis. His hands, however, didn't fare so well. They are septic, with bacterial inflammation throughout his hands and up into his wrists. If we don't have to amputate his hands, he'll be lucky. For now, we have him on IV antibiotics and topical antibiotics. Do you know who did this to him?"

"Yes," Ellie replied. Then she added, "The police have been looking for him, but nothing has turned up yet." She didn't know how lying to the doctor was going to help anything. It just came out that way.

"Have the police gotten a statement from you as to how you found him?"

"No, sir," Tyler said. "We've been waiting, but no one has shown. We assumed the nurses called it in. I think they're all busy with the storm."

After the doctor left, Ellie brought out her phone again and checked for a signal. Still no service. She had been trying to reach Major ever since they handed Dawson off to the nurses. She knew that he was capable of handling Oswald, and yet an uneasiness hung over her. She shouldn't have gotten him involved. The handcuff key was still resting at the bottom of her pocket, but that didn't mean Oswald wouldn't try something. Hopefully Major had already gotten to the police.

For now though, there was nothing else to be done. They would have to wait out the storm from within the bowels of Lee Memorial Hospital.

———

It was fascinating, really. In all his years down here, he had never experienced the phenomenon with his own eyes. The waters of Manatee Bay were nearly gone. Only brown sand laced with thin streaks of algae sat where the water was supposed to be, like the tides had short-circuited and once water had reached low tide it just kept draining.

It was perfect.

The waterline was now thirty yards out. He guided Oswald into the sand, and it displaced slightly around his feet as he crossed it.

Oswald's jaw had finally loosened, and he was busy pleading. "You can't do this! Your neighbors are going to see you." Any other day, the man might have been right. But today he was not. He didn't know that every neighbor on this street had already evacuated. He didn't know that there was no one left in the entire neighborhood, not even a gerbil or a parakeet. Oswald also didn't know that when you looked east out of Manatee Bay there was nothing but naturally pristine water and mangroves for two miles and, with the weather like it was, there was no concern of a boat passing unexpectedly. No, they were all alone. Just the two of them. Ringo nudged his hand into Oswald's back, pushing him along as the younger man tried in vain to provide rational solutions to the disagreement that stood between them. They splashed through a few puddles as they finally neared the edge of the water. After they'd gone a little further, Ringo shoved Oswald one final time until the water was at their knee caps.

The wind had died down some. The rain, for now, was a light drizzle. Ringo looked out across the shallow water. He took in a deep breath, inhaled the brackish odor of an empty ocean bed. He took a couple steps back. "Please, Eli. Get down on your knees."

"M-m-m-man, th-th-th-there's a better way, Ringo." When Oswald got down on his knees, the water reached up to his chest, and he winced as the salt water washed over his bad hand. He brought his cuffed hands up in a pleading defense.

Ringo held the gun at his side, held it in a loose grip, like it wasn't even there. He looked down on Oswald. The man's black hair was matted to his scalp, half of it drifting into his eyes. His nose was swollen, and blood, crusty and moist, spread around his lips and his chin.

"Eli," he said softly. "When I was a boy, oh, I don't know, maybe about ten or eleven, I was walking through a forest in Ohio, just near where I lived, when I came out into this clearing. In the clearing was a flock of blackbirds—must've been a couple thousand of them. They were all laid out over this field; couldn't even see the dry grass. Just blackbirds as far as the clearing went. And you know what? Every last one of them was dead. And when I say dead, Eli, I mean they had been lying there for days. Stank to high heaven and flies buzzing in ecstasy. Now, I have no idea what happened to those poor blackbirds, how they got there. But I do know one thing. That was just surely the sorriest sight I ever did see. And you, Eli Oswald, happen to be the second sorriest."

"I didn't mean nothin' by it all, I swear! I swear I'll do right by you and help with whatever you need. I swear!"

"I'm not looking to extract any promises from you, Eli. What's done is done. The final act, closed curtain, after-party; all over."

"Ringo...Ringo," he choked. "I can pay you. You want money? I can tell you where to get it."

Ringo knew it would come to this. If they had it, money always became a topic for discussion at the very end. When the one about to die could no longer see a way out, he turned to the only thing he thought he had left. Ringo had been ready for this. He played along. "Where?"

"Get me out of here and I'll take you to it."

Ringo didn't smile. Not this time. "Eli, do you think I am a stupid man?"

"No. No, of course not."

"But you think I will let you take me to your money so that you can find a way to escape?"

"No, I just—"

"Then tell me where it is, and I will reconsider. Tell me where it is, and I'll call Chewy to go retrieve it. If it's there we could very well have a deal."

"Okay. Okay, yeah." Oswald struggled on his knees, expressed a breath of relief. "It's ugh, it's in my hotel room. At the Purple Parrot. Wrapped up in the toilet tank."

"How much?"

Reluctantly, Oswald said, "About sixty thou."

"The Purple Parrot, you say?"

"Yeah. It's up near Sweetwater."

"Thank you, Eli," he interrupted. "I do hope you're a man of your word. This brings our relationship to a close, and your days which the Lord has numbered are now complete."

"Please no! I...I don't wanna die!" He shuffled on his knees through the water toward Ringo's feet. "Please...please…" he said in crying whispers.

Ringo despised the pleading tears of cowardly men, men that couldn't—wouldn't—take their medicine. They repulsed him. Men who could inflict the grossest forms of violence on others but folded beneath the promise that it would be turned back on them. He tucked his gun into the rear seam of his cargo shorts and stepped in behind Oswald, laying two strong hands on his shoulders. He leaned in, said, "You reaped. Now you sow. You sow a reaping. I'm the Reaper." Then he heaved Oswald's head beneath the water.

The brackish, bitter tide found its way into Oswald's mouth and up through his nasal passages. He could feel strong hands lace their fingers around the back of his head like wicked roots, wrapping into his hair, forced down by sturdy trunks above.

Memory rumbled through him, accompanied by the salty, briny taste of the ocean, and as the last of the oxygen was milked from his bloodstream and his CO_2 levels began to rise, he saw King, the brown Cocker Spaniel he had as a child. That was, until the day the King chewed through his old man's wallet, leaving the leather in a soggy heap under the dining room table and the cash in tiny pieces all over the floor. His father had taken the dog out back near the tree line and beat it until there was no more yelping, no more breath in the small animal. Oswald had watched the entire thing from the living room window, scared to venture out lest he suffer half the fate of the dog. His father had barreled back a few minutes later and, without looking at his son, said, "Don't ever ask me for another dog." Then his father went to the refrigerator, grabbed a Budweiser, and set himself into his easy chair.

Now, King was running toward him, his ears flopping lazily around his head, his tongue hanging out, his eyes locked happily on the master he hadn't seen in over thirty years. But then, slowly, the dog's eyes turned a bright green and then shifted into a deep red, and Oswald remembered that he was dying, that in this moment, *he* was King, his life being taken by the hands of a violent man.

He felt the fingers on the back of his head relax. This wasn't supposed to be the way it all ended. He had years to go, a new posse to recruit. He and his brother Drew had even talked about maybe going on a cruise. What cruise line had they talked about again?

That question was the last thought Eli Oswald ever had.

CHAPTER FIFTY-THREE

At eight o'clock in the evening, an hour after Doctor Flynn had spoken with Ellie and Tyler, as Ellie flipped through a year-old copy of Better Homes and Gardens for the fourth time, and as Tyler was dozing off next to her, the door to the hospital waiting room opened, and Major stepped through, soaking wet, rain water still dripping off his shorts.

Ellie came to her feet. "Major? What are you doing here?"

His pupils were dilated with concern. All he said was, "Have a seat, kiddo."

He took the chair next to her. Tyler rubbed his eyes and leaned forward.

"What's going on?" she asked. Something was wrong; that much was clear. "Where's Oswald?"

"That's why I'm here. That Oswald. He's...uhh…"

"What?"

'Well, he's gone."

Her stomach clenched. "What? Gone? What do you mean?"

"Well, he got away—Ellie, I'm so sorry. I didn't think he would make run for it."

"A run for it? He escaped?"

"Yeah."

Ellie closed her eyes, heard Tyler whisper, "Oh, no."

"I took him back to the house with me to get a few things, and then, on the way back out, he just bolted for it when I was leading him back to the truck."

"Bolted? Where?"

"Toward Manatee Bay. With all the rain I lost sight of him almost immediately. He could have doubled back." He shook his head. "I just don't know."

Ellie slicked her hands down her face and moaned. "Okay...Okay…" She sighed long and slow.

Tyler put a hand on her knee. "He can't get off the island, not in this weather."

"Well, that's what I want to talk with you about," Major said. He took in the empty room and then turned back to his niece. "I need to call the police, Ellie, and let them know. They need to know that guy is out there."

She nodded pensively.

"But first…" he said, "I was thinking the three of us could come to some sort of agreement."

She cut her eyes back to him.

"What do you mean?" Tyler asked.

"Ellie, you...took that man's thumb off, didn't you?

"Yes."

"Anyone see you do it?"

"No, we were at Jean's cabin."

"And if memory serves me right, law enforcement tends to frown on that kind of thing."

"Major, I'm fine with taking responsi—"

"No." He said it flatly, as if what Ellie was trying to

say wasn't an option. "Tyler, son, correct me if you feel differently here, but I want to propose that you and I have no idea how that man lost his thumb. I don't recall Ellie ever saying how it happened."

Ellie sat up. "Major, I—"

"I'm game," Tyler said. "I don't have the foggiest clue what happened. Could have lost it changing his bicycle chain for all I know."

"No, you two."

Major, ignoring her, said to Tyler. "Maybe it was penance for what he did to Ronnie's friend."

"*No*, you two. Once they find him, he'll just tell them the truth."

"And who's going to believe him over you?" Tyler said.

"I don't want to lie. I'm not sorry for what I did."

"I'm not sorry for what you did either," Tyler said. "I would have done the same thing had I, you know, tracked down a psycho on the front end of a hurricane."

Major slicked a hand across his still wet face. "Ellie, you did the right thing. I'm not going to see you have to lawyer up because you went and saved Ronnie's friend's life."

"I'll have to anyway. Oswald isn't going to forget this anytime soon."

"It's going to be Oswald's word against yours. Let him try."

"I don't want you guys lying for me."

"Well," Tyler stretched his arms out and yawned large. "I don't guess you have a choice there, Julie Jangle."

She slapped him on the shoulder. "Major, they're going to wonder why you came here first."

"Sentries are gone from the bridge now. All the phones are down. Cell and landlines. I knew the hospital would have some phone or radio system operational."

"You've really thought through this."

"So we're agreed."

"Warren, you've got my ballot," Tyler said.

"Thanks, you guys," Ellie said softly.

Major put an arm behind her and brought her in close, kissed the top of her head. "All right," he said, "I'm going to make the call."

When he was gone, Tyler said, "He's a good man."

"Yeah. The best."

CHAPTER FIFTY-FOUR

THE STORM WAS OVER.

Hurricane Josephine had, in the late evening hours, continued a turn out into the Gulf of Mexico, the outer edge of its eye missing Lee County's barrier islands by thirty miles. Before moving out to sea, it had torn across Marco Island and up into southern Naples, leaving nothing of Major's Marco Island marina but piles of fractured pine, naked pilings, and punctured fiberglass.

Ellie, Tyler, and Major had spent all night in the hospital's waiting room, wind and rain lashing at the windows and making the lights flicker, and Tyler being the only one to find a couple hours of sleep. As soon as the winds began dying down, the FBI and the Sheriff's Office initiated a systematic search of the island, allowing no residents to return until Eli Oswald had been found. No one seemed to mind the inconvenience, as they were all a little wary of the idea that a high profile madman might be hiding in one of their attics or boathouses. Just as the sun was coming up, and with tailing winds still reaching upwards of fifty miles an hour, the Coast Guard had, at the bequest of the FBI, undertaken a search for Eli Oswald, focusing their attention on the eastern side of the island near Manatee Bay, the general area that Major had seen him run off toward. Less than an hour into the search, they found his body in a cluster of Rag Island mangroves.

Ellie, dog-tired and without cell service all night, was startled when her phone rang. It was Garrett, calling her personally to inform her that Eli Oswald's body had been found. Garrett said someone had relayed that it had been her who had located and grabbed both Oswald and Montgomery. "That's the kind of thing that made me bring you on in the first place," he'd said, and then added that when the FBI brought her in for questioning later that day he planned on being present to ensure they let her off easy. When Ellie hung up and informed both Major and Tyler of Oswald's fate, they all sighed in collective relief.

The authorities' initial conclusions held that, due to the lower water levels brought about from the reverse storm surge, Oswald had fled into the empty bed of Manatee Bay and had possibly tried to skirt around Dobbs Preserve. When the waters quickly returned, Oswald had probably been caught up in a rip current, the handcuffs making it difficult to swim. That was the preliminary assessment, and no one expected any extended investigation to conclude otherwise.

Early that afternoon FBI had brought in Ellie, Major, and Tyler and questioned them in turn.

Ellie, leaving out any mention of the paperwork Mark had provided her, claimed that she had recalled something Drew Oswald had told her and followed it up on a whim. She had grabbed Oswald and utilized previous training to question him and get him to give up Dawson's Montgomery's location.

Did you torture him? Was taking his thumb a part of that?

"It was not."

What happened to it?

"It was like that when I found him."

Did you ask him about it?

"I did. A couple of times. He wouldn't tell me, and honestly, at the time that was the least of my concerns." Reminding herself that Dawson was alive mitigated against the opprobrium she felt about lying to the good guys.

You couldn't stop and use a payphone to alert us you had Oswald as well as a lead on his kidnap victim? You couldn't use someone else's cell phone?

"I figured if mine wasn't working no one else's was either. And I wasn't going to spend precious time trying to locate a payphone."

What about the sheriff deputy at the Matlacha Pass Bridge? You couldn't have notified him when you went back on the island?

"I didn't see him out there."

What about coming back out? On your way to the hospital.

That, she had to own. "I should have. To be honest, the rain at the time was severe and didn't exactly allow for much of a conversation. It was my understanding that the nurses had a protocol to alert the police when a patient comes in like Mr. Montgomery had.

They questioned her for two hours, Garrett sitting beside her the whole time.

They believed her.

There was no CCTV footage from the gas station where Ellie had picked him up. She had checked before Oswald came out with his Funyuns and his Jim Beam, before she escorted him to her truck. He had been under the bed cover all the way back in to Pine Island, so there was no way for a traffic camera to pick him up. There would be no way for them to confirm that his thumb had already been severed and wrapped in gauze when she grabbed him.

One of the FBI agents, an Agent McLusky, who smelled a little like Funyuns himself and sweat too much, wanted to charge Ellie, claiming she had not followed a citizen's protocol for handling a wanted fugitive and that she had been reckless and maverick.

Ellie had liked that last one. She had been a maverick. It had been her who had saved Dawson Montgomery's life, so that moniker was just fine with her.

After they had Ellie's statement, it had been Major's turn. He spent over an hour with the FBI. He had, after all, been the last person to see Oswald alive and had taken responsibility for a known fugitive. Major had been clear that it had been his own suggestion to take Oswald off Ellie's hands, and he had done so with the conviction that doing so would be the best the thing for Dawson Montgomery.

Why did you stop at your house? Why didn't you go straight to the police?

I wasn't expecting to have a criminal riding back off the island with me, and there were a few sentimental things I wanted to get from my house.

Why were you even on the island at all?

So Major told them the truth about why he had been at the bar that afternoon, that he hadn't emptied the safe since Mango Mania and it held a fair amount of cash he didn't want to be out of.

Did you have anything to do with the death of Eli Oswald?

No, of course not.

They believed him too.

Tyler stood up under questioning as well, relying how Ellie had called her and asked him to prep the Bertram for her. He hadn't known until she arrived at the marina just what was going on and by that point felt it his civic duty to help get Mr. Montgomery.

You could have called the Coast Guard at that point. They could have gone out.

"With what phone? They were all down by that point."

There would, of course, be additional questions over the next few weeks from other agencies and lawyers who drew their paychecks from Uncle Sam. Other than that, the ordeal was behind them.

Pine and Sanibel Islands had seen wind gusts upwards of a hundred miles an hour that left trees and telephone poles strewn about like discarded pencils. Watercraft were found festooned in mangrove swamps and coves throughout the county, and a few of the boats at The Salty Mangrove's marina were no longer in their slips, having broken free of their mooring lines. Major's Bertram, as it turned out, remained in its slip and made it through without any more damage than that caused to the propellers as Ellie brought it back across the sound in receding water.

For those who had re-entry decals, entrance back onto the island occurred late that afternoon, with county cleanup trucks leading the way, removing trees and fallen branches from the roads and checking for loose and fallen electrical wires.

The peaceful quiet that typically held Pine Island in a sleepy trance was replaced with the constant buzzing of chainsaws cutting into fallen trees and the groan of Bobcats clearing debris into towering piles. Palm fronds and string lighting had been ripped off The Salty Mangrove's tiki hut, and the backside of the restaurant was now missing, but, overall, Major was happy to discover that the damage hadn't been any worse.

As fate would have it, Hurricane Josephine had docked a center console Cobia in the Berensons' living room. Two months ago, after a Cessna loaded with cocaine crashed nose-first into the Norma Jean pier, one of its wings had ended up in the exact same spot, taking the place of the Berensons' Pottery Barn coffee table.

As of a couple hours ago, Ted Berenson had left a voicemail at Pine Island Center asking for the first available realtor to give him a call.

Now, a full day after the storm had passed, with pockets of sky beginning to clear, Ellie and Tyler were moving sandbags from her back porch to Tyler's truck. The waters hadn't reached over the canal's seawall, but the sandbags were heavy with rain water. Tyler paused at the corner of her house.

"Hey, Ellie?"

"Yeah?"

"You did good. You know that, right?"

"Sure, why?"

"All this about Oswald and how it all went down. You being let go from the DEA, him dying."

She shrugged. "Oswald made his own choices. What happened to him is a sad ending to a sad life, but I'm not going to feel guilty about it."

"Well, I'm not either but," he looked down on a thumb and rubbed at it. "I just hope I'm never on your bad side."

She smiled and they both reached down and grabbed up a couple more sandbags. Tyler winced.

"You all right?" she asked.

"Yep. Just a little sore." He started walking to his truck.

"From what?"

"Nothing."

"Tell me."

He set the heavy load on his tailgate and mumbled something.

"What's that?" She chucked her sandbag into the truck.

He mumbled a little louder, still not enough for her to hear clearly.

"Geez, Tyler. What's the deal?"

"My stomach muscles. Okay? They're sore."

"Sore? What, did you start doing sit up—" and then she smiled. "You're sore from throwing up." It wasn't a question.

"Can we talk about something else now?"

"Certainly not."

"You're a pain sometimes." He winked at her.

They returned to her backyard which was littered with debris: roof shingles, branches, leaves, a rogue panel of corrugated steel, a splintered two-by-four, and an unopened, but punctured can of Folgers dark roast. Ellie's house had fared well, only suffering a fractured window pane at the front and a fallen line of gutter at the back. A brown and white koozie lay half-tucked beneath a fallen palm frond. Ellie reached down and picked it up, examined it.

"Oh, look. It's a koozie from The Perfect Cup." She

held it out to Tyler. "See, this is how you do a koozie. Notice how it doesn't say 'The Perfect Coup.'"

Tyler rolled his eyes and grabbed up another sandbag.

WHEN TYLER LEFT AN HOUR LATER, Ellie took a long, hot shower and changed into comfortable cotton shorts and a Salty Mangrove t-shirt, then poured herself a glass of merlot and put Dylan's *Blood on the Tracks* on her father's old vinyl record player. She tucked herself into the corner of the couch, and Citrus jumped up and laid his head on her lap.

She pet his head as she enjoyed her wine and thought over the events of the past week. Her sister and niece were back, she had been asked to turn in her contractor's badge with the DEA, and then, through sheer tenacity and persistence, she had found both Eli Oswald and Dawson Montgomery. From what the doctors were now saying, it looked as though Dawson would be keeping both his hands and would be out of the hospital in the next few days. He was going to need a lot of therapy though.

Oswald had been served up a plateful of justice by Mother Nature. Ellie didn't expect to shed any tears over ol' Jimmy Jangle. No, but she might shed some for Ryan Wilcox. Quite literally, the last few days had been a whirlwind, and Ellie had hardly made time to think about the fact that Virgil had reconnected with her and dropped a bomb in her lap. Now as she sat in the comfort of her living room, his words echoed, chilling her. *I think I'm being framed for something. I think...well, I think we all are.*

For three years now she had wanted to be wrong in thinking that some of what TEAM 99 had done was unsanctioned, and she had tried to convince herself over the last few years that the hit in Saint Petersburg had been an isolated event. But she couldn't do that any longer. Not after what Virgil had said, not after she witnessed that unalloyed fear in his eyes and after she learned that Ryan Wilcox had been killed. But now, as Dylan intonated "Idiot Wind" and Citrus slept beside her, it was beginning to look very much like she had been right.

Her father was alive, doing something for someone, somewhere.

Ryan, her only line back to her father, had been murdered.

Virgil had gone off to Arizona to see what else could be known.

Someone was setting them up to take a fall.

And so, with Virgil's disconcerting words on the forefront of her mind and the last of the merlot on her lips, Ellie decided it was time to start finding some answers.

CHAPTER FIFTY-FIVE

WHEN CHEWY ENTERED RINGO'S OFFICE AND STOPPED in front of his boss's mahogany desk, Ringo asked him what life coach he was listening to. Chewy, who wasn't one to manifest anything that could be deemed emotion, took pause, mildly surprised by the question. "Actually...it's music."

"No kidding?"

Chewy shrugged.

"What band?"

"Not a band. Vivaldi."

"Now you're talking." Ringo pulled open his center desk drawer, removed an envelope, and handed it to Chewy. "Take this to the post office if you would."

"Of course."

Ringo shut the book he was reading and leaned back in his chair. "Chewy, what made you come work for me?"

Chewy and Ringo didn't get personal very often; their engagements, for the most part, remained business-related. Not superficial, just business. Chewy considered the question. It had been ten years since he came on with Ringo. Initially, he received small shipments—Ringo didn't do big ones back then—and took them to a buyer on the other side of the state. That was it. Pick up, drive, and hand off. A caveman could have done it. But it had been steady work, and Ringo paid him well.

While Ringo waited for Chewy to answer, he said, "You remember when I first met you?"

"I do. It doesn't seem so long ago."

"No, it doesn't. You were angry back then, remember? Hot temper."

He did remember. And if Chewy was honest with himself—and his prophets of personal power told him that doing so was the first step to growth and change—Ringo had become the greatest influence in his life. Ringo had accepted him, even back when he was a twenty-five-year-old punk who was mad at the world. Ringo had seen something in him and gave him a chance, and there had never been a time when Chewy felt disrespected or untrusted by the man. Ringo had been good to him. Very good. "I had gotten a job down here as a trawler hand and got a drink at The Salty Mangrove one night. That one old man started making fun of me in my coat. He couldn't believe someone would be wearing a coat during a record breaking summer."

"Stu Dudley," Ringo huffed. "I'm glad that bastard bit the dust. He was a mean old coot. Spent a lot of money at my bar though. You stood out. You and that wool coat of yours."

Chewy fixated on the edge of the desk as he stared into the past. "You offered me a job. I thought you were going to have me flip burgers."

"I have a confession to make," Ringo said. "Something I've never told you. That first run that you made across the Glades. The stuff that was in the suitcases. It was baking soda. It wasn't coke."

Chewy shrugged. "No matter. I delivered it. That's what you asked me to do."

"I had to test you. You did well. But you need to know that there is no one I trust more than you. Not even Andrés. And I trust Andrés very much."

"Thank you, Ringo."

"You're a good man, Jared."

Chewy paused. The nickname had developed during his time working for Ringo. No one had called him by his real name in years. It sounded good, personal.

"We've come a long way, you and I, and I confess that it is due to my failed discernment that we have had a couple setbacks of late. But now that Eli Oswald is gone and César is out of the picture, we will be on the fast track to success. Wild Palm is working out better than I imagined."

"It is," Chewy agreed.

Ringo removed his fedora, the white one with the black band, and stood up. He set the hat on the desk. "My marina on Marco Island did not fare well. I'm going down there to monitor the cleanup. I'm not sure when I'll be back. My schedule is quite off these days. I don't like it." He turned to leave and then stopped. "Oh, I almost forgot. Quinton will be back in a couple weeks."

At this, Chewy's brows lifted. "That's good. He's been greatly missed."

"Yes," Ringo nodded. "He certainly has. His return will be the dawn of a new era for us. It will be good."

"I'm sure he has much to share with us. Ringo, if I may, what are we going to do about your—"

"Let me deal with that."

"She's getting close, Ringo."

"Yes. I know. Leave that to me. I'm working on it." He stared out the office window with a soberness that Chewy had seen only once before.

"You love her," Chewy noted.

"Yes. I do." *More than you can possibly know*, he thought. *All three of them*. And that was why, now, as he contemplated the heart-wrenching decision he had made this morning, his stomach soured. It was nearly unbearable, thinking about it, deciding to do it. But it had to be done. They were all now too close to what he was doing here, too close to the life he was leading as Ringo. For the moment, he brushed such harrowing thoughts aside.

Chewy took notice of the sudden change in Ringo's complexion. "Are you okay? You don't look well."

Ringo nodded vaguely.

"Is there something I can do to help?"

Ringo was silent for a while, pondering a question he had not considered before in such a context. "Yes," he mused. "Yes, I think there just might be."

CHAPTER FIFTY-SIX

THE CABIN SAT HIGH UP ON THE FOOTHILLS AND looked out onto Humphreys Peak, the highest natural point in Arizona. Before today, Ethan Bradford, known by his former teammates as Virgil, had never been to Flagstaff. Now that he was here, he was beginning to think that Cicero might be onto something. The high altitude and low humidity meant that the early evening air was cool and dry, and being this far out of town made one feel the good kind of isolation that came with being all alone in nature.

Virgil turned off the winding mountain road and onto a gravel drive that led up to Cicero's cabin. He had spent the last week trying to fill in knowledge gaps left wide open when Ryan Wilcox was killed. Ryan had been the one and only connection he had into the unsettling revelations developing around TEAM 99's past. Pascal —Ellie—had known nothing of these recent developments. Perhaps Cicero would. Maybe Ryan Wilcox had reached out to him as well before he was murdered. If he hadn't, then Cicero and Virgil could work together to find answers. Cicero was brilliant with a keyboard and, given the right equipment and enough time, could research and uncover anything. Virgil recalled that Mortimer used to refer to Cicero as a digital archaeologist.

Virgil parked his rental car next to a dark blue Pontiac Bonneville that had a sign on its roof reading "Albert's Pizzeria."

Virgil stepped into the crisp mountain air and walked up three porch steps before arriving at the cabin door. He knocked, and while he waited he turned to look at the view. Panama was great, but this...this was in a different class altogether. Getting no answer, he knocked again, but this time the door gave and creaked on its hinges as it moved back a few inches. His brows drew together. He pushed the door open and cautiously peered inside. No one, no sound. Instinctually, he brought out his 9mm from the back seam of his cargo shorts. He pulled the slide back, and the crisp sound of metal on metal followed as a round entered the chamber. He trained the gun out in front of him and went in.

A framed poster of Jack Bauer—gun raised, face set as hard as a flint, Eiffel tower in the background—hung adjacent to the door. Had Virgil's spidey sense not been tingling at this moment, he would have allowed himself a laugh. He went down a short hallway, and when he turned the corner he saw his old teammate lying on his side in a pool of blood. Virgil made small steps toward him, scanning up and across the cabin. Ten feet behind Cicero the back door was open, and long streaks of blood led out over the threshold as if someone had dragged themselves across it. His eyes followed the streaks until they came to rest on a body lying at the tree line ten yards off the back porch. Cicero had fallen where he had been injured. A clean pool of dark blood had gathered around his head and neck. A pepperoni pizza lay behind him, folded haphazardly like a taco, its box upside down on the other side of the room.

Virgil put a knee on the floorboards, but his eyes kept scanning the house and the open back door. "Are you alone?"

Cicero tried to speak, but the only thing that came out was a slow trickle of blood from the corner of his mouth.

Virgil stood back up and spent the next minute clearing the cabin. Finding no one else, he rushed back to his old teammate and alternated his gaze between Cicero and the body outside. Assessing Cicero's wounds was simple enough. His throat had been cut. That was all. He lay still with his eyes fixed on the ceiling.

"Can you talk at all?" In response, Cicero, moving slowly, turned his head. It rolled only a few inches, and his eyes went the rest of the way. Virgil followed his gaze underneath a hutch. Something flat and shiny lay there. Virgil scrambled over and snatched it up. It was a phone. He came back to his old friend. "Hang in there, buddy. Hang in there. Is this yours?"

Cicero slowly moved his eyes left and then back to the right. He gagged and tried to cough. Virgil surveyed the gash in his throat. He had to get his head up so the blood could drain.

But suddenly, Cicero's breathing became shallow, halting. He swallowed weakly and tried to speak with great effort. "V..V..." He left hand dragged along the floor and stopped. "Vir....Vir......." and then his eyes closed, and he was gone.

Virgil called out to him, laid a hand on his head and called his name again. Nothing. He fought back tears and the urge to scream as a canvas of raw anger unfurled across his chest. He closed his eyes for a brief moment, and when he opened them tey were full of revenge.

He stood up. The phone required a thumbprint to unlock. Cicero had indicated it wasn't his. His weapon in one hand and the phone in the other, he cautiously made his way out the back door. He got down behind a thick porch post and listened while searching the forest and the scattered boulders on the hillside above. He heard nothing, saw nothing. Other than the high pitched screech of a mountain chickadee further in the trees, all was quiet. He quickly took the three steps off the back porch and followed the trail of streaked blood to the body at the tree line.

It was a woman. She was lying on her back, her dead eyes staring blankly into a muted sky, orange with dusk. She wore a red "Albert's Pizzeria" polo on which a large button was pinned that read "Your Door in 33 or it's Free." She had three gashes in her abdomen from where Cicero had retaliated.

In a flash of coherence, Virgil saw what had happened. The pizza delivery lady/ assassin had gotten the drop on Cicero, had sliced him before he could react but then underestimated his will to square up even after he was mortally wounded.

Virgil brought out the phone and, grabbing the lady's hand, pressed her thumb onto the lower section of the glass. Nothing. He grabbed the other thumb and tried that one. It worked, and her limp hand thumped onto her leg when he let it go. He held the phone in front of him and scanned the contents. His eyes stretched into wide, dumbfounded disbelief. He scrolled down, and his heart thumped in his chest as a nightmarish dread enveloped him.

Then, with no warning at all, coming from somewhere deep in the woods, a bullet screamed into his shoulder, hurling him onto his back. The phone scattered across a carpet of pine needles, and Virgil writhed on the ground, the pain in his shoulder like a hot poker fresh off the fire.

He winced through the agony and grunted as he forced himself to stand back up. He ran for the tree line and weaved around trunks, cradling his elbow in a hand to keep his shoulder from jostling. He had been foolish. Of course they would send two people; one to fulfill the primary engagement, one for backup should something go wrong. The backup would have seen Virgil's car coming up the road and waited for his moment. Seeing Cicero like that had messed Virgil up, clouded his thinking.

A muffled *snap* sounded through the woods. Virgil didn't feel the bullet, only its effects. His left knee exploded, and he tumbled forward, his forehead just missing a large rock as he came down. He bellowed out a muffled, frustrated scream through clenched teeth. It felt like someone had detonated a bomb behind where his knee cap had just been. His breathing was now coming in ragged gasps. He glanced down. The top half of his shirt was soaked in his blood, and his left leg was slick and shiny with red. His head started swimming, and he focused on controlling his breathing. Shock was setting in, and when it rose into its fullness, he would lose his will to press on. He swiveled onto his stomach and brought himself up on his right elbow just as another bullet slammed into the boulder on his right, missing his skull by an inch.

He had to keep moving.

He'd been wrong, what he told Ellie. He told her they were being framed. But that wasn't right. The remaining members of TEAM 99 were not being set up.

They were being exterminated.

What he had just seen on that phone called for the systematic elimination of the remaining members of TEAM 99. Cicero had been first on the list. Virgil, the fourth.

He scrambled forward, shredding his elbow on skree and pine cones for twenty yards before he stopped abruptly. The forest before him descended into a sharp decline, filled with boulders and trees and scrub. He swiveled his gaze. Whoever was behind him would keep advancing. His phone was in the car.

He had to alert the others, warn them before it was too late, before they ended up like Ryan and Cicero. But right now his only thought was to warn the next one in line, the one the exterminators would come for next.

Pascal. Ellie's face was pulsing through his mind like an ambulance siren.

He had to tell her.

And so, with his sight beginning to blur and his chest heaving in great ragged breaths, Virgil pushed off and tumbled down the ragged slope just as another bullet ripped into his shoulder and exited through his collarbone.

VACANT SHORE

Read on for an excerpt from **Vacant Shore**, book 4 in the Pine Island Coast Florida Suspense Series

———

Ellie had watched Major drive off two minutes ago. Now, she knew he would have stayed had he known what had been waiting for her.

She peered cautiously around the wall of the fishing shack. Her breathing hijacked when she saw the man who was standing against the far wall, facing the doorway, a gun trained in her direction.

"Hello, Ellie."

She stepped into the doorway and couldn't speak for several moments, just stared at him, blinking. Ordinarily, she would have ducked back behind the wall for cover. But she was too stunned to do that. For a brief moment, she thought this was some kind of inappropriate joke. But his eyes held a coldness she had never seen in them before, silently telling her that this was the furthest thing from a joke she had ever experienced.

*Her brows lowered and drew together. "I...don't understand."
She searched all that she knew for a rational explanation. Some
surfaced, but they all disappeared before his frozen disposition and
the gun he had on her. Up to this point she thought she had pieced
together who was behind everything, who was calling the shots.
Now, she wasn't sure of anything at all.*

*He flicked the muzzle toward a side wall and told her to sit
down against it.*

*She had never felt as disoriented as she did in this moment.
Not even that fatal, misguided afternoon when Assam Murad and
his family were murdered by God knew who. At least in that situation there had been the possibility that something could go wrong.
But this? She hadn't planned for this at all. Her thoughts swirled,
muddled, like they were caught up in a tornado intent on sucking
the coherence out of everything it touched.*

*She did as she was told and slid to the floor, pressed her back
against the wall. "Why?" she whispered, half to herself and half
to him. But it all ran deeper than that. Deeper than a simple 'why'
and even, for now, even superseding the 'how.'*

*She looked at him, her confused eyes searching his,
"Why **you**?"*

Vacant Shore

Will be available in August-September

JOIN JACK HARDIN'S VIP READER GROUP

You'll be the first to get access to new short stories about characters in the Pine Island Coast world, notifications of upcoming releases, and overall just have a jolly old time.

https://jackhardin.lpages.co/vip/

BE SUPER COOL. LEAVE A REVIEW

If you enjoyed this book and only write a review every so often, would you consider leaving one being for Bitter Tide?

When you do, your awesomeness meter will rise. You can do so by visiting the book's sales page on Amazon. Thanks so much.

GRATITUDE

I want to thank author Don Rich for his help with the Bertram scene. Any errors, of course, are mine.

I'm working as fast as I can to get book 4 (Vacant Shore) ready for you.

In the meantime, head on over to Amazon and get to reading Don's *Mid Atlantic Adventure Series*. You can grab them up on Amazon.

AUTHOR'S NOTE

Pine Island and Matlacha are truly a paradise of their own. But, as with any good fiction, I have taken certain liberties with the local culture and location, while doing my utmost to stay true to it. In *Bitter Tide*, I took the most license with Mango Mania, which occurs in July rather than late August, and is hosted in Cape Coral, not the southern tip of Pine Island.

Made in the USA
Middletown, DE
30 September 2021